LEGENDS OF KAIATAN

A FANTASY FAIRYTALE COLLECTION

UNEXPECTED HEROES
BOOK 6

MARTY C. LEE

Bookaholics Press

Book design & publication by Bookaholics Press LLC, Provo, Utah
Edited by Martha Rasmussen
Front cover design by Lara Wynter
Maps by Michelle Allan and Naomi Rasmussen
Author photograph by Melissa C. Baxter

ISBN-13: 978-1-950230-22-8 (epub)
978-1-950230-40-2 (paperback)
978-1-950230-24-2 (large print)
978-1-950230-25-9 (hardback)
978-1-950230-59-4 (audio)

Published by Bookaholics Press LLC
Provo, Utah bookaholicspress@gmail.com

Contact the author at MCLeeBooks.com

For Andrew Lang and other collectors of fairy tales who shaped my childhood imagination.

CONTENTS

DEAR READER

Welcome to the world of Kaiatan!

If you've been here before, maybe to read about some Unexpected Heroes, then what you need to know is that these stories all take place long, long before then. In fact, they're so old that the stories have passed into legend. You might recognize them and think you know what happened, but here are the *true* stories.

If you've never been here before, I could give you a lecture about this not being Earth, which is pretty obvious if you notice the colors of the sky and ocean. I could talk about the four different countries and the four races: the winged Iojif, the gilled Nokai, the shapechanging Darrendrakar, and the desert Iskrins.

Or I could just throw you into the world and let you see it for yourself... That sounds like more fun. Just remember, these tales are all from far back in the misty reaches of time.

Come find out what really happened...

Marty C. Lee

RESCUE

1. DISASTER

(AKASHA, IOJ)

As soon as she received word, she set off to rescue him.
The Legend of the Flute Player

I*'ve been captured.*

Fala Ilmarinen stared blindly at the dirty, crumpled letter in her hands. The messenger had brought it in that state, though the wax seal had somehow still been intact. Now opened, the broken seal taunted her with the shadow of her broken betrothal.

She wept silently. Not broken yet, but it was only a matter of time.

A breeze trickled through the large, unshuttered window of her bedroom, tickling her feathers and tempting her with a good flight. Fala absently spread her wings to catch the draft, without taking her gaze from the trouble in her hands. The day was warm and sunny, too lovely for such bad news.

The crooked letters on the parchment wavered in her vision. *Zafrir Kyveli is holding me in his fortress.*

If Avari didn't come back before the wedding, the marriage contract would fail. What would her family do? Her parents had tried for years to find her a suitor, but no one wanted a plain girl with boring brown sparrow feathers and no riches to bring to the union. If Masiela House hadn't decided they wanted the small piece of land by the river badly enough to exchange their youngest son for it, the Ilmarinens would have quietly sunk into obscurity and starvation.

And now that stupid feud with Kyveli House would ruin everything. She had never gotten a straight answer among the rumors about the cause of the quarrel. If it was too horrible to talk about, what would the Kyvelis do to her betrothed?

The breeze ruffled her plain brown hair, too straight and fine to stay properly pinned back. She was homely, old, boring, and poor. She would die a spinster, which would bother her less if it involved more time and food. Her parents had been quietly declining for years, and though she had hidden the latest inventory report from them, she knew starvation was around the corner.

Someone in my House betrayed me, so I can't ask my family for help.

Fala had always known this marriage was less urgent to the Masielas than to her family. In fact, she was sure they agreed to a wedding rather than an outright purchase of the land only because her dower would cost them less, since their son himself theoretically made up the difference in value. They certainly didn't esteem the union enough to introduce the bride and groom to each other. But she hadn't known they prized Avari so little they would abandon him to Kyveli House. But who was actually responsible, the head of the House or someone else? And why?

Please send someone to rescue me.

Fala dropped the letter into her lap and buried her face in her hands. Avari had obviously forgotten — or never paid attention to — the resources of her family. The entire household consisted of herself, her elderly parents, and one equally elderly cook who also did the gardening and stayed partly from loyalty but mostly because she had nowhere else to go.

Perhaps Avari expected Fala to hire someone. A bitter laugh escaped. If she had money for a mercenary, she would have enough to buy food. As if to punctuate her thoughts, her stomach growled. Downstairs, the cook would serve herself and Fala's parents. Fala, as usual, would skip lunch. She no longer bothered with a pretext but merely stayed away from the kitchen until dinner. The less she ate, the longer their small garden could feed them. When winter arrived in a month or two, their meager food stores would keep them alive for only a few weeks.

Until Masiela House revealed Avari's absence and canceled the marriage contract. Then Fala would still have to sell the land, desperate enough to take whatever price she could get. The Masielas might even purchase it for less than her contracted dower, leaving her with no marriage, no home, and nowhere to go.

How long would her family last then?

Fala wiped away despairing tears and jumped to her feet. Angrily pacing from one side of her tiny bedroom to the other, she tried to think. She couldn't ask Avari's family for help without knowing who the traitor was. Her family was out of the question. Hiring someone was impossible. And without the marriage to save them, her parents would die.

But she could do nothing about it. No woman could travel alone for hundreds of miles and expect to arrive safely. The Kyveli wouldn't listen to a mere woman, either.

If only she were a man — a warrior. Better yet, the leader of an army.

She paused in front of the mirror. She knew why the Masielas wanted the marriage, but why had Avari agreed? He wasn't getting anything from the deal but an unwanted wife, as plain as a man.

As plain as a man... Fala squinted at her reflection, then yanked her skirt backwards between her legs to mimic pants.

As plain as a man... And after years of cleaning, gardening, wood chopping, and everything else, she was nearly as strong as an ordinary man, though not as much as a warrior.

Wild hope ran through her heart like a tornado, and she took a deep breath to calm herself. She must think this through very carefully. One step at a time.

First, could she disguise herself well enough?

Fala turned sideways and pulled her dress tight. Hmph. Two years of no lunch made that easier, too, though it had never been much of an issue. For the first time, she was thankful for her height and resemblance to her father. If she cut her hair, she would easily look like a boy. Her lip quivered, and she bit it firmly. It wasn't as if she had any beauty to ruin.

Second, food. Easy enough. Her work in the garden had taught her edible plants, and in the past two years, she had used her father's slingshot to hunt small game.

Third, what reason would she give for traveling?

With no goods, she couldn't pass as a merchant. She couldn't pretend to be a messenger lest someone try to hire her. Her gaze fell on the music stands crammed into the corner. Though most of her skills were practical, meant to care for a household, she had taken music lessons until the family finances withered a few years ago. The harp was too large to carry, but either her lute or the recorder from her earliest lessons would allow her to request shelter as a traveling musician, which would also reduce the amount of time she must spend hunting food.

Fourth, how would she defend herself and free Avari?

She had no weapons. Well, just her slingshot. Fala rolled her eyes. More likely, she would have to find a way that didn't rely on weapons at all, but actual plans would have to wait until she arrived and gathered more information.

She had little chance of succeeding, but if she stayed here, her family had no chance at all.

Fala hurried downstairs. After stopping in the hall to calm her breath, she poked her head into the kitchen with what she hoped was a sunny smile. Her parents sat at the table, picking at their old bread and leftover salad.

"Mother, Father, I need to make a trip to prepare for the wedding. I'll be back as soon as I can."

She waved cheerfully and rushed away before they could ask questions.

Her father's closet yielded an outgrown pair of pants and two old shirts loose enough to aid her disguise. He only had one jacket, but she grabbed it anyway. If she wasn't back by the time the weather cooled, he would have bigger problems than no jacket.

Fala dashed back to her room and cut her hair to just long enough to tie at the back of her neck. Though her hair and wings were an ordinary brown, she wanted no clue to her actual identity. She managed to blacken her hair by herself, but she couldn't possibly reach all of her wings. She almost gave up in tears before she remembered the feather-painting salon in town.

After carefully dressing in her father's clothing over a figure-flattening vest, she found a bag in her closet and added a comb, soap, fishing line, and a blanket. With a bit of food and a musical instrument, it would be heavier than she had anticipated. So, her recorder instead of her lute, then. Besides, the recorder wouldn't lose its tuning. She slid it inside and flew out the window toward town.

To her surprise, the salon accepted her male guise and took her order without a sideways glance, welcoming her to town as if she were a newcomer or traveler. Was she so ordinary that no one remembered her face? Perhaps, or this might be proof her disguise was as effective as she hoped. Who would expect a proper young lady to be dressed like a man? Fala spoke as little as possible to avoid breaking the illusion. It took the last of her tiny savings, but her wings were soon dyed black to match her hair.

Next, she went to the city library. Though it was much smaller than the Great Library in the capital city of Vasi, it had a decent map collection. She traced the way between Akasha and the Kyveli lands, noting landmarks, obstacles, and potential places to stay as she traveled. Even by wing instead of foot, it would take her days if everything went perfectly, or weeks if she had to spend much time foraging or dodging danger.

A librarian started blowing out lamps, and Fala returned the maps. She headed for the door, then paused. Night had fallen, but with no money, she couldn't rent a room in an inn, and she certainly couldn't go home looking like this.

Perhaps it was for the best. If she left now, no one would see where she went. She tied her jacket firmly shut and walked north out of town, flapping her damp wings. By tomorrow, her feathers would be dry enough to fly.

Alone, unarmed, and without supplies. Desperation swamped her like a cold downdraft. She must be crazy, but what else could she do?

Halfway through the night, Fala climbed a tree and wedged herself into an uncomfortable fork in the branches. Blue dawn woke her from poor sleep, and she painfully worked herself out of the tree. Edible weeds made a scant breakfast, and by the time the sky lightened to day's apricot, she was ready to go. Since her feathers were dry, she sprang into the air and flew northeast.

Below her, the hills of home flattened into the wide plains of central Ioj. Every few hours, she landed by water to drink and forage and stretch her tired wings. She had never flown this much, and every muscle burned and cramped. If possible, she would have flown for the morning and made an early night of it, but she didn't have time. Aching though she was, she must keep going.

At night, she landed in a village and nervously offered music in exchange for dinner and a place to sleep. The local inn, a room behind the stables that sold food and drink, accepted with no questions.

After playing for an hour or two, Fala gulped a mug of hot onion soup and rolled up in her blanket in the farthest corner of the dirt floor. Though she listened breathlessly for anyone to discover her disguise, the sounds in the inn merely changed from stories and bragging to dish-washing and snoring, and eventually exhaustion won over her sore muscles.

She left early the next morning, flying all day between rests. That night, she again bargained for food and shelter. This time, the innkeeper cheerfully questioned her about her journey and asked her name.

Fala blinked, blowing a quick tune on her recorder to demonstrate her skills while she thought quickly.

"I'm Marin," she finally said, hacking her family name short, then deflected any further questions by asking the innkeeper's favorite songs and complimenting the scent of dinner before she settled in the corner to play for the customers.

Dinner was a delicious lamb roast, and in the morning, the innkeeper gave her a loaf of bread for breakfast and an open invitation to return if she passed that way again.

With a full stomach, the flying was easier despite sore muscles, and Fala made good progress all morning.

Around noon, when she was looking for water and a place to stop, she spotted three people riding horses below her. Though common for freight, not many Iojif rode horses rather than fly, and Fala swooped in a circle to watch. After a few minutes, she noticed the two pursuers carried weapons. It was not a race below her, but a hunt, and the first rider was the prey!

Then the lead horse stumbled and the quarry fell off, rolling across the ground with a crunch Fala heard even from high above. Without a thought, she whipped out her slingshot and aimed a pebble at the flank of the first hunter's horse. It whinnied and bolted, dumping its rider, who promptly sprang into the air and flew off with a worried look at her over his shoulder. She aimed her next rock at the last rider's weapon hand.

Judging by the pained scream and the dropped weapon, she hit her target. He galloped after his companion.

Fala circled again, scolding herself for idiocy. How did she know whose side she should be on? If anyone's at all! Perhaps she had just saved a criminal from law officers.

Below her, the quarry moaned, and his wings twitched awkwardly. If he was a dangerous criminal and she landed within his reach... But he needed help, and she was the only one here.

Stupid, she was stupid. Nonetheless, Fala landed nearby and cautiously approached. "Can I help you?"

He jerked to look at her, then winced. "Are you why they left? Then you have already aided me."

He rolled to a sitting position, though his creamy wings hung badly and one was spotted with blood.

Fala stepped closer, curiosity burning. "Why were you riding horses? What did those men want?"

The man grinned crookedly, even as he tried to straighten his wings. "I broke a wing in my youth and have ridden horses ever since. I've made such a profit breeding horses that my neighbors decided to steal them. Alas for me, I was in their way when they raided my stables. Alas for them, I was riding my best stallion. Oh, where is he?" He craned his neck.

Fala pointed. "Two of your horses are still running loose. Will they go home by themselves, or should I try to catch them?"

The man untied a small pouch from his belt and offered it to her. "Sugar makes good bait. If you can get any of them back here, I can ride home."

She took the bag and flew toward the closest horse, the famous stallion. He had already come to a stop, and with the help of the sugar, she tempted him back to his owner.

While the man worked to remount, she tracked both of the other horses, since the other assailant had apparently abandoned his mount and flown after his accomplice. When she returned with both horses in tow, their master nearly cried, petting their glossy hides and cooing to them.

"My name is Sahali," he said. "Come back with me. Let me reward you for your good work this day."

Fala shook her head. "I need no reward." Her stomach growled, and she amended her statement. "I could use some food, actually. And a chance to rest my wings."

Sahali laughed. "Those I have in abundance. Come, my young friend, keep me company and ease your wings on the way."

He coaxed her onto the back of a horse, though he kept the reins in his own hands to ease her nervousness. While they rode slowly back to his estate, they chatted. She again gave her name as Marin and told the same story of traveling entertainment.

After reaching Sahali's house, he fed her a generous meal while his injuries were treated, then loaded her bag with food and yet again begged her to name a reward.

And how could she accept payment for something she had done by reflex? Fala shook her head. "I need nothing else."

"I value my horses more than a bag of food," Sahali said wryly, "much less my life. At least take this ring from me in token of friendship." He pulled a plain gold signet from his finger and pressed it into her hand, curling her fingers closed around it. "If ever you need me, you have only to return it to call me to your side. Don't bother to argue, for I won't take it back."

Reluctantly, Fala dropped it into her pocket. Shouldering her nicely heavy bag, she nodded. "As a token of friendship. Good flight, my new friend."

"Good flight." Sahali clapped her on the shoulder and backed up to let her spread her wings.

In a moment, Fala was back on her way. All that fuss for a couple of pebbles in the right place. If only the rest of her mission would go so easily. Despite her worries about the future, a smile tugged at her lips.

2. TRAVELS
(NORTHEAST ACROSS IOJ)

On her way, she had many adventures.
The Legend of the Flute Player

T wo days later, Fala calculated she was almost to the Kyveli province. At least, she thought she recognized the fork in the river from the map she had studied in the library. The thought of stopping early was so tempting she almost landed immediately. Instead, she swooped lower to double-check her position, and movement in the water caught her eye. If fishing was easy here, a stop would be worth her time. Even if it took her the rest of the afternoon, she could camp early and leave in the morning with a full stomach.

But she'd never seen a fish with such vibrant light green scales and a... wing? Someone was drowning!

She folded her wings and dove nearly straight down, landing on the riverbank with a thump. The river-soaked wing thrashed above the water again, as did a small hand.

Fala dumped her pack on the ground and rummaged through it. Rope, rope, why didn't she have rope? The wing submerged, and the hand clenched on air, grasping for nonexistent help. No time. Fala whimpered and grabbed her fishing line. She made a loop in one end and tried to throw it around the waving hand, but without a weight to direct it, the line wafted to the wrong place.

As she pulled the rope back for another try, the hand disappeared again.

This time, it didn't surface.

No, no, no. Fala jerked the line around a tree and waded into the water.

The river was cold, much colder than the air, and she immediately started shivering. Within a few steps, the water rose to her thighs, then her waist, and still she couldn't see the green wings. As the river reached her shoulders, she waved her arms through the water, blindly searching.

Nothing. Nothing. Had she failed? Was the child swept away already?

Still nothing.

Something brushed by her, and she clenched desperately at the bit of fabric. Please, let it be the boy. When she dragged her heavy catch to the surface, it turned out to be a sleeve. She gasped with relief as another yank found his shoulder, and a third hauled a small head above the river current. The child's eyes were closed, and as Fala lifted the youngster higher, water ran from his mouth. Was she too late after all?

"Come on," Fala pled, pulling on the line with one hand while she propped him against her shoulder with the other — no, her, since she was wearing a pretty blue dress. "Wake up. Breathe!"

She paused for a moment to beat the girl's back.

Nothing.

Pulling harder and angling through the icy current, she slogged toward the bank. It felt like an eternity before she reached the shore, but it couldn't have been more than a few minutes since she first spotted the drowning girl. Too many minutes?

Please, Irajahan, spare her life, she prayed.

As soon as her feet hit solid ground, Fala heaved the girl onto her stomach and pressed on the child's back between the vivid green wings. "Breathe!"

An appalling amount of water streamed from the girl's mouth with every compression, but finally, no more came. Fala pushed once more, sobbing with frustration and sorrow.

"Breathe," she begged.

The girl didn't move, and her cold body was so still.

Fala let go and covered her face. She had been too slow. She should have had a proper rope. She should have moved faster. This was her fault.

The girl coughed, and as Fala dropped her hands to stare, the child gagged and spit up more water.

"Mama," she wailed, then coughed again.

Oh, Irajahan, thank you, Fala prayed, wrapping the girl in her blanket. She picked up her bag and cradled the child in her arms. Which way was home? But while Fala turned in circles, panicked shouts came in the distance. That way, then. She shrugged the girl higher and trudged away from the river, following the noise.

Within a few minutes, a tall man swooped from the air. "Aerilyn," he gasped, reaching for the child.

"Are you her father?" Fala shifted the child into his arms. "She fell into the river."

"No, her uncle, Esen. You saved her? Please come with me." He clutched his niece tighter and bellowed, "Solana, over here!"

Fala clutched the strap of her bag. She couldn't afford attention, especially when her wet clothes clung to her. As she edged backward, a pretty woman flew down and wrapped her arms around Aerilyn and her uncle, kissing the girl's face and sobbing. Both siblings had matching green wings, darker than the child's. Esen muttered something, jerking his chin toward Fala, and the lady turned, one hand still clutching her daughter.

"Thank you, thank you. She slipped away, and I didn't realize—" Solana's lip trembled, and she clamped her mouth shut for a moment. "Thank you for my daughter's life. Please, come to the house and get dry." She let go of her daughter only long enough to grab Fala's arm.

"You're welcome," Fala said, "but really, I'm glad I was there. If you'll give me back my blanket, I'll be on my way."

She tugged the front of her shirt away from her chest, hoping the wet fabric hadn't already betrayed her gender.

"I can't give it back to you all wet," Solana insisted. "Surely you can stay for a few hours to dry?" She glanced at the afternoon sun. "Or stay the night? Please, let us thank you properly."

Fala tugged on her shirt again. The longer she stayed, the more likely her disguise would be discovered. The wind picked up, and her wet clothes chilled almost instantly. She shivered, teeth clacking together, and reconsidered. With clothes, jacket, and blanket wet, she would never get warm. As long as she was careful, she could surely manage a few hours of company while she dried. After all, the patrons at the inns had never guessed, nor had Sahali.

"Thank you," she stuttered. "I accept your hospitality for the night. My name is Marin."

"Oh, good." Solana beamed and turned to murmur to her daughter, but she kept one hand clutched firmly around Fala's shivering elbow.

As they walked, they were joined by more relatives and servants who had been searching for Aerilyn. Some of them stayed close, on foot or wing, while others flew ahead to prepare.

The house was nearby, nearly hidden from aerial view by a grove of trees. It was smaller than Sahali's mansion, and she was ushered into a warm, sunny kitchen instead of a parlor. Though perhaps that was more because of the water dripping from her clothes rather than any informality. She didn't care why, only that it was warm. By now, she was half frozen, and her teeth hurt from chattering.

Fala stood awkwardly by the door, dripping cold, muddy river water onto the gleaming floor. A horde of relatives and servants streamed through the kitchen and into different rooms, shouting instructions and gathering food and blankets.

As soon as the little girl was carried farther into the house, Fala was shown to a steaming washtub behind a screen by the fireplace. A brother or nephew or servant or whatever offered to help "Marin" with "his" bath, and Fala shook her head as vigorously as she could manage, clutching her bag to her chest. Hot water sounded almost painfully wonderful, but she couldn't ruin her disguise now.

Though she meant only to hide anything her wet clothes might reveal, the man raised his eyebrows and stepped back. "No one will touch your things. You can spread your clothing on the chairs or screen to dry."

Heat rushed to Fala's cheeks. "But what should I — I don't have — I mean, a shirt, but—"

She inhaled to make herself stop babbling. To add to her misery, something delicious-smelling was making her stomach rumble loudly.

The man blinked, then smoothed his face to a polite mask. "I would be happy to bring you something to wear while we launder your clothing."

And what choice did she have? If she caught pneumonia, who would rescue Avari and save her family?

Fala choked down her fear of discovery and said, "Thank you."

When the man left, she carefully arranged the screen to block all views, then scrambled out of her wet clothes. After tossing her jacket and outer clothes across the top of the screen to be washed, she hung her vest and underclothes by the fireplace. With a sigh of anticipation, she folded herself into the hot water.

After rinsing her wings of dirty river water, she let them hang over the edge of the tub and immersed her body. Gradually, her shivers eased and her sore muscles relaxed. Her eyelids dragged with exhaustion, but she couldn't sleep... yet...

She woke some time later in cool water and with the lovely smell tempting her nose. Looking frantically around, she discovered no one in the kitchen, though her dirty shirt and pants had been replaced by another outfit. She had a clean pair of underclothes in her bag, but only one vest. Reluctantly, she put on the damp vest before donning the new pants and shirt. At least the screen had protected her ruse. Her gender, anyway. Her feathers had faded to the deepest charcoal gray instead of true black, and though she couldn't see her short hair, she feared the same was true of it.

As soon as she pulled back the screen, scraping it on the stone floor, the kitchen door opened. Solana and her brother entered. While Solana ushered Fala to a chair, repeating her earlier thanks, Esen dished up a large bowl of steaming vegetables and spiced meat. He placed it in front of Fala, then sat across from her with Solana.

Barely able to restrain herself long enough for a muttered, "Thanks," Fala dug in to the food, closing her eyes in sheer delight. The vegetables were crisp-tender, and the juicy meat was perfectly savory. If she wasn't careful, she might drool on the ironed tablecloth. Even better, the bowl was piled high, and a nearby platter held bread so fresh it still steamed.

She'd thought she could handle scant food supplies on this trip, since she commonly ate only two meals, but it had proven harder than expected. Her foraging barely supplemented her inn dinners, and all the flying burned energy she wasn't replacing fast enough. Forgetting her company, she shoveled food into her mouth so fast she nearly burned her tongue.

The siblings merely watched her eat, not speaking until she finished a second bowl.

"How can I reward you for saving my daughter?" Solana asked.

Fala shook her head. "Anyone would have helped."

Solana frowned. "There must be something."

Fala shrugged, and the damp vest shifted against her skin. She glanced at Esen, who wore a lovely embroidered vest properly over his shirt. "I could use a vest? An old, plain one is fine."

Esen laughed until Solana touched his hand.

"Certainly," she said. "And you may keep the clothes you are wearing, also."

"And we'll send you with food, if you like," Esen offered, handing Fala a spiced sweet roll. Despite his earlier laugh, which had sounded more surprised than mocking, his eyes were kind.

"Then I shall count myself rewarded indeed." Fala bowed her head in thanks.

"If you ever need somewhere to stay," Solana offered, "you are welcome back here."

"Or if you need a job," her brother added.

A contract was a contract, and the Masielas would enforce it. Fala shook her head, but said, "Thank you," then attacked the roll.

Fala slept on a cot in the kitchen and left early in the morning. Her pack held her own freshly laundered clothes and blanket and a new vest of plain sky-orange but fine stitching, with Solana's crest embroidered discreetly on the pocket. An extra bag of bread and dried meat and fruit was slung across Fala's chest. As she flew away, Solana and Aerilyn and the rest of the household waved.

All day long, Fala flew. Her rest stops were shorter, thanks to the food from Solana, and her muscles ached less after the hot bath. By nightfall, she was within sight of the Kyveli lands, but not quite close enough. Reluctantly, she landed in a small town on the outskirts of enemy territory and wound her way through the market-day crowd to the inn.

At the door, two burly men shoved past her, arguing in loud voices. Forced off the threshold by their flapping wings, she fell back against the building and covered her head.

After a long moment, they were gone, and Fala slowly unfolded herself. As she struggled free of the shrubs that had grabbed her ankles, a sparkle caught her eye. She leaned over and dug through the twigs and dirt until she uncovered a pin shaped as a House crest. Unlike the plain steel one she had left on her dressing table, this one was gold and silver and decorated with colored jewels. It was beautiful and obviously very expensive.

Fala hid it in her fist and wrestled free of the shrubs. Now that the doorway was clear, she made it inside the inn with no troubles. A server directed her to the innkeeper, and she ran through her familiar audition for music in exchange for food and shelter.

Once they had struck a satisfactory bargain, she showed the innkeeper the jeweled pin. "Do you recognize this? Do you know where I could find the owner?"

The innkeeper's eyes shone with greed. "I can return it for you." His fingers twitched impatiently beneath her hand.

Fala pursed her lips. "I think I would prefer to handle it personally."

He glared at her. "I'll tell him you have it!"

She dropped the pin into her jacket pocket. "That will be quite satisfactory, thank you."

The innkeeper huffed and showed her to the corner where she could play her recorder.

Before Fala's dinner break, a tall Iojif with bright red wings entered, spoke briefly with the innkeeper, then headed directly for Fala with two armed guards following.

"I hear you stole something of mine," he commented mildly, though his hand was on his dagger.

"I *found* something," Fala said. "If you can tell me what it looks like, I would be happy to return it to its rightful owner."

She tightened her hand on her recorder and took half a step backward. Even if her slingshot were within reach, it wouldn't help against the slender swords the guardsmen carried. Had the innkeeper really reported her as a thief?

The red-winged man unbuttoned his jacket to reveal embroidery across his chest. "I lost a gold and silver pin with this crest."

"The innkeeper saw that much," Fala said. Perhaps this was some plan between the two men to take what did not belong to them, and intimidation was part of the scheme. She squared her shoulders before continuing.

"Can you prove it belongs to you instead of someone else in your House?"

The man frowned but waved off his guardsman's reflexive step and tapped a spot on the embroidery. "The jewel here, fell out last year. And my initials are on the back. SK, for Siroko Kyveli."

Kyveli! Fala gulped. Not the right Kyveli, but still, proof she was getting close... With shaking hands, she pulled out the pin and examined it. Yes, the tiny jewel was missing, and when she examined the back under the lamp, she could barely see "SK" engraved in the gold. So not a plot with the innkeeper, though he was glaring at her from the bar.

Siroko raised an eyebrow.

Fala nodded. "It is yours, sir." She dropped the pin into his outstretched hand and picked up her recorder to play.

"Is that all?" Siroko asked.

Fala lowered her instrument. "I'm sorry, sir, that's all I found."

She cast another glance at the innkeeper. How could she prove she had discovered nothing else?

"I mean, don't you want a reward?"

Fala sighed in relief. "For returning your own belongings? Wouldn't anyone do the same?"

Siroko looked toward the innkeeper and grunted. "Perhaps, perhaps not."

He waved at a server and ordered three dinners, then sat at a nearby table with his guards.

Fala shrugged and returned to playing, though she kept one eye on the armed guards and their frowning, red-winged master. She had returned his pin, so he couldn't report her as a thief. Perhaps he was staying around because he liked music.

Some time later, a server came to tell her it was time for her break, and he set her dinner at Siroko's table. One guard pushed out a chair for her and glared. The steaming food was too tempting, and she sat, digging in as rapidly as she could move the spoon. If the Kyveli wanted to yell at her for something, he could do it while she filled her belly.

Siroko said nothing until she finished eating, then he leaned back, balancing on two chair legs. "I find I can't leave without giving you a reward. That pin is a memento from my father, and I treasure it. Tell me what I can do for you to avoid a shameful debt on my House."

"Kyveli House?" Fala gulped. "There is one thing."

Siroko barked a laugh. "I thought there might be."

"If you know Zafrir Kyveli, tell me what kind of music he likes? I'm heading in his direction next."

Siroko's chair thumped to all four legs. For a moment, he merely stared at her, eyebrows knotted. "What kind of music he likes? I asked you to name a reward."

"Yes, that would help me the most." She sat on her hands to keep them from twitching. If she knew how to please Zafrir, it would give her an actual chance to free Avari. Perhaps. At least it was more of a plan than she'd had before.

Siroko examined her from head to wings, eyes narrowed. Finally, he laughed. "Very well, little man. I will grant your reward."

He sent a guard for parchment and ink and wrote a list of songs. "Here you are, Zafrir's favorites."

He handed her the rolled parchment, then stood. His guards flanked him as he held out his hand. "Let me shake the hand of an honest man."

Thankful as never before for inheriting her father's blunt fingers as well as his thin figure, Fala accepted Siroko's hand clasp. His firm grip lasted only a moment, then he and his guards swept out of the inn. Left behind in her hand was a Kyveli pin of gleaming silver, beautifully crafted though it had no jewels.

Fala sucked in a shuddering, thankful breath. With this on her shoulder, Zafrir would surely let her in.

3. ENEMY
(KYVELI PROVINCE, IOJ)

She played her flute for the enemy for three days.
The Legend of the Flute Player

After Siroko left, Fala played the songs on his list, practicing until they were smooth and nearly perfect. Though she had somehow expected a Kyveli to have sophisticated tastes, most of the songs were common ballads of love and family and adventure. At the end of her shift, she slept in a dark corner, dreaming of freeing Avari and saving her family.

Early in the morning, Fala left the inn without breakfast or directions, as the innkeeper refused to stretch his bargain to a bite of food or a scrap of information more than agreed, merely glaring at her as he pushed her out the door. Instead, Fala found a baker setting up his market stall and offered to help for a slice of bread. The job went quickly, and she was soon on her way with half a loaf of day-old bread and instructions to the home of Zafrir Kyveli.

It wasn't far, and as long as she reached it before the dark clouds hovering over her turned into a storm, she would arrive today. Once safe from prying eyes, Fala stopped long enough to pin the Kyveli crest to her jacket.

The first two hours went well enough. The cloud cover made the air refreshingly cool, and Fala's stomach was full. Then the clouds gathered faster, piling like a haystack at harvest. Though she had never been a particularly swift flyer, she flapped her wings hard instead of letting herself coast. If she didn't beat the storm, she would have to wait until tomorrow to continue, and she was too close to wait. Muscles protesting, she flew faster. Above her, the clouds gradually grew darker, and the apricot sky deepened to rust.

Landing would be safer. But she wouldn't melt in a little rain, and she could *see* the Kyveli fortress from here. She was almost there.

A crack of thunder made her flinch. Fala whimpered and stroked harder. Rain was one thing, but lightning was a much bigger problem. Landing in the middle of nowhere was suddenly dubious safety. She needed shelter, and the closest was the fortress.

Another crack of thunder, and lightning illuminated half the sky. Too close, much too close. She could smell the hot whiff of the lightning. Fala tucked her wings and dove to a lower altitude. Pushing her aching muscles as much as possible, she flew toward the stone garrison.

Lightning shot past her, close enough to make her hair stand on end, and thunder exploded in her ears. Fala dropped until she was skimming just above the ground.

Then the thunder and lightning rocked the sky almost continually, as if the gods were playing drums and cymbals. The clouds split open, and freezing needles of rain stabbed her face and wings. Visibility shrank to nothing. Fala flew blindly, slowing to prevent herself from slamming into the stone walls that must, Irajahan willing, be somewhere close.

For a long minute, she felt lost in the gray rain. Only her aching wings told her she was still moving. Her hair was plastered across her eyes, despite her new, shorter style, and rain stuck to her eyelashes, blinding her even more. The frigid rain cooled the air to near-winter temperatures, and her soaked jacket was useless.

Then a dark mass rose in the grayness, and Fala jerked to the side, stumbling to her feet and letting her exhausted wings fold. In front of her was a gray stone wall, but not far to the left was a large wooden gate. She staggered sideways and pounded on the logs, shivering.

"F-fair winds," Fala shouted upward, stammering through her frozen lips. "Is a-anyone home?"

No one answered, but the gate creaked open enough for Fala to slide through.

On the other side of the gate, armed guards waited. Fala raised her shaking hands and let them search her, though once they saw the crest on her shoulder, they searched casually enough that they didn't break her disguise.

Bless Siroko for giving her the pin.

One guard pointed toward the inner building. "Hurry inside." He dragged her by the elbow, nodding to the servant who ran to meet them.

Bless the storm for making them cold and anxious to hurry.

As the guard went back into the rain, the servant threw a blanket around Fala and escorted her to a steaming bathhouse, tutting all the while. Just before he shut the door, he said, "Take your time, kinsman."

Bless Siroko twice. Fala choked back a laugh — or was it a sob? — and locked the door.

The warm bath did much to restore her, and the dry clothes from Solana did more, even with her wet feathers. When she emerged, a warm bowl of soup finished the job. She told the helpful servant that she was making her way as a musician, and he promptly examined his schedule and assigned her a time to play during dinner. Until then, he assigned a young boy to show her around. At first, Fala let the boy lead her wherever he liked, but eventually she asked about the Kyveli captives.

The boy blinked. "What captives?"

Fala shrugged. "I suppose I assumed you have enemies, since you live in a fortress. Battles mean captives, sometimes, don't they? Dungeons or unassailable towers? It all sounds so exciting."

It all sounded terrible, but the more information she could gather, the better chance she had of rescuing Avari.

The boy frowned. "Sometimes, but the only dispute we have right now is with the Masielas, and that is no battle." He brightened. "Oh, we do have one hostage, I suppose. The youngest Masiela is staying with us to encourage his parents to keep their word. I suppose he's the closest we have to a prisoner, but he's kept in a nice room and comes for meals with the family. You'll see him then. He's not very exciting."

Trying to hide her excitement, Fala nodded and changed the subject to a weapons display on the wall.

A t dinner, Fala was seated at a lowly table across the room from the family. One of the side tables held guards in matching livery, except for one seat occupied by a dark-haired and handsome man wearing an unchained manacle on one ankle. Avari! He picked at his food and glared at everyone. He seemed uninjured, and his hands and bright blue wings were free.

Fala pursed her lips. He didn't seem in much danger. Though perhaps she didn't know the whole situation, and of course, losing one's freedom was a problem all by itself. Whatever the case, if he was trapped here, he couldn't fulfill his marriage contract with her.

Once she gulped her delicious meal, she was escorted to a corner near the main table so she could play while the family finished eating. Three small children sat between a lovely, pink-winged woman and a stocky man with maroon wings who looked utterly unremarkable except everyone jumped to obey his slightest whisper. This must be Zafrir, the man who held Fala's fate in his hands.

She took a deep breath and started with the first song on Siroko's list.

To her disappointment, no one seemed to notice her choice. She finished and moved to the second song, and the third. Still no reaction. But when she began the fourth song about heart's desire, the Kyveli lady smiled at her husband and twitched an eyebrow in Fala's direction. Zafrir smiled, turning from an unremarkable man into a very charming one, and winked at his wife.

Bless Siroko thrice. With a lighter heart, Fala worked through half her list, switching to other songs when Avari left with guards.

When the servant returned to escort her to a room, he passed on the thanks of the lord and lady.

Fala lay fully dressed in her bed in the male servants' barracks with a wisp of hope cautiously winding around her heart. Her dreams were once again of freedom.

I n the morning, she rose and went to the kitchen for breakfast, then volunteered to help with chores until it was time for her to play again.

With a peculiar look, the head servant asked if she would like to spin.

Without thinking, Fala made a face. Spinning was so boring. Even weeding was better, since it was out in the sunshine. Nonetheless, she should accommodate her hosts. She opened her mouth to accept the request, but the servant was already talking.

"Yes, that's what I thought. I told them they were being silly. Let me show you to the garden, then? Or would you prefer weapons practice?"

"The garden is fine," Fala said. Who was being silly? About what? As they passed the spinning room, she glanced in and saw only women, not even a single young boy helping with the carding or winding. Why would they ask her to spin if it was strictly a woman's task here?

Oh no. She gulped. Someone suspected her disguise. Had she done something in her sleep? Talked in her regular voice, perhaps? Fala squared her shoulders and tightened her jaw. She would have to be especially careful to look and sound like a man. Though they seemed to treat their hostage with kindness and were unlikely to harm her for her deception, she couldn't afford to be evicted before she rescued Avari. Or arrested and held captive with him, and then her parents would truly be helpless.

Fortunately, she was used to the hard labor of gardening, and she attacked the weeds with a hoe and all her energy, sure that while she worked, she would not look feminine.

At lunch, she played first and again saw Avari. She was still eating when he rose to leave, but she grabbed her bread and followed some distance behind the last guard. By feigning interest in the wall decorations, she trailed them long enough to locate the hall where he was imprisoned, but that was as close as she could get. A burly guard with sky-orange wings crossed his arms and glared at her until she turned around and left.

Fala spent her afternoon unloading supplies for the kitchen, thankful for the adversities that had hardened her muscles.

At dinner, she played the other half of Zafrir's favorite songs, and this time, he tapped his finger to the beat.

She slept in the same barracks as before, ignoring the speculative looks from some servants. *I'm a man,* she chanted mentally, *just an ordinary man. No need to look at me.* Grumbling in a low voice, she turned her back and pulled her blanket over her head.

T he third day, she walked to breakfast in a crowd of servants, male and female. Just outside the kitchen, the cook was cursing a deliveryman. The entire hallway was covered in dried peas. The women in front of Fala squealed and picked up their skirts to watch their feet. As they minced across the peas, the men stomped forward with their usual heavy tread.

As she reached the peas, Fala happened to glance at the cook, who was watching her with narrowed eyes. Not the other servants, just her. Ah, another test, then. What had she done to make them suspicious?

Fala let her gaze drift casually past the cook as she strode firmly on the peas, crushing them underfoot as the men did. As soon as breakfast was finished, she grabbed a hoe and escaped to the garden.

At lunch, she again played Zafrir's favorite songs, and he nodded at her as he left.

Though she frequently approached the corridor that held Avari, she could never get past the guards. While she chopped wood, she tried to determine which window was his from the outside, but she never saw him. Without more time to research and plan, she couldn't rescue him that way.

During dinner, Fala eavesdropped with great interest as Zafrir and his wife discussed Avari. It seemed that hostage or not, his family was not willing to fulfill their bargain. Their most recent letter invited Zafrir to keep Avari and consider it payment enough.

And what about the marriage contract? Did they plan to break that, too, or did they think Fala would join Avari in captivity? Neither of those would help her family. No, she had to free him, somehow.

What if Masiela House didn't keep the contract even if she freed Avari? No, they would, because they still wanted her family's land. As long as she had something they wanted, they would keep the bargain. Wouldn't they?

She had to believe it, or her family was already lost.

The Kyvelis, unsurprisingly, didn't find it satisfactory to support their prisoner forever.

"And we can't hang the mite-infested scoundrel," Zafrir muttered with a nasty look at Avari, who was dropping bits of unwanted food onto the floor.

Eventually, the discussion trailed into nothing, and after a final round of his favorite songs, Zafrir rose, his wife hanging on his arm.

"I wish to thank you for your playing, Marin," he said to Fala. "Do you plan to stay with us long?"

Fala squeezed her recorder and tried to sound unconcerned. "Not long, no."

"Too bad. I would love to add you to my household, kinsman."

His wife nodded encouragingly.

Fala touched the Kyveli crest on her shoulder and gathered her courage. This was her best chance to save Avari and her family. "I'm afraid I must leave, but if I have pleased you, I would ask a boon."

Zafrir raised an eyebrow. "You have lifted my cares from me for a few days. If your boon is reasonable, I will grant it. Do you want a purse? New clothes? A fine lute?"

"Thank you, sir, but I would most like a companion in my journeys. I'm afraid I get lonely as I travel."

Zafrir narrowed his eyes. "I will not send a woman with you. My trust only goes so far."

"Oh, no, sir," Fala blurted, stifling a laugh. "But — I heard you talking about your hostage. If — if you no longer want him, might he keep me company, instead?"

Zafrir stared, then threw back his head and laughed. When his wife tugged on his elbow, he calmed to a mere chuckle.

"You want my hostage?" he asked. "To drag him through a life of travel and hardship, hunger and work? Well, why not? He has proven useless at encouraging his family's integrity, and I certainly don't want to keep him. Yes, I agree. We will have him ready for you in the morning, whether he likes it or not." He waved his arm at a guard, who trotted away.

Fala nearly sagged with relief. "Thank you, sir. This means more to me than you know."

Zafrir snorted. "You might not be so grateful after a few days in his company. If you get tired of him, feel free to bring him back and stay with us."

He clasped Fala's arm firmly, then turned to deal with his impatient children. Fala nearly danced to bed, only restrained by the knowledge that she couldn't afford to let anyone suspect her more, not when she was so close to success.

In the morning, she arrived early for breakfast, then packed her things. She was all ready when the guards dragged Avari outside, whining and sagging in their hands.

The guards wrestled Avari into a pack, then locked a leather cord into his manacle and gave Fala the free end and the key. They loaded their crossbows and threatened to shoot Avari if he landed while still in their sight. Zafrir and his wife called "Good flight" as Fala and Avari flew away.

Fala concentrated on flying calmly, though she wanted to bolt at full speed. Soon, she could tell him he was free. To preserve her reputation, she couldn't tell him who she was until the journey ended. If nothing else, gratitude should make him keep his bargain with her family.

In a couple of weeks, they would both be home, and their wedding would proceed as planned. Her family would be saved. And as she and Avari grew to know each other, they might love each other, in time. If not, a steady framework of appreciation and hard work and companionship would make a good marriage.

Once out of sight of the fortress, Avari yanked on the leash and tried to free himself. Fala held on, but the leather tangled around her legs and she spiraled out of control. Still connected, Avari fell with her.

Desperately, Fala let go of the leash and let herself spin. The leather slid around her legs, burning through her pants, but it finally worked free. Fala snapped out her wings and grabbed for the leash at the same time. Her wings caught air, slowing her just enough for her to land heavily on her feet instead of her head. Avari jerked at the end of the leash, then landed roughly and stumbled to his knees.

"You idiot," Fala hissed. "What are you doing?"

Avari grabbed a stick from the ground and lunged at her. She danced back too slowly, and he stabbed her ankle.

"Ow," Fala howled. "Stop!"

"I've had enough of being a prisoner," Avari screamed, scrambling to his feet and yanking on the leash.

Fala let go. "I was freeing you, stupid!"

She limped back, hands held out to show she had no weapon. Broken feathers in black and bright blue littered the ground.

"I'll make you let me go," Avari screamed, then stopped and stared at the freed leather at his feet. "Freeing me? But why the leash, then?"

"So the Kyveli wouldn't suspect," she said. "Idiot."

Keeping one eye on him, she crouched to examine her ankle. It didn't seem broken, but blood was running into her boot. And it hurt more than anything had ever hurt her before.

"But aren't you a Kyveli?" He stared at the silver crest on her shoulder.

"No. I got this from... a friend and let them assume what they liked so I could rescue you." Fala removed the pin and tucked it in her pocket.

"Oh." Avari sagged, letting the stick fall. "So I can leave you now?"

"If you want. Do you know your way home?" Fala rummaged through her pockets, then pressed her handkerchief to the wound.

"Why would I know the way?" Avari asked. "I have people for that."

Fala snorted. "Then perhaps you shouldn't attack your guide." She tried to tie her handkerchief around her ankle, but it was too small.

Avari sighed loudly. "Here."

A large embroidered handkerchief appeared under Fala's nose. She took it, and after folding her own into a pad, tied his around the whole mess. It still hurt, but at least it wasn't ruining her boot anymore.

Fala picked up a few broken feathers, stood, and glared at Avari. "So, do you want me to take you home or not?"

"I should have a cook and half a dozen guards and—" He inhaled and then sighed. "Yes, I want to go home."

Please, Fala thought, but she let it pass. "Then let's get going."

"Aren't you forgetting something?" Avari asked, shaking the leash.

"I'll remove it when I'm convinced you can behave." As Fala sprang into the air, she thought she saw Avari stick out his tongue, but surely a grown man would be more mature.

Fala flew slowly for the rest of the day, pacing their flight by the number of complaints from Avari. Apparently, his best pace was about half as fast as she had come on her own, and she was no athlete. She couldn't tell if he *couldn't* fly so fast or if he just didn't want to. Even so, they reached her last inn stop shortly after dark.

As soon as she unlocked his leash, Avari marched to the largest, fanciest inn and demanded a room. The innkeeper told him the price, and Avari waved at Fala with a bored look on his face.

Face burning, Fala pulled him aside. "I have no money. You will need to pay."

"But, but—" Avari spluttered. "I have no money. I never carry my own funds."

Fala squeezed her eyes shut. "Do you trust me?"

"Why should I?" Avari asked.

"Do you have a better idea?"

Avari folded his arms and pouted.

"Then follow me." Fala led the way to a smaller inn down the street, though not the one she had stayed in before. She wished she could find Siroko to thank him for all his help, but Avari would certainly not let her talk to any Kyveli.

"Sit there and *be quiet*." She pointed at a chair in the corner and glared fiercely until Avari complied.

A few minutes of bargaining with the innkeeper led to sleeping space for both of them, though the second space took the place of dinner. All they had to eat was a bit of leftovers from the lunch the Kyvelis had sent with them. Breaking the news to Avari was more unpleasant than her empty belly, and she finally ordered him to be silent so his complaints wouldn't scare off her audience.

After her music shift, they rolled up in their blankets on the floor, and Fala went to sleep despite Avari's muttered curses and criticism.

In the morning, she had to shake Avari awake and drag him from the inn before he annoyed the servants with his comments. Once again, she helped a vendor set up his market stall in exchange for breakfast. It tasted fine to her, but Avari's acid commentary made it clear he felt abused.

She tried to increase their flight speed, but Avari trailed behind until she slowed again. He also insisted on rest breaks twice as often as she planned, and every time they stopped, he wanted to eat. Fala did her best to find edibles, but feeding *one* was hard enough. Most of the time, she gave him the food and went hungry herself.

Even that didn't spare her from his whining. He complained about everything. His wings were tired. He was hungry. His family didn't love him. He had been cruelly imprisoned and held in terrible circumstances.

Fala barely hid her scoff. Even at the servants' level, the Kyveli fortress had been very comfortable.

And then Avari told her about his arranged betrothal. "My family is making me do it," he protested. "I don't want an ugly girl, but they want her land. It's not fair."

No, Fala thought, not fair for anyone. She tightened her lips and ignored the pang of his insults. Perhaps she wasn't actually ugly, but she was plain, and he felt no love to blind him to her faults.

"Why did you agree then?" she asked.

"I'm tired of living under my parents' wings. I want my own house and my own life."

"What about your new wife? Won't she be part of your life?"

Avari snorted. "She'll have her own room and her own servants. I won't have to look at the ugly thing."

Fala choked back a gasp. Her ankle wound was suddenly only the second most painful experience in her life. She knew she wasn't Avari's first choice but hadn't realized he hated her. He didn't even *know* her. Unfortunately, she didn't see a way to escape the contract. If the Masielas were willing to sacrifice their own son to an unwanted marriage, they certainly wouldn't care about her feelings.

"I never want to see her," Avari continued. "She didn't come rescue me when I wrote to her."

"What did you expect her to do?" Fala blurted. "One woman, alone."

"That's not *my* problem," Avari said. "My problem was the Kyvelis, and she didn't care enough to help me."

Fala flew in silence for the rest of the day, though Avari continued to complain.

4. HOMEWARD
(AKASHA, IOJ)

When they arrived home, he censured her for abandoning him, not realizing who saved him.
The Legend of the Flute Player

At nightfall, she found shelter and food for them in the tiny temple of an equally tiny village with no inn. The fresh bread tasted wonderful to her, but Avari loudly protested the lack of butter and honey or meat.

After another day of flying, Fala realized they would reach Solana's house by evening. The woman would surely give them shelter, if Fala was willing to submit her friends to Avari's poor manners. While she was still debating, they flew over the house, and Esen flew up to meet them.

"I thought I recognized those black wings," he called. "Come for dinner. Solana and Aerilyn will be overjoyed to see you again."

Before Fala could think of an excuse to decline, Avari flew after Esen, and she could only follow.

The entire household ran outside when Esen bellowed the news of their arrival. Fala was embraced and welcomed until her ears rang. When she finally got free, she discovered Avari watching sulkily, though Esen stood politely nearby, introducing him to everyone.

"You're just in time for dinner." Solana took Fala's arm and urged her inside.

After a quick wash of hands and face and a brush-off of their clothing, everyone sat to a generous meal, nearly a feast to Fala's shrunken stomach. Avari gulped his food without a word of thanks and grabbed seconds and thirds without waiting for them to be passed to him. Fala hoped she had misheard his mutters about households improperly headed by women instead of men. Everyone certainly heard his complaints about the way "Marin" had botched his rescue and treated him badly.

Solana ignored Avari's bad manners and spoke kindly to Fala. "Did you accomplish your mission, then?" Her gaze flickered to Avari, but she kept smiling.

"Yes," Fala said, "and I thank you again for your help."

"It was little enough to repay you for saving my daughter."

"How could a weakling like him save anyone?" Avari said.

Solana frowned at him. "He saved you, it seems." She turned to smile at Fala. "Now that you are free, I will renew my offer." She left it thankfully vague as she refilled Fala's glass.

Fala shook her head with regret. As much as she would like to join Solana's household, she could not abandon her parents or break her marriage contract.

Avari belched and raised his hands. "I'm inviting you all to my wedding in a month." He beamed at everyone and bowed his head regally.

"That... is thoughtful." Solana raised her eyebrows and glanced at Fala, who winced.

"Yes, isn't it?" Avari grinned and stood. "Now, where's my bed?"

Esen narrowed his eyes, but at a finger twitch from Solana, he led Avari from the table.

"And do you wish to stay in his room?" Solana asked Fala.

Fala set down her fork carefully. "No, thank you. I'm satisfied with the cot in the kitchen."

Solana nodded as a small smile curved the corners of her mouth.

Everyone continued eating and talking, and Fala gradually relaxed in the companionship despite the perpetual cloud of her upcoming marriage. By the time the others left and she took a hot bath and rolled into bed, she felt happier than she had in months — years, perhaps.

When Fala woke, it was late morning. She had somehow slept through the early bread-making, and hot loaves now steamed temptingly on the counter. Breakfast was fresh fruit, scrambled eggs, and hot bread with honey, served by Aerilyn's small hands and accompanied by the little girl's proud smile.

They chatted sweetly as Fala ate, and she gave the girl a black feather as a memento. She offered one of Avari's pretty blue ones, but Aerilyn turned up her nose. By the time Avari stumbled out of bed and demanded food, Fala was cheerful again. Even the discovery that her wings and presumably her hair had faded another shade couldn't depress her mood.

Fala and Avari left soon afterward, food supplies replenished, and whenever Avari complained again, particularly about his unwanted marriage and ugly bride-to-be, Fala retreated to her newest pleasant memories.

That night, Fala again bargained for shelter at an inn, including a small dinner to preserve their travel food. By the time she finished her shift, Avari had vanished. Upon questioning a server, she learned he had gone upstairs with a woman of questionable habits.

Well, Fala wouldn't drag him out of *that* mess. He could deal with his own problems. She slept soundly without his snores and mutters in her ear, and woke early enough to charm her own breakfast from the innkeeper.

By the time Avari staggered downstairs, reeking of alcohol and stale perfume, Fala was ready to leave. Fortunately for her, his sour stomach kept him from asking for breakfast until their first rest break, when he had to be satisfied with cold sausage and cheese.

Their pace continued to be twice as slow as Fala's trip out, and it was four more days before she saw Sahali's horse pastures below them. Again she debated the wisdom of introducing Avari to her new friends, and again the choice was taken from her. At the sight of the large house, Avari spiraled down and landed on the front lawn, bellowing for the master of the house.

To Fala's great embarrassment, he overrode Sahali's warm welcome with demands for food and shelter for the night. Though Sahali furrowed his brow and compressed his lips, he invited both of them to stay.

Avari commandeered a fine room and demanded a bath and a meal in his room. Sahali complied silently, then showed Fala to a room overlooking his horses.

"But I do hope you will join me for dinner?" he asked.

"Gladly, as soon as I clean up a little." When Sahali turned to call a servant to prepare a bath, Fala assured him, "No, a basin of water will do. No need to worry about me."

She washed her face and hands, beat the dust from her clothes, and brushed her hair thoroughly before joining Sahali. They had a quiet meal by a large window where they could watch the sunset throw blue fingers across the apricot sky before the blue darkened to purple and then black. By the time the stars sprang to life, Fala couldn't hide her yawns anymore, and her friend walked her to her room.

Unfortunately, Avari came to breakfast. Though Sahali sang Fala's praises and told how she had saved him and his horses, Avari countered every accolade with a complaint about the way he had been treated. Eventually, Sahali fell silent and let Avari grump unopposed.

As Fala and Avari prepared to leave, Sahali clasped her shoulder. "Let me know if I can do anything to help you."

"You can help *me*," Avari said. "In one month, come to my wedding to celebrate my freedom." After rattling off the details, he added, "My bride is ugly, but I will feed you well to compensate for the sight." He slapped Sahali on the back and sprang into the air.

"I'm sorry," Fala whispered.

Sahali sighed. "As am I, my friend. Come visit again when you are no longer needed to guide that one."

The marriage contract meant she would never be free of Avari, but Fala nodded. She spread her wings and flew after Avari, heart so heavy she wondered how the air could hold her up.

Their journey home took another week, and every day was a misery. Avari made enemies wherever he went, and Fala was heartily sick of apologizing for him. When she finally delivered him to his parents' house, she nearly danced with relief.

"I've decided you deserve a reward," Avari announced grandly.

"I—" she started, but he kept talking.

"You, too, may come to my wedding." He smiled broadly and clapped her on the back. "Everyone knows when and where it is."

And before she could think of a proper reply — any kind of reply — he disappeared into his house. Shouts echoed through the windows, though they seemed more surprised than happy.

Anxious to reassure her own parents, Fala flew away before anyone could stop her with thanks. Unless they were all like Avari, in which case waiting for thanks was useless.

But as soon as she entered her own house, her parents fell into her arms, weeping with joy.

Home, she was home. If only she never had to leave again.

After swearing her parents and the cook to secrecy, she told them the whole story, including how badly Avari had behaved on the way home. Her father wept, and her mother threatened to go punch Avari.

"You can't," Fala said wearily. "I still have to marry him."

"We'll break the contract," Mother fumed.

"Then what? We'll be out of food before winter ends, or faster if he takes me to court."

"He said he will lock you in your room," Mother complained.

"He was supposed to save you from poverty, not imprison you," Father said.

Fala shrugged. "At least I know what I'm getting into now. A month ago, I would have been caught off-guard and heartbroken."

"It's still not fair," Mother muttered.

No, not fair at all, but what choice did she have?

Fala and her family spent the next month washing the dye from her wings and hair and applying creams to her wind-chapped skin. Though they could do nothing about the length of her hair, they changed the cut to be more feminine and hunted through the remnants of her mother's jewelry box for any hair ornaments too worthless to have been sold.

Every day, Fala considered running away, but without some way to support her family, her parents would starve. Her impending marriage approached like an unavoidable tornado, and her panic rose daily.

The fatal day arrived much too soon. All morning, Mother and the cook fussed with Fala's once-again-brown hair and her fluffy orange dress and veil. As they worked, Fala played with the ceremonial fan. Absent-mindedly, she worked the broken feathers from her trip into the back of the fan where she would be the only one to see them during the ceremony. The black and bright blue contrasted starkly with the wedding orange and white.

"There, you're ready." Mother stepped back and tilted the mirror so Fala could see.

Even in the finery, Fala was homely. She closed her eyes and pressed a hand to her aching chest. For the rest of her life, she would be Avari's ugly wife, useless and unwanted. Dressed or not, she was definitely not ready, but she had no more time. For comfort, she slipped Sahali's ring and Siroko's silver crest into her pocket, then added Avari's newly washed handkerchief to return to him. Once the wedding was over, it would be too late for him to argue about her reputation, and since he already hated her, the revelation would make no difference to her fate.

Her hands shook. No matter what she did, her husband would lock her in her room. How was her sham of a marriage a fair reward for rescuing Avari? All by herself, she had saved him, and for what? So her parents would be safe. That was what mattered. And really, being separated from Avari was better than being around him every day.

After another glance in the mirror, she whirled for her closet and retrieved Solana's orange vest.

"If we cover the crest, may I wear this over my dress? Please?"

She had once been brave and competent, and if she wore the vest, perhaps she could make herself remember it.

"But your pretty dress," the cook protested.

Mother raised a hand. "It's well cut and prettily sewn, but it's a man's vest, Fala. It would ruin what figure you have."

Fala slipped it on and buttoned only the bottom button so the top of the vest curved around her small bosom.

"Like this, perhaps?" She pressed her quivering lips tightly. "Please? It's the right color." She squared her shoulders. Brave and competent.

Mother sighed and reached for the jewelry box. "I suppose we could pin our own crest over the embroidery."

The adjustment took far too little time, and within minutes, they had collected Father and left the house.

Their small procession walked down the street to the temple where her groom would meet them. With every step, Fala yearned for freedom. At the side door, she waited outside while her parents and the cook entered.

The door closed, and Fala waited, breath growing short. She had saved Avari, but where was her own salvation?

The music started, and the door opened. Across the temple, another door swung wide to reveal Avari, resplendent in his fancy orange garb and bright blue wings.

Fala choked off a sob and stepped forward to her doom, fan shaking in her hands. The far side of the temple was full of the Masiela family, servants, and friends. On her side, her parents tried to smile at her from the row in front of Fala's new friends. Arms folded, Sahali watched silently next to a few from his household. Solana sat in the middle of her family and frowned, shaking her head almost imperceptibly. She probably agreed with Avari's opinion of his ugly wife. And why not?

Gaze fastened on Fala, Solana tapped her upper chest, then bent her fingers toward herself. Oddly, the gesture looked like she was summoning Fala. Oh, wouldn't that be nice? Fala would much rather go home with Solana than marry Avari, but she had to fulfill the contract. For her parents, she could do this.

An idea hit Fala so hard she stumbled. Was the contract open to one change? As she approached the altar, matching her steps to Avari's, she thought furiously, staring at the black and blue feathers on the back of her fan. She pressed her elbows against the orange vest. Brave and competent.

Bride and groom reached the middle and turned to face the priest, a fourth-rank Tempest in honor of the prominent Masiela family. As Avari puffed out his chest, the Tempest opened his mouth to start the ceremony.

"Wait," Fala blurted.

The audience gasped. Avari turned toward her, eyes wide. The priest's eyebrows rose, and he closed his mouth with a snap.

Fala straightened her shoulders under the weight of all the stares. "I don't want to marry Avari."

Indignation and insult twisted Avari's face into something ugly. "I don't want you, either, but we have a *contract*," he hissed under his breath. "The only thing you should say today is yes."

Fala slapped the fan on the altar, black and blue side showing. "I saved you when no one else would, and in return, I want my freedom."

Avari turned purple and shouted, "That wasn't you. A *man* saved me, and he had black feathers, not brown. You could have picked up that feather in the street." He lowered his voice to an angry whisper. "Now shut up and stop embarrassing me. When I get you home, I'll teach you to behave properly."

Not a chance. She wouldn't take lessons from someone so ill-mannered, and she wouldn't agree to this marriage.

"I have witnesses," Fala said. "I can prove my story."

Solana jumped to her feet. "I will witness for her. I recognize her as Marin, who saved my daughter from drowning and brought Avari to my house." She tapped her chest again, emphatically.

Fala finally realized what she was saying and removed her own House pin to reveal Solana's embroidered crest beneath it. How Solana had already recognized her, she didn't know, but the question must wait until later.

"Solana's brother gave me this vest," she said.

Esen rose. "I confirm it was my vest."

Avari spluttered, and half his family jumped to their feet to protest. Fala's parents leaned forward anxiously.

From her pocket, Fala took the ring and held it toward Sahali, speaking louder than the crowd. "Will you identify this as the ring you gave the person you knew as Marin?"

With a half-smile, Sahali came forward and minutely examined it. "This is indeed the ring I gave my friend Marin after he saved me from robbers." He patted Fala on the shoulder before he returned to his seat.

"All lies," Avari protested. "I don't know how you bribed them, but my rescuer was disguised as a Kyveli."

Fala took the silver crest from her pocket. "You mean I wore this?"

"Coincidence," Avari said, but his shoulders hunched. "None of this is real proof."

Fala shook out the handkerchief. "You gave me this yourself when I rescued you from the Kyveli fortress."

Avari turned purple again. "How did you steal that?"

He lunged, and Fala stepped backwards.

"I have more proof," she said.

Avari spluttered incoherently, waving his arms in frustration.

The priest waved Avari to silence. "You interest me, daughter. Go ahead."

"Will you please ask Avari where he stabbed his rescuer?"

The priest flinched. "He stabbed his rescuer? That hardly seems proper thanks."

He turned to Avari, who looked side to side, obviously trying to decide if the truth or a lie would serve him better. Hoping he would fall for the ruse, Fala rubbed her elbow as if it ached.

Avari grinned. "I admit I stabbed my rescuer, but it was a misunderstanding. And I hit his *ankle*."

Fala slipped off her low boot and raised her skirt a few inches. "There is the scar from Avari wounding me."

Everyone leaned forward to look. The priest bent and examined her ankle closely. When he stood straight again, everyone held their breath to listen.

"I can confirm the wound," the Tempest said.

"No," Avari howled. "He was a *man*."

"You spent the entire trip complaining about your ugly bride," Fala said, "and how you had to marry her for the sake of her land. You told me in detail how you planned to lock her in her room after the wedding and never look at her again."

The crowd gasped, and the priest frowned. The Masiela family glared at Avari, who stared in open-mouthed shock at Fala.

"You?" he croaked. "But you're just a woman."

Fala clenched her shaking hands and addressed the priest. "I can't — I won't marry him. I know we have a contract, and I'm willing to make a small adjustment to it. If the Masiela family gives me the amount that would have been my dower, they can still have the land and the house. I will take my family elsewhere."

She glanced at her parents, who shrugged. Behind them, Solana smiled and nodded. On either side of her, Aerilyn bounced on the seat and Esen grinned. Fala had no doubt the invitation would include her parents and their cook. No one would starve in her friend's house.

Ashen-faced, Avari glanced at his family. His father nodded firmly, jaw clenched and eyes narrowed.

"Fine," Avari blurted. "But you will need to remove your family yourself. We won't help you."

His father covered his eyes and shook his head.

"Agreed," Fala said. "I'm sure I can hire a cart and horse."

In the audience, Sahali waved a finger and smiled.

Avari glared at her. "And you need to be gone in a week."

His relatives groaned, but Fala merely nodded. The furniture would mostly stay behind, and they had very little left to pack.

Avari folded his arms and sulked.

The Tempest unrolled the marriage contract on the altar and read through it, occasionally drawing a line through clauses.

After a few minutes, he gave the pen to Fala. "If you would sign again, please."

After checking the changes, she signed with a flourish and held the pen toward Avari. He glared at her and refused to take it until his father prodded his arm. While Avari signed, scratching so hard he tore the paper, Fala's father approached for his turn. After him, Avari's father signed, making it all final.

Fala's wings twitched with the urge to fly. Mere gravity had no chance to hold her now.

She kissed the priest on his cheeks. "Thank you."

Avari snatched the modified fan from the altar and tore it in half before his family marched him toward the opposite door.

Fala danced from the temple with her parents. As the door closed, she pulled her family in for a hug.

"We did it," she said. "We're free."

Free from an egotistical idiot and an unwanted marriage. She was still brave and competent, even in her stupid fluffy dress.

"But what do we do now?" Father asked.

"We'll figure it out," Mother said.

Fala squeezed them tighter. "I already know."

The door opened again, and a stream of people exited, laughing and babbling. While most of them walked down the street or flew away, two joined Fala's family.

"I can bring you a horse in a few days," Sahali said. "That will give you time to pack."

"That's perfect, my friend." Fala clasped his arm, then slid his ring onto her finger. With no need to hide anything now, she was free to be herself and do as she pleased.

"My invitation is still open," Solana said hopefully.

Fala wrapped an arm around the woman's shoulder. "I saw that in the temple, and I accept."

Solana whooped and threw her arms in the air. Nearby, Esen and Aerilyn cheered.

Overflowing with happiness, Fala tilted her face to the warm sunshine. Now this was a lovely day. With her family now safe and settled, perhaps she would have time to decide what she really wanted from life.

If you like this story, you might like the traditional Earth fairytales:
The Lute Player
The Canary Prince
The Twelve Huntsmen
Kupti and Imani
The Hoodie-Crow

FATED

1. PROPHECY
(VASI, IOJ)

Upon hearing the destiny of his daughter, he vowed to change it.
The Legend of the King Who Hated Fate

I rajahan, the Almighty God of Air, leaned over the crib set at the back of the glittering throne room. "Isn't she beautiful?"

The king and queen of Ioj beamed at him as he cooed at their daughter, Hasana. Their royal finery gleamed with silk and jewels in colors that complemented their feathered wings. Even so, they were outshone by their immortal guests, whom they watched anxiously.

"She looks like every infant," Resef rumbled softly. The God of Fire let the newborn clutch his pale finger.

"She is beautiful." The Goddess of Earth nudged her brother, then touched the baby's curls. With her brown skin and ash blonde hair, Darravani looked entirely the opposite of the tiny girl, whose dark hair contrasted her soft peach skin.

Makanavailea laughed. "I approve of the pink wings." The Goddess of Water smoothed her own pink and purple dress and tossed her rainbow-striped hair over her bare golden shoulder.

Irajahan sneered at her. "I don't need your approval, Makana." His flighty sister never had any opinions worth the air they took to express.

"I was just thinking what a beautiful queen she will make," she said. "Her pink wings next to her husband's gray and black."

Irajahan frowned. "Hasana is not betrothed."

"Oh, certainly not yet," Makana agreed. "They're only babies, after all. And his parents' farm is too far away."

"Farm?" Irajahan blurted. "My favorite great-great-great-great—" He tried to count the generations on his fingers and gave up. "My granddaughter won't marry a peasant!"

The king and queen gasped and leaned toward their daughter as if a threatening peasant might appear from nowhere.

Makana shrugged one shoulder and tickled the baby. "I am the Omniscient. But if you don't want details, I won't bother you with them."

And he was the Omnipotent, Irajahan fumed. No one told him what to do.

After a moment of thought, he forced a smile to his lips. "Please, tell me more. Where can I find this boy?"

Resef's eyebrow twitched, and Darravani pressed her lips together. They both looked at Makana.

Makana winked at them, then smiled at Irajahan. "I'd be happy to."

Irajahan smirked. Of course she would — everyone was always happy to do what he asked.

His two oldest siblings said their farewells and left, then Makana told Irajahan where to find the boy and how to identify him. He thanked her graciously, forcing the words past the bile in his throat.

When she dove off the high cliffs into her ocean below, Irajahan reassured the king and queen that he would take care of everything. Spreading his mirror-bright wings, he sprang into the air and headed for the farm.

When he arrived, he found the farmer and his wife in the fields, plowing and sowing with five children in tow. Five! Did they think they were ducks? A basket sat at the edge of a field, and inside was yet another child, a tiny infant with black-striped gray wings and black hair. And *this* boring thing was supposed to marry his darling descendent? Not a chance.

He slapped on a smile and marched toward the farmers, spreading his arms in greeting. "Fair winds!"

He patted a toddling urchin on the head, then slipped his hand behind his back to wipe it on his robe. Ugh. He'd have to burn his clothing when he got home.

The farmers dropped to their knees, as they should. "Fair winds, My Lord Omnipotent," the man stammered. "What brings you here?"

"You have such beautiful children. How do you feed them all?"

The farmer's wife blushed. "We work very hard, Almighty."

"Mmm, indeed. Well, let me make your life easier. I'm looking for a boy to raise in the palace, and you seem to have plenty. With one fewer, the food will stretch farther, yes? I'll take the littlest one; he's too young to help you work." He dusted his hands together and beamed at them.

"Oh, no, Omnipotence," the farmer said. "We love our children and want to keep them *all*."

Irajahan frowned. "Nonsense. What kind of love lets your children starve?"

"But we aren't starving," the wife said, head bowed low.

"Not *yet*," Irajahan growled. He sent power into the sky, and the pale apricot darkened to rust as clouds rushed over the farm. Thunder rolled, and lightning cracked. "But what if your crop failed? We wouldn't want to risk your children."

The peasants flattened themselves to the freshly tilled earth, gray and black feathers quaking. "No, Almighty."

Irajahan relaxed his grip on the storm. "But no need to worry. Let me take your youngest son, and I will give you enough gold to feed the rest of your family for years. I promise to take care of him."

Tears in their eyes, the farmer and his wife poured kisses on their infant son. They packed a few of his things around him and handed the basket to Irajahan.

He sprang into the sky, arms full of a baby whose life would change this day.

Once out of sight, he swooped low over the river and dropped the basket.

"Oh, no," he cried. "My hands slipped! Poor baby! What have I done?"

That would take care of *that* peasant. He would never grow up to sully Irajahan's beautiful princess.

Irajahan would send a servant with a double portion of gold to the farmers and explain about the terrible, terrible accident.

He wouldn't tell Makana anything. If she was so Omniscient, she could discover it for herself.

For the next twenty years, Irajahan secretly gloated whenever he saw Hasana Senjyor. Even though she would never know, he had protected her from Makana's evil declaration. His power would always beat her professed knowledge. After all, this wasn't the first time he had tricked her.

The lovely baby grew into a gorgeous young woman, and before he quite realized how the years had flown, it was time to arrange a marriage. Irajahan and her parents, the king and queen, invited prominent young men from all across Ioj to come meet the princess. But months passed, and no one caught her interest.

To distract himself from the infuriating waiting, Irajahan started eavesdropping on his officials. Though he had trained his people to handle everything without bothering him, he periodically reminded them they worked for *him*. He listened to his priests chatter, he monitored the courts, and he snooped on the king and queen. It was all very boring, but if he turned invisible, the hum of conversation made a good background for a nap.

One afternoon, a loud wail interrupted his sleep in the courtroom. He stretched and yawned, then dropped his invisibility to see if the chaos was interesting enough to fend off boredom for a few minutes.

At the front of the room, the priest serving as judge leaned back from the old woman kneeling at his feet.

"But he is innocent," she cried, "and my only son. If you put him in prison, I will have no one to tend my garden and herd my goats. I will die!" Her pale blue wings fluttered unevenly, and her brown eyes filled with tears.

Behind the old woman, a young man stood between guards, his lapis-blue gaze fixed on his mother. His hair was black instead of the red-blonde showing among his mother's gray, and his wings were gray with black stripes.

Gray and black! And though they were common colors, the young man looked nothing like the old woman.

Irajahan jerked to his feet and strode forward. "You say he is your son, but surely you are too old to be his mother. Why, he is a mere stripling, eighteen at most." He held his breath and hoped.

"Twenty, Almighty." The young man bowed low.

A clap of thunder sounded in the clear sky, and Irajahan tightened his self-control as panic swirled.

Tears ran down the ugly, wrinkled cheeks of the woman. "He is my adopted son, My Lord Omnipotent. I found him as an infant, floating on the river in a broken basket. I thought I saw someone else in the water, but when I reached the bank, nobody was there and the basket was flooding. If I had not rescued him, he would have drowned."

Then this was the infant from Makana's prophecy! His meddling sister must have saved him! Irajahan ground his teeth. Unbelievable! "How unfortunate."

She nodded vigorously. "Yes, wouldn't it have been? So I took him in. I found his name written in his shirt and tried to find his parents, but nobody in the area was missing an Arcelio, and I'm afraid I can't reach all of Ioj. But please, Omnipotence, release him! Our neighbors lied because they want my land, small though it is, and know that if my son is gone, I must sell. He is innocent. I beg you, help us!"

Irajahan clenched his fists behind his back. If only he could execute the boy! He snatched the court notes and read through them. The entire case rested on the testimony of the neighbors, with no actual evidence the boy was involved. Even if they were telling the truth, it was a matter of theft and vandalism, not worthy of death.

He glanced at the judge, who had leaned forward and was patting the crone's hand on his knee. Then her pleas had softened the court's heart — or judgment — and if Irajahan ruled against the boy, he would be seen as a tyrant. But neither did he wish to turn the boy loose.

Irajahan forced a smile and spread his mirror-bright wings. "Since the truth of this case can't be determined, the court chooses a middle path of mercy and repentance. The boy shall serve me for a year, and half his wages shall go to the neighbors. At the end of a year, he may return to his mother."

By the end of a year, Irajahan would no longer have a problem. He might have failed once, but he would win in the end.

The old woman threw herself at his feet, weeping. "Thank you, merciful Omnipotence."

The upstart knelt in proper respect. "Thank you. I will serve you well."

Irajahan shook himself free and escaped for a nice flight above the palace, winging between the lightning strikes he could not aim at his annoying sister.

When he finally landed, he commanded the king and queen to send their daughter far away, under the pretext of meeting young men who could not make it to the capital city. Once he got rid of the nuisance boy, he would summon her back and see her married to someone worthy.

He assigned the boy to the army, hoping a training accident would take care of him.

A month later, the captain sent Irajahan a glowing report of the twit's courage and natural talent, suggesting he should train as an officer.

Irajahan replied, agreeing it was a possibility, but the young man should prove himself first. Perhaps the captain should send him on a challenging mission and see if he was resourceful enough to accomplish it. Then they could discuss a promotion. He suggested the most dangerous mission he knew and sealed the letter in triumph.

In a few weeks, the captain wrote again. *Arcelio not only accomplished the main goal of the mission, he surpassed expectations. Then the modest young man sent the reward to his mother and went back to work. His troop favors him, and indeed, so do I. Now, if My Lord Omnipotent agrees, is an excellent time to take advantage of his skills and promote him so he won't want to leave at the end of the year.*

Irajahan ground his teeth. Obviously, he couldn't trust anyone else to take care of his problems. He replied, pressing the quill pen hard enough to scratch the parchment. Certainly, the captain could promote the twit — er, the amazing young man. In fact, assign him to serve around the temple, as a sign of favor.

That would give Irajahan more opportunities to — *reward* him properly. He sent the letter and started plotting.

His first chance occurred a month later, when he was sitting on the temple roof enjoying the breeze rustling his feathers. Arcelio walked around the corner and stood below, talking to a fellow guard. Irajahan dug at one of the slate tiles until it came loose. With a scraping clatter, the tile slid to the edge and fell off.

Irajahan rushed to look down. "Oh, no," he called. "Watch out below!"

Two guards looked up at him, standing on either side of the broken shingle.

"No harm done." Arcelio waved graciously. "I'll send the roofers to check for any other problems." He clapped his companion on the shoulder and flew away.

Irajahan flopped on the roof and sulked. Was it impossible for the boy to stand still for a few seconds?

Well, if he couldn't catch him off-guard while he was awake, Irajahan would have to make other arrangements.

He waited until a natural storm blew in a week later, then paced the roof until night fell. When the last light flickered out, he stretched his power into the cloud and redirected the next lightning bolt, just a little. It struck the middle of the guard barracks with a thunderous crack. Within minutes, smoke drifted gently from the shingles.

Irajahan grinned and went to bed.

In the morning, he dressed in a boring robe and appeared in public ready to sorrow for the lost lives. To his surprise, the city hummed with gossip and laughter. An ash-streaked crowd was already hard at work, tearing down the burned barracks and cleaning the debris. No bodies lay in the street. No one was crying. Half-dressed soldiers directed the efforts.

And Arcelio was helping! Though his uniform was ashy and spotted with burns, it was neatly buttoned. Even his hair was finger-combed.

Irajahan clenched his fists and glared.

The guard captain rushed to him. "Don't worry, Almighty. We can rebuild the barracks, and we lost no soldiers. Thanks to Arcelio, we even have few injuries. Everyone will be back to work within a week."

He continued gushing about Arcelio's courage and alertness, explaining in far too much detail how the oaf had woken at the scent of smoke and hurried everyone from the building.

"Even when the fire was burning the walls, he returned to the barracks again and again until every guard was rescued, dragging the last of them over his shoulders. And he won't take credit for it, claiming someone woke him and warned him of the fire, though no one will admit to doing so."

Irajahan clenched his fists. Someone warned him of the fire? It must have been Resef, interfering where he had no right!

The captain kept babbling. "What a modest hero! How lucky we are to have him in the guard! How wise of you to recruit him!"

Irajahan folded his arms across his stomach to stop himself from vomiting. "Yes, yes, wonderful," he muttered.

"I decided to save time and send the reward directly to his mother," the captain continued.

Irajahan almost punched the smug smile from the captain's face, but then his ongoing nausea gave him another idea. "Yes, indeed. I, too, shall reward him. I know you guards live on basic fare, so I'll have a feast sent from the temple."

The captain bowed low, wings spread. "An excellent gesture, Almighty."

Irajahan walked through the crowd, encouraging everyone who was helping. He congratulated Arcelio through gritted teeth, then flew home to speak to the temple cook.

When the feast was ready, Irajahan packed it in a basket with his own hands, subtly adding his own slow-acting ingredients. He included a congratulatory letter and sent the package with a servant.

Two hours later, the basket returned to the kitchen, plates scraped clean and a thank you note tucked in with the utensils. Irajahan went for a long flight to celebrate his hard-earned success, happy that the nuisance would be dead by the time he landed.

While flying over the city the next day, he spotted a familiar pair of gray and black wings. With a tornado ripping through his heart, he thumped down beside Arcelio and greeted him with a smile.

"And how did you enjoy your feast?" he asked.

Arcelio turned red and rubbed his toe on the cobblestones. "Sorry, Almighty. A hungry dog approached as I was unpacking the food, and I couldn't stand his pitiful eyes. I'm afraid I gave it all to the poor beast. But I thank you for the honor." He bowed low and stayed that way until Irajahan flew away.

Lightning sparked in Irajahan's veins. It seemed this needed a personal touch. He couldn't be seen to be involved, but there were other ways. And considering the unnatural luck of the fool, perhaps he should make doubly sure.

Back at his temple, he wrote two letters. The first addressed his favorite governor in the far north. Though he was too crude to rule in the civilized southern provinces, he was unfailingly loyal to Irajahan and knew how to keep a secret.

His hand shook with glee as he wrote. *Behead the messenger who brings this letter, secretly and at once. Ask no questions and tell no one. Irajahan.* He sealed it and sent it to the barracks with instructions to have Arcelio deliver it to the far north.

He would have to deliver the second letter himself, dropping it into a certain bandit's den that lay on the way to the northern province. *The messenger with black and gray wings carries a fortune.*

With a little luck, the bandits would take care of the upstart. If that failed, then the governor would take care of Irajahan's problem.

2. DESTINY

(FAR NORTH, IOJ)

Three mysterious strangers helped the boy.
The Legend of the King Who Hated Fate

A rcelio buckled his pack between his wings and patted his chest pocket where the letter lay hidden. Irajahan had promised a special bonus if he delivered the message safely, and Mother could use the gold to hire help until he returned. Though her letters to him were always optimistic, he could tell she was having a hard time. Both of them could hardly wait until his year of punishment was finished.

The letter was confidential, for the eyes of the governor only, and Irajahan warned him that if he tried to open it, he'd be struck by lightning. As if Arcelio would be so dishonorable.

The trip would be long, but his wings were swift, and he carried plenty of supplies. Though he wouldn't offend his fellow guards by saying so, it was a relief to spend time alone after months in the crowded, noisy barracks. Mother's goats were never so chaotic.

He patted his pocket again, then spread his wings and flew. The wind ruffled his hair as the fancy buildings dwindled to miniature below him. After circling the city to gain height, he turned northward, ready to fly all day at this pace.

At nightfall, he stopped at a small inn and paid for a room and two meals. Dinner was filling, though bland compared to palace fare. After sleeping on a thin, hard cot, Arcelio woke anxious to leave.

After a quick breakfast of hot eggs and toast, he thanked the innkeeper and left. The next two days were similar, but on the fourth day, he couldn't find an inn and had to beg shelter from an old woman.

"I'm sorry," she said, "but you shouldn't stay here. Bandits live nearby. They don't bother me because I have nothing worth taking and am too frail to be a danger to them, but you wouldn't be safe."

Arcelio smiled warmly and offered her money, though not enough to rouse suspicion when she spent it. "Please, just for the night. I'll leave early, and you needn't feed me."

The old woman's hands quivered, and she reached for the coins. "You can stay in the goat shed, if you like."

"I like goats." He patted her hands and headed out back.

The goat shed was old and creaky, but hay lined the walls for extra warmth. Arcelio scrounged a few bent nails from the ground and reinforced the most rickety spots, then ate some bread and cheese from his pack and curled up with both goats. With all of them together, the shed stayed warm enough.

Shaking woke him suddenly in the middle of night. The goats baaed and scattered, and he crawled from the rattling shed as quickly as possible.

"Help," someone called, and more voices echoed the plea.

Arcelio tried to get to his feet, but the ground shook again, knocking him flat. When the earthquake finally stopped, he staggered upright and ran for the old woman's shack. To his surprise, she was already outside and uninjured, struggling to light a lamp with shaking hands.

"You need to go now," she urged. "Don't wait for morning."

"Help," someone called again.

Arcelio scanned the area, thankful the large moon was full, but he could still see nothing. "Nonsense. You can't help whoever that is by yourself."

"Go," the old woman said. "You mustn't be here when they get free."

"Who? Free from what?" Arcelio took the lamp and the coil of rope from her shoulder and headed toward the cries for help.

"Go!" She nearly wept as she hobbled after him.

"How can I leave them in danger?" he asked, but her frown remained.

Not far from the house, they found a new gully, broken edges still crumbling. Somehow, the earthquake had split the ground so the ravine was wide at the bottom but narrow at the top. Twenty feet down, a dozen or so men tried to climb the overhanging sides, only to retreat when the slope leaned backwards. One flew to the top, but the opening was too narrow for wing strokes, and he had to land again.

Arcelio dropped to the ground and carefully leaned over the edge. "Don't worry; I'll get you out. Give me a minute to anchor the rope."

Without waiting for an answer, he hopped up and returned the lamp to the old woman, despite her repeated plea to leave. He set his jacket neatly on the ground where he could monitor it and the precious letter. After tying the rope around the closest sturdy tree, he threw the loose end into the chasm and braced himself.

"I'm ready," he bellowed. "Send the first person."

The rope jerked, and soon a dirty head popped over the edge of the gully. The man pulled himself up and lay panting, dark blue wings twitching. By the time the next two reached the top, the first had recovered and was glaring at Arcelio while the old woman whispered frantically and clutched his arm.

Soon, everyone rested safely on solid ground.

"Well, I'm back to bed." Arcelio turned to retrieve his jacket, but two of the men grabbed him.

"Where's the gold, messenger?"

Arcelio raised his eyebrows. Surely these were the bandits the old woman had mentioned. "If you are desperate, I can give you a coin or two. I have a little for my traveling needs."

"That's not what we was told," they grumbled.

One of the men patted Arcelio's pants pockets while another headed for his jacket.

"Leave that alone, please," Arcelio barked.

"Ah ha!" Rough hands emptied all his pockets, and his money vanished. The precious letter was passed from hand to hand.

"He saved you," the old woman quavered. "I couldn't rescue you from that chasm. How long would you have stayed there? Let him go!"

"He don't got much gold," one of the men grumbled. "We was lied to."

The letter passed to the second row of men.

"Take the money," Arcelio said. "Give me back the letter, and I'll go. I won't mention we met." Still the bandits glared at him, and fear chilled his veins for the first time. "My aged mother is waiting for my return," he said, hoping for mercy.

Hands from the back of the crowd, so dirty they were several shades darker than normal Iojif skin, took the letter and moved out of sight. All Arcelio could see was the ash blond hair of a tall bandit, bent to look at the message.

But Arcelio didn't have time to worry about bandit hygiene, even if the envelope got smudged. He squashed the panic rising in his chest. "Please don't try to open the letter or the wrath of Irajahan will strike you."

"He did save us," a bandit muttered. "We wasn't never going to climb out of there."

"Twice, if he's right about Irajahan striking us," another grumbled.

The letter reappeared and made its way forward through the crowd.

"Eh, take it and leave." The bandit with dark blue wings shoved the message at Arcelio while another bandit handed back his jacket.

The letter seemed whole, and the seal looked intact. Arcelio breathed a sigh of relief and shook his head. What had he been worried about, anyway? No mortal could have harmed Irajahan's message.

"Thank you. I'll leave after I help find the goats."

"No, no," the old woman said. "They'll come back in the morning by themselves."

Arcelio shook himself free and approached the old woman. "Thank you for your hospitality." He glared at the bandits. "If anyone around here is thankful they aren't still in a hole in the ground, they should make sure your goats get home. Good flight."

He grabbed his pack from the shed and flew off before the bandits could change their minds.

The next few days were spent hungry and cold, since he no longer had funds to pay for inns, but they were otherwise uneventful. Soon he could see the great forests of the north, and if he flew a little higher, he could spot Darrendra beyond the trees.

One more day took him to his destination, and the sun remained high in the sky when he landed in front of the governor's large estate. A guard soon came to greet him, and Arcelio asked to speak to the governor.

"He's out on business," the guard replied. "But you can wait here for him. I'll bring you food and water, or whatever you need."

Arcelio unbuttoned his jacket, brushing his fingers across his secret pocket as he did. Yes, the letter was still safe.

"Food and water would be appreciated," he said. "Would anyone mind if I took a nap under the trees?"

The guard quirked an eyebrow. "Why would they?" He left, returning soon with the promised supplies before departing for his own duties.

Arcelio ate everything with relish, then relaxed in the shade and went to sleep.

When he woke, the sun had sunk to late afternoon, and a pretty young woman was examining him from her seat under a nearby tree. Her dark curls were piled on top of her head in a fancy hairstyle that looked like it would fall apart if she flew, and her embroidered pink dress was two shades darker than her wings.

He sat up, and she held a finger to her lips.

"Shh; they haven't found me yet," she whispered.

Arcelio leaned back against the tree and crossed his ankles. "Who are *they*? Are you running away?"

She shrugged. "I'm still here, aren't I? Who are you?"

"Arcelio."

"Arcelio who?"

"Arcelio of no known House. Who are you?"

"Hasana." Her cheeks turned as pink as her wings.

He winked. "Hasana who?"

She raised her chin. "Hasana Senjyor."

Arcelio leaped to his feet and bowed to his future queen. "Princess. I thought you were in Vasi."

"Sit," she hissed. "They'll see you."

Reluctantly, he sank to the grass. "But will they cut off my head when they find me sitting in your presence?" Or if she told them he had winked at her.

"If you stay down," she said, "they won't find either of us. My parents sent me here for a visit. Where do you come from?"

Arcelio looked toward the mansion again to make sure nobody was watching. "My home or recently? I grew up in a tiny, mundane village, but I've been working in Vasi for a few months."

Hasana waved her hand dismissively. "I've seen Vasi. Tell me about your home."

Obedient to his future queen, Arcelio shrugged and described the little hut he lived in with his mother. When he mentioned the goats, Hasana insisted on hearing all their names and how to milk them. After telling about his rescue and adoption, he explained his current employment. He tried to skip the fire and bandits and other dangers, but she always asked questions until she got the whole story.

"And why are you here?" Hasana's face beamed with curiosity.

Subtly, he brushed his pocket, which crinkled. The letter was still safe. "I have a message for the governor."

"Ooh, exciting! What does it say?"

"I don't know, and it's for his eyes only."

He frowned sternly, but she merely laughed and launched into a new set of questions. They chatted for another hour before someone from the house finally headed toward them.

Hasana held her finger to her lips and dashed from tree to tree until she reached the house and slipped around the back. She was safely out of sight when the uniformed servant asked Arcelio to follow him.

They walked through the tall entry hall of the mansion and wound through one room after another until they arrived at a spacious office. Behind a polished wooden desk, a stout man with dull green wings frowned at a stack of papers.

"Fair winds," he grunted. "You have a message for me?"

Arcelio pulled the letter from his chest pocket and handed it over. "I'm afraid the journey was a bit rough on it, but the seal is intact. Shall I wait for a response?"

"Yes, yes." The governor broke the seal. His eyebrows rose and his eyes widened, though his mouth remained stern. "I can see why Irajahan had *you* deliver this."

Arcelio nodded. "He said he wanted someone outside palace politics."

The governor grunted again. "He could have told me sooner. It would have saved me the trouble of throwing all those dinner parties."

"I — I'm sorry? Dinner parties?" Arcelio shook his head, thoroughly confused. "Should I take a reply?"

The governor folded the letter and stared at Arcelio. "Don't you know what's in this message?"

"The Almighty said it was for your eyes only."

The stout man leaned back in his seat and examined Arcelio from head to toe. Arcelio squared his shoulders and pressed his hands flat against his legs to keep himself from brushing at his travel dust.

"Huh. Well, orders are orders." The governor pulled a bell cord, and when a servant appeared, he said, "Please escort the princess to my office. Mmm. And my wife. And prepare a room and a bath. Quickly!"

The servant bolted, and the governor continued to stare at Arcelio.

"What's your name, boy?"

"Arcelio."

"Arcelio *what*?"

"Just Arcelio. I'm a foundling."

The governor twitched an eyebrow and opened the note again. After rereading it very slowly, he folded it and leaned back, hands clasped over his stomach.

Finally, after way too many tense and silent minutes, the servant returned with the princess on one arm. Holding his other arm, a middle-aged lady with a pleasant face wore a sober dark blue dress, but it was embroidered with silver thread, and jeweled silver combs decorated her hair.

The princess perched on a cushioned chair while the teal-winged lady swept around the desk and pressed a kiss to the governor's cheek.

"What do you need, dear?"

"How soon can you plan a wedding? Only the minimum, please, none of your grand plans."

She sank to a chair and tapped a finger on her cheek. "The minimum? We have a priest on the estate, so that's easy. A dress would take at least a week, and a dinner party would take a few days to prepare."

"Too long. Don't you already have a dinner party planned to torture me?"

She laughed. "Not to torture you, but yes, we have one tonight. You need to hurry and dress for it, actually."

Arcelio edged for the door, but the governor motioned him to stop.

"And don't you already have the princess's wedding dress finished?" the governor said. "Or did I misunderstand all that excited babble last week? I haven't seen the seamstress haunting us since then."

The princess and the governor's wife both shot to their feet. "The princess's dress?" overlapped with "*My* dress?"

"But I'm not getting married yet," the princess protested. "I haven't found a husband."

The governor unfolded the letter. "According to Irajahan, you have. 'Marry the messenger who brings this letter to the princess, at once. Ask no questions. Irajahan.' It seems clear to me."

Arcelio staggered against the door frame as the princess and the lady erupted into questions and objections.

Marry the princess? *Him*?

The servant shoved a chair against the back of Arcelio's knees, and he gratefully collapsed into it. He pressed his shaking hands to his forehead and tried to make sense of it all. Why would Irajahan wish him to marry the princess?

The governor rose to his feet and bellowed, "Quiet!" When the ladies fell silent, he took a deep breath. "I obey orders, and these are as clear as a warm current. Hasana and Arcelio will marry. Tonight. And I don't want to hear another word."

Hasana rushed to Arcelio and knelt beside his chair. "Did you know about this?"

He shook his head numbly.

"Do you want to marry me?" She bowed her head and picked at her sleeve, but when she peeked at him, her hazel eyes gleamed.

"I — I like you," he murmured, "but who am I to marry the princess?"

He was a nobody from the country. He even slept with the goats when they were close to kidding. She was the first person to ever talk to him as if he were important. Except his mother, but she was naturally biased. Certainly, no beautiful young lady had ever liked him.

She shrugged one dainty shoulder. "With no House, you could be anyone. Perhaps Irajahan knows. For whatever reason, he thinks you are the right person." She ducked her head again.

Arcelio scrubbed his hand across his face. "I certainly can't disobey the Omnipotent. If you will take me, I agree. I will be the best husband I can be and try to make you happy every day."

She raised her face and smiled at him. Taking his hand, she rose to her feet and drew him with her. "As My Lord Omnipotent commands."

The governor clapped his hands. "Take this young man to his room and let him bathe. Bring him appropriate clothing. Call for the priest. Set the table for dinner. Dress the princess in her wedding gown. Hurry!"

Arcelio hurried after the anxious, wide-eyed servant, up a grand flight of stairs to a room as large as his mother's entire hut. A steaming hot bath was followed by clothes so fancy the servant had to help him dress while he lectured him on the marriage ceremony as if he were a country bumpkin. He *was* a bumpkin, since half the instructions were new to him.

The servant slapped an orange-feathered fan into his hands and rushed him downstairs to a gilt chapel where the priest and Hasana already waited. She wore an orange dress so fluffy he had to stand three feet away and stretch his arm to hold her hand. Before he had a chance to change his mind, the ceremony was finished and he was married to a princess. How would he ever explain this to Mother?

Arcelio and Hasana were escorted to dinner and seated at the head of the longest table he had ever seen in his life, longer than the barracks tables. The spotless white cloth was covered with shiny china and so many sparkling silver utensils that he could have used a different one for every bite. Or so he thought until servants began carrying in a seemingly endless stream of food. Desperately, he copied everything his bride did, too nervous to notice what he was eating, though everything tasted delicious.

They had just started dessert when a howling wind circled the mansion and the windows darkened. The priest that had married them rushed in, robes hiked to his shins, and whispered frantically to the governor, who summoned his clerk with a jerky motion. Before they finished their conversation, the double doors flew open, slamming into the walls with a resounding crash.

In the doorway, Irajahan stood, arms still spread. Lightning sparked around him, reflecting in his impossibly huge silver wings that stretched past the doors and down the hall.

Everyone lurched to their feet, and half the chairs toppled. Hasana squeezed Arcelio's hand, wide-eyed and quaking. Though he squared his shoulders, his own feathers puffed with fear.

The priest fell to his knees on the polished marble floor, wings crimped so tightly that Arcelio's ached in sympathy. The clerk edged his way to the back door and fled.

"Fair winds," the governor choked, creeping halfway to the door. "You honor us with your presence, Almighty. Please sit and—"

"What. Did. You. DO!" Irajahan bellowed. Wind rushed through the room, flipping the tablecloths and rolling crystal glasses.

The governor wavered on his feet and gasped for air as the currents tightened around him in a swirl of dust and power. "Your instructions—" he choked.

Irajahan's face turned purple. "My instructions? MY instructions?"

The clerk skidded back into the room, a familiar dirty letter in his hand. He looked at Irajahan and cowered against the wall. The governor beckoned for him, but the clerk didn't move.

Arcelio squeezed Hasana's hand until she whimpered, then stiffened his spine and forced his feet to the clerk. He took the letter and walked toward the far end of the room, sliding his feet when the air pressure threatened to blow him off balance.

Ten feet from Irajahan, he could go no farther. He held the letter toward his god, one arm shielding his eyes from the wind and rage. "Here, My Lord Omnipotent. I delivered your message as commanded. If you let him speak, the governor will testify it was still sealed, despite the troubles I encountered."

The governor frantically nodded.

Wind knocked Arcelio to his knees and snatched the letter, whirling it directly to Irajahan's hand. The God of Air read the message, face turning impossibly darker. The parchment crumpled in his hand, but the wind died to a fitful breeze and the lightning faded to mere sparks.

"Tell me of your journey," he commanded, folding his wings enough to pass through the doorway.

Without rising, Arcelio began the story. He got to the bandits before Irajahan interrupted.

"Bandits attacked? How did you defeat them?"

"Oh, no, Almighty. They didn't attack. An earthquake trapped them in a ravine, and I pulled them free. In gratitude, they let me go unharmed."

"An earthquake!" Thunder cracked in the room, rattling the windows. "Darr—" Irajahan's chest heaved, and he bared his teeth. After a minute, he smiled painfully. "Daring of you to risk yourself to help bandits. And did anyone touch the letter?"

Arcelio bowed his head. "I'm afraid the bandits did hold it, but they didn't open it, Omnipotence. I examined it before I flew on. And the rest of my trip was uneventful. The letter never left my possession afterward."

"A mere touch from—" Irajahan pressed his lips together and glared at Arcelio.

Arcelio clamped his wings tight across his back. Was his god truly upset someone had touched his letter, even though it arrived safely and unread? What harm had been done?

And yet Irajahan examined the letter as if he had never seen it, tracing the words with a trembling finger that sparked miniature lightning and left scorched holes in the parchment.

Now free of his imprisoning currents, the governor approached. "It was still sealed when he gave it to me, My Lord Omnipotent. I recognized your handwriting and fulfilled your commands immediately. Please, what did we do wrong? We wish only to serve you loyally." He knelt and pressed his forehead to the ground.

Irajahan said nothing, but the air crackled.

Hasana edged forward and knelt beside Arcelio. "Please, Omnipotent, spare my new husband. We tried to obey your will, as always."

"*My* will," Irajahan roared, crumpling the letter again.

Everyone in the room sank to the floor with terrified whimpers. The priest who had married them crawled on his elbows and knees until he was even with the governor.

Irajahan glanced out the window, and his mouth moved as if he was talking, though he made no sound. Anger flashed across his face, then surprise. His eyes narrowed, and his skin turned purple with rage.

The air pressure grew and grew, until Arcelio gasped for breath, struggling to inflate his chest against the force. Hasana wavered beside him, and he put an arm around her shoulders.

Finally, Irajahan's expression settled into chilly determination. A cool breeze swept in, and the storm pressure collapsed.

"And such is fate." He nearly spat the last word. "But what have you won with your manipulations?" He didn't seem to be talking to those who trembled before him.

Raising his voice, he said, "Behold your next queen and her husband, a common man of the people. After her reign, the hereditary crown shall end. All noble ranks shall end. Ioj will become a land of equality where anyone can rise to influence. Only my priests shall permanently stand above the people. All others shall be appointed from the people to serve at my pleasure."

He turned and stalked out. Nobody moved until they heard his wing-beats outside and the windows shone with sunlight. Slowly, servants picked up chairs and cleaned spilled food and drink. The governor's wife rushed to his side.

Arcelio and Hasana helped each other to their feet, and without thinking, he drew her into his arms. She stiffened briefly, then relaxed before he could let go.

She stretched to kiss his cheek. "Fair winds, husband."

"Fair winds, Princess. I'm sorry I cost your children the throne."

She shrugged. "Our children. And it's more a burden than anything."

He searched her face for hidden distress but found none. "I can't wait to introduce you to Mother. She'll love you."

Tentatively, he leaned down and pursed his lips, and after a moment, she lifted her mouth for a sweet kiss.

A thought struck him, and he gasped.

"What's wrong?" Hasana asked, looking quickly toward the door.

"Wait until I tell Mother we're moving to the palace!" He raised an eyebrow. "Do you have a shed for goats?"

I f you liked this story, you might like the traditional Earth fairytales:
    The Fish and the Ring
The Story of the King Who Would Be Stronger Than Fate
The Devil with the Three Golden Hairs
The Story of Three Wonderful Beggars

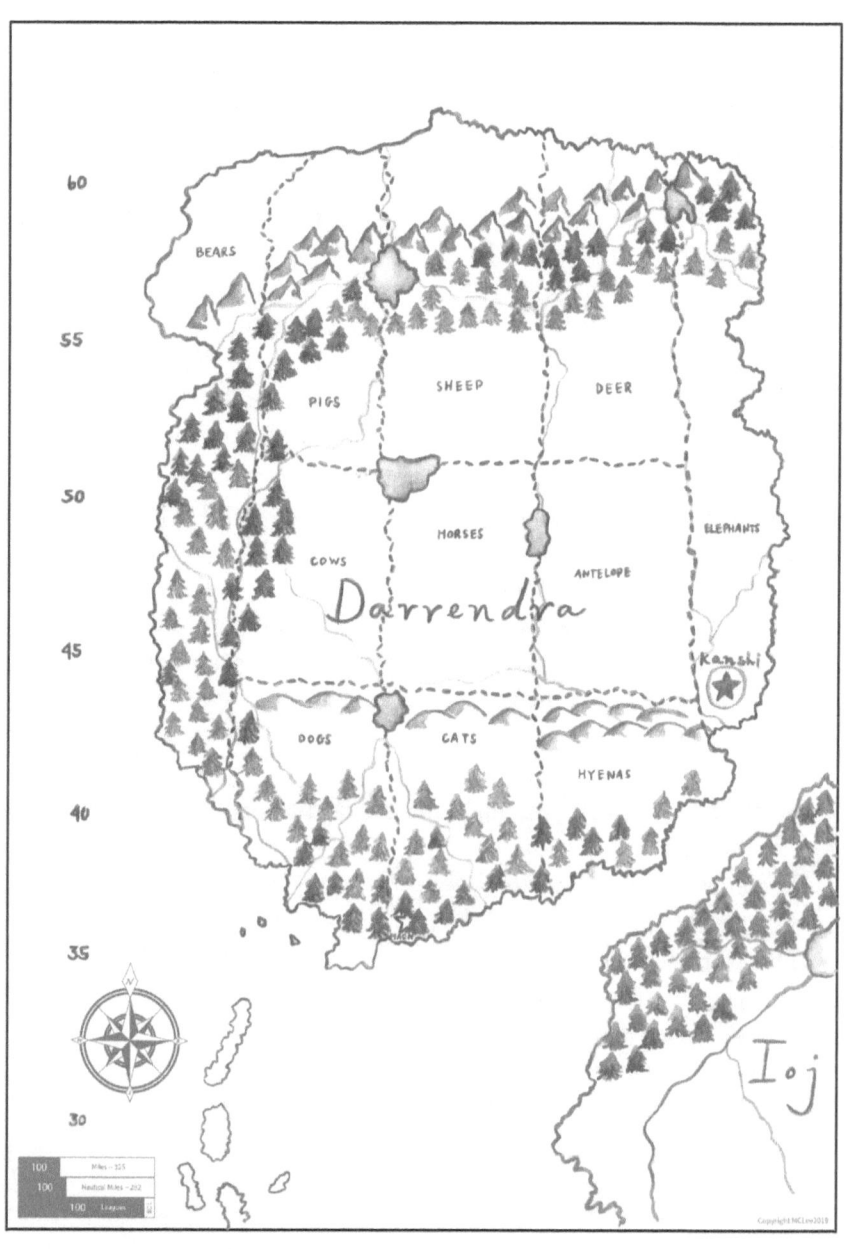

RED

1. MEETING

(CANID TERRITORY, DARRENDRA)

She met a stranger in the woods.
The Legend of the Red Cape

"Keep well, Grandmama. Eat your soup and take your medicine." Zienna Erroldin leaned down for a hug.

Eyes twinkling, the elderly woman tweaked her nose. "Be sure to stay on the path. You know how close it runs to the border. Don't talk to any strangers."

Zienna picked up her basket and edged toward the exit. Not that she was likely to meet any strangers. Sadly, few other Canids traveled in their quiet section of the woods, except for the occasional trader. Adults worried about how close they were to the Bovid border, but any Cow would need a safe-conduct pendant to pass the guards and get across the border into Canid territory. Since nobody dangerous or unreliable was given a pendant, any foreigner she met would be trustworthy and boring.

But arguing was useless. "Yes, Grandmama. I already promised Mama."

"And hurry home."

"I will." Zienna opened the door and stepped outside, choking back a sigh.

If she was old enough to visit Grandmama alone and bring her food and medicines, why wasn't she old enough to be trusted to take care of herself?

"And keep your siblings out of trouble."

"Yes, Grandmama. I love you." Zienna closed the door, hiding the sight of the worried face on the pillow.

She barked a soft laugh and leaned against the house for a moment. Keeping the little ones from trouble was nothing but a dream. It would be easier to chop down an oak tree with a butter knife. She had been in charge of her six younger siblings for almost four years, starting when she was as young as the boys were now, and she had never yet managed to have a day free of chaos.

Which meant Grandmama was right about one thing. Zienna *had* better hurry home, before her nine-year-old brothers got bored of watching their five-year-old sisters and abandoned them in favor of mischief. Why Mama thought the boys were responsible enough for anything, let alone taking care of three little girls, was a mystery.

She adjusted her empty basket so it wouldn't bang against her leg and set off on the track for home. Though it was only a winding path between the two small villages, it was used enough for the forest undergrowth to be trodden into dirt. To keep travelers from getting lost when the path was buried under snow, trees were periodically marked with directions. But now, spring flowers bloomed on the ground and trees alike. The scent of cedar and pine was underscored by apple blossom and new grass, and Zienna skipped cheerfully toward home.

Her second favorite part of running errands was the chance to be outdoors in the warm sunshine and sweet air, alone with her thoughts, and she frequently mentioned that to Mama. She did not reveal her favorite part, which was the thrill of freedom from her pesky little siblings and the endless chores they created for her.

As she skipped, she occasionally passed people in the forest, pruning trees or gathering mushrooms and spring greens. Even when she recognized them, she didn't waste her solitude on conversation, though she did wave and call greetings as she bounced along the path.

Halfway home, a flash of red caught her eye. She turned to stare, and a man stepped from behind a tree. Though his tunic was printed in the typical Darrendran bright geometric patterns, his cape was dyed a startling solid red. She had never seen so much scarlet in one place, and she tried not to wince.

"Good to see you," he said in their traditional greeting, flashing his teeth in a wide grin and waving at the gardeners in the distance.

He seemed friendly, but she didn't recognize his face, and she would certainly remember that red cape. Even though she knew she had nothing to worry about from strangers, especially with other villagers within sight, Zienna took a step backwards. "Good to see you."

"What are you doing this fine morning?"

"Just going home." She pointed through the trees automatically.

He strolled closer, hands behind his back. "What luck! I'm afraid I got a bit lost and could use a native guide. Would you mind walking with me?"

Something about his scent bothered her, but the forest odors were too strong for her to identify without shifting. She tried not to roll her eyes. Canids from other villages almost always smelled different, of course.

Nonetheless, Zienna backed up and dropped her basket from her arm to her hand so she could swing it freely.

"Follow the marks on the trees," she explained. "You are between two villages. Try that one." She pointed the opposite direction from home.

He read the signpost on a nearby tree, then squinted the direction she had pointed. "Oh, but I think I need to go to Admiel. Wouldn't you like company on such a fine day?"

His continued contractions bothered her. Why would he use such familiar language with someone he just met? And if he wanted a guide, why wasn't he asking one of the adults working within sight?

She took a step backward. "I really must go now."

"What is the hurry? Why not pick some flowers for your mama?" He waved his arm at the spring blossoms and took a long step toward her.

She whirled and ran, boots thumping on the dirt path. Around the next turn, she passed a group of familiar villagers and waved but didn't slow. Maybe their presence would scare off the stranger and give her a chance to escape.

After a few minutes, no sounds of pursuit followed her, and when she dared look, the flash of red was gone. So maybe he had given up following her, after all. Who was he, and what was he doing here? Curiosity itched at her, but not enough to go back and question him.

Zienna slowed to a fast walk. Sometimes she thought she glimpsed red behind her, but she could never see it when she stopped to scan the woods.

None too soon for her nerves, she reached her village and hurried through it to her small cottage on the other side. Home was safety, even though they lived closer to the border than any other family. But was she safe? She looked behind and saw only trees and houses and pale green seedlings.

She heard nothing but her siblings. Though they had left the shutters closed as Mama ordered, their playful squeals and shouts carried past the far edge of the garden. One more reason to appreciate her quiet walks among the trees. They didn't bother her with conversation or hurt her ears with howling. At most, they *barked* a little. She snickered. She would have to remember to tell the joke to her siblings, sometime when they were being good, or she needed to bribe them.

After scanning her surroundings again, she pressed the latch and leaned against the door to open it. But it didn't move. She pushed harder, and something scraped against the floor, but the door only opened a crack. Trouble, as usual.

"Roukan!" she shouted. "What did you put against the door?"

The shouting faded into giggles.

"Kanagan! Olkan! Open the door!"

"We can't open the door to strangers," Olkan shouted. Hoots of laughter followed.

Zienna glanced around the yard again. Everything looked normal, but the hair on her arms stood on end. "You know it's me. Open the door."

"Prove it," Roukan said. "Maybe you're a big bad monster waiting to eat us." More giggles.

Zienna growled. Little brothers were so stupid! "I know you recognize my voice."

"Maybe you're a monster who ate honey to soften your voice," Kanagan said. "Maybe you're only imitating our very annoying sister."

Zienna banged her head on the door.

"Is there a monster?" Tikani asked, voice quavering. The three little girls started crying.

"Stop crying," Roukan demanded, but the girls only sobbed harder.

"We don't want a monster," Nashoba whimpered. "Where's Zienna?"

"Where's Mama?" Honi begged.

"Mama went to town to talk to the elders," Kanagan said, "but Zienna is at the door."

Zienna took a deep breath and pressed her face against the crack she had managed to open. Softly, she sang Mama's favorite lullaby, the one she always sang to the little ones when she tucked them into bed.

"There's no monster," Olkan said, but the girls kept wailing.

"I want Mama," Tikani sobbed.

"I want Papa," Nashoba cried.

"Papa went hunting." Roukan had to raise his voice over the noise. "But don't you hear Zienna?"

The girls' sobs grew even louder. Someone groaned, and then something scraped across the floor inside.

Zienna kept singing while the door swung open, spreading her arms wide. Her sisters ran past the boys and threw themselves on her, clutching her legs. She embraced them, glaring over their heads at her little brothers, who were still pushing the tall clock back to its place beside the door.

When she finished the song, she kissed each girl and pried her loose with assurances there was no monster. After closing the door and putting away her basket, she stuck her hands on her hips and surveyed the house.

It looked like an earthquake had hit while she was gone. Drawers and chests hung open, their contents missing. Empty cupboards gaped at her. Furniture was overturned, and the feather-stuffed mattress drooped naked over the side of Mama and Papa's bed frame. Even from below, she could see the children's mattresses piled in a heap in the loft. Dishes and pans and clothes and blankets littered the entire house. Everything was splotched with gray and brown and black. All six children were filthy, covered in dirt and ashes.

"What did you *do*?" she asked, but she knew they wouldn't answer even before they shrugged, faces falsely innocent. "Never mind. Let's clean before Mama and Papa get home. Whatever is dirty, put it into a separate pile."

Zienna cracked open one shutter by the front door just enough to allow sounds of Mama's return to warn them of her approach, while still blocking sight of the mess. The girls ran to gather all the clothing strewn across the floor, while the boys collected dishes, picked up toppled chairs, and put away tools.

Zienna swept the ashes that had somehow been scattered from the fireplace. With every pull of the broom, she thanked Darravani the fire was not needed on the warm spring day. But every time she got a pile of ashes ready to pick up, one of the children walked through it, arms full of pans or clothes. They apologized for not being able to see above their loads, but she still had to sweep all over again. By the time she finally got the mess confined to a bucket, she was as dirty as the children, and the pile of soot-marked clothing was knee high.

She wiped an ashy hand across her sweaty forehead and surveyed the pile with dismay. It would take hours to wash it all. Papa probably would be gone until nightfall, but Mama would surely be home before they finished. And even though it wasn't her fault, she was sure to get the blame.

Zienna groaned and slumped into the nearest chair. "We should start laundry before Mama gets home, or we'll really be in trouble."

"No," Kanagan moaned.

"And baths."

"No!" Olkan yelped.

Zienna stuck her hands on her hips. "Yes. Do you want Mama to see you like this?"

"But baths are terrible," Roukan whined, flopping onto the dirty floor.

"We can do laundry first," Zienna offered. "You can run around on four legs for a while, then you'll have something clean to wear after you bathe."

Kanagan grinned. "What about *your* dress? You can't wash clothes with paws."

Zienna stuck out her tongue at him, but he had a good point. "I don't need a full bath. If I wash my face and hands and..." She surveyed the house for *anything* clean. "If I wear Mama's nightdress, then I can wash my dress, too."

While the children stripped and shifted into wolf puppies, she hauled in buckets of water from the well and poured half the water into the large pot hung in the fireplace. She washed her hands and face and slipped Mama's nightdress over her head. It was much too large, but at least it covered her. The little girls shifted back long enough to add Mama's frilly cap, tying it firmly with many giggles.

The puppies were still dragging their dirty tunics and dresses to the pile of laundry, one mouthful at a time, when they heard footsteps clacking along Mama's fancy stone walk. Zienna sighed. She hadn't even lit a new fire yet, so Mama wouldn't be able to tell they were going to do the laundry, like responsible children. Why couldn't she have at least waited until they had one batch hanging to dry?

"Mama's home," Roukan said.

Zienna headed for the door.

"No," Olkan whispered. "Let's surprise her."

Kanigan squealed. "Everyone hide."

Before Zienna could stop them, the kids vanished. Roukan swept pans from the cupboard and jumped inside. Nashoba ran for the fireplace and somehow scrambled up the chimney, which explained the ashes all across the floor. Olkan huddled beneath the overturned wooden half-barrel they used for a washtub. Kanagan dove under the table, pulling the long table-cloth to touch the floor. Tikani wiggled under Mama and Papa's bed. Honi ran to the tall clock beside the front door and somehow squeezed in and closed the case again.

In seconds, they were all out of sight. No wonder Zienna could never find them during hiding games!

"Hurry," Kanagan hissed, then pulled his head back behind the tablecloth.

Zienna looked at herself in Mama's nightdress and laughed. This might be funny, after all. And if she could make Mama laugh enough, she might forgive the children for the mess. Quickly extinguishing the lamp, she scrambled into Mama and Papa's bed and pulled the covers over her head.

The footsteps stopped on the doorstep, then Mama knocked instead of entering. She must be giving the children a chance to behave before she opened the door.

Zienna smothered a giggle and tried to relax under the messy blankets as if she were nothing but a stray pillow. She assumed her siblings were also watching to know when to emerge, though from her long experience with them, she wouldn't be surprised if they already had a signal arranged. The miscreants seemed to have plots for every possible variety of trouble.

The latch clicked, then the door slowly opened. Feet thumped on the floor as Mama walked into the house.

Silence. Mama must be in shock at the mess, even though they had cleaned most of it. At least the floor was swept, or poor Mama would have a heart attack. Now all they needed to do was distract her from the chaos long enough to apologize and promise to clean it all.

If they all jumped out at once, Mama should give a satisfying scream. Was it time? Zienna peeked from under the covers.

But the person in her house was the stranger in the red cape.

2. CAPTURE
(CANID TERRITORY, DARRENDRA)

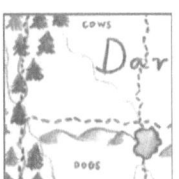

The stranger followed her home.
The Legend of the Red Cape

Z ienna smothered a gasp. What was the stranger doing in her house? He must have followed her, and it couldn't be for any good reason.

Her heart rate sped, and her breathing sounded much too loud to her own ears. *Oh, please, let the children stay hidden.*

Why wasn't Mama home yet?

Fear shifted Zienna to her wolf form without a conscious decision. As fur sprouted and her bones realigned, she bared her much longer teeth in a silent snarl under the pile of blankets.

"Is anyone here?" the stranger asked.

Without Mama and Papa, Zienna was the only one who could protect her siblings. And she had no weapons besides her teeth, and no way to call for help.

Worse, she was trapped in Mama's nightdress, which was loose enough it didn't split despite Zienna's shift. The cap was tied so well that it stayed on, though her wolf ears poked from beneath it. If she tried to spring out and bite the intruder, she would trip on the long hem and land on her snout before she could even reach him.

After a moment, his feet tapped on the floor, one step at a time, slowly enough that she knew he was scanning the room.

Her hair stood on end. Where was Mama? She wanted to cry like her little sisters, but that would only give away her hiding place. But Zienna couldn't hide forever, or the intruder might find her siblings. She must distract him before the children lost their nerve and made a noise that drew the man's attention.

As the footsteps slowly approached the bed, she took a deep breath and flung back the covers.

"Who are you?" she growled.

Without the lamp, the room was dim, lit only by the sunlight through the open door, but she had not been mistaken. The intruder was clearly the man who had talked to her in the woods. That solid red cape was unique.

"Oh." The man stopped walking. "Good to see you. Um, what a deep voice you have. I was looking for a woman, not a wolf?" He squinted at her cap and nightdress.

As if she would admit she was a little girl to a strange man in her house.

"I am the only one here to greet you," she said as gruffly as possible.

If she distracted him long enough, maybe Mama would arrive.

"You have very big eyes." His own were growing wider and wider, and he shuffled from one foot to the other.

"The better to see you." She rolled her eyes, sure he would laugh at the ridiculous statement but still trying to stall.

He took a step backward, fidgeting with the edge of his stupid red cape.

Behind him, Honi cracked open the clock case. As she silently snuck out the open door, Zienna glared at the stranger to keep his attention on her. Hopefully, her little sister would go for help, but even if she didn't, at least she was out of danger. One down, but five to go. Unfortunately, the others were farther into the room, well within sight if the man looked away from her.

He stared at her cap again. "And your ears..." he whispered.

The more he talked, the more his accent sounded not quite right. She already knew he wasn't local, but now he didn't even sound Canid, even though he obviously understood her speaking in both two-legger and four-legger dialects. Of course, languages could be learned. And now that he was closer, she could tell he had no safe-conduct pendant. He had sneaked across the border against the law. Trouble, for sure.

Oh, Mama, come home now.

"I can hear your accent, you know," she said. "Big ears are good for that."

This conversation was absurd, and surely he would realize it at any moment. And what would she do then? He was twice her size.

But she couldn't abandon the rest of her siblings, and she couldn't run on four legs in this stupid nightdress.

Kanagan peeked from behind the tablecloth, and she stuck out her tongue at him and twitched her head toward the door.

The stranger flinched. "Oh, what a big tongue." An embarrassed flush colored his cheeks.

Instead of running for the door behind the stranger's back, Kanagan ducked back under the table, and Zienna nearly wept.

"The better to speak to you," Zienna said tartly.

If only Kanagan had understood her signal to escape! But in a minute, the cupboard door cracked open, and Kanagan dragged Roukan silently under the table. In another minute, the laundry tub tipped up, and Olkan joined the other boys.

Yes, he had understood her after all! Now, if she could keep the intruder's gaze on her long enough for them to sneak out, four of her siblings would be safe.

Tikani couldn't escape while he faced the bed, nor could Nashoba climb down the chimney without being caught, but if the boys could leave, they would go for help and take Honi with them.

Zienna grinned at the stranger. Would pretending to be friendly distract him long enough?

The stranger coughed and patted his knife. "My, what... big teeth. And so shiny and... sharp."

She stopped grinning. Apparently, she didn't look friendly.

Halfway out from under the table, Olkan caught his paw on the tablecloth. The dishes piled on top slid toward the edge, clinking softly. Olkan shook his paw, and the cloth jerked downward. The dishes clattered to the floor, and her brothers raced for the open door as if their tails were on fire.

Oh no! Zienna sucked in a breath and jerked upright.

The stranger whirled to look at the boys, and Zienna leaped from the bed. Attack was the only way to protect her brothers now. Landing next to the red-caped man, she stretched up on her hind paws and leaned toward his face.

"If you do not leave, I will EAT you," she snarled.

The stranger screamed and fell backward.

Tikani squirmed from under the bed and scrambled for the open door. Her puppy howls echoed in the small house.

As the red-caped man floundered, struggling to rise, Zienna tried to run past him. Her paws tangled in Mama's nightdress, and she fell on him instead. His breath whooshed out, and for a second, he lay still as she struggled to free her feet. But she was caught! She clawed at the tangling fabric, growling in frustration.

He sucked in a breath and pushed her off, screaming in her ear. They both rolled in opposite directions, and the nightdress bunched around her neck. Paws now free, she bolted for the door.

But the stranger had done the same, and they collided in the doorway, both of them howling and shoving to exit the house.

As she struggled, her siblings shouted to each other. One voice was high above her. On the roof? What were they doing? Her fur stood on end. Why hadn't they gone for help, or at least run away to save themselves?

Despite her attempts to exit, the stranger in the red cape shoved her aside and dove out the door, rolling past the threshold and flopping down the front step. Within seconds, he jerked upright and whirled back toward Zienna, a long knife in his hand.

She tried to run, but Mama's nightdress had fallen around her legs again, and she couldn't move.

To her horror, Honi and Tikani ran at the man, barking and nipping at his ankles, driving him backwards. They were so tiny in comparison, only shin-high. The man slashed down, but the pups were too short to hit. But how long could their luck last? If nothing else, one strong kick from the man's heavy boots would crush the pups.

Zienna screamed, "Run!"

Suddenly, Roukan shouted, "Now!" and the ground rose around the stranger, jerking him into the air.

Honi and Tikani sat on their haunches and panted, tongues hanging from their mouths as they stared upward. They bumped their heads together and nodded with a satisfied jerk.

Zienna collapsed across the doorway and blinked. That was no earthquake. Somehow, her siblings had rigged a trap, and now the man was suspended in a net. His knife lay on the ground below him, fortunately.

And where were the rest of her brothers and sisters?

While Tikani barked at the captured stranger, Honi ran to Zienna and licked her face, nudging her into action. Gathering her courage, Zienna forced herself to be calm. After a few deep breaths, she shifted back to two-legger. She scooped up Honi and walked into the yard, looking for the others.

On the roof, Nashoba bounced much too close to the edge, tail wagging in excitement. Somehow, she must have climbed all the way up the chimney and exited onto the roof.

Zienna groaned. If Mama discovered the puppies were climbing on the roof while she was watching them, she would be confined to the house until she married. Maybe she could get an early release by pointing out they were still alive.

Perched on nearby tree branches, her stark-naked brothers pulled on the rope attached to the net, hauling the red-caped man even higher.

"Let me down!" the man shouted. "You can't do this to me."

Zienna sighed. If she didn't have to be in charge of her siblings anymore, she could survive losing her errand privileges.

She rubbed her forehead. "I'm impressed, boys, but why do you have a net?"

Roukan cackled, and Kanagan swung his feet from his seat on the branch.

"Oh, you never know when it will be handy." Olkan wrapped the line around a branch and tied it snugly.

Honi licked Zienna's cheek frantically.

"Oh, I see," Zienna said, suddenly remembering all the prior pranks from the boys. "You were waiting for me to pass this spot, were you? You thought I might enjoy learning how to fly?"

All three boys howled with laughter.

"Get down here and either shift or get dressed," Zienna commanded, tapping one bare foot on the flagstones. She pointed at the roof. "You, too, Nashoba. All of you."

She put Honi on the ground and stood guard until all six children shuffled into the house. Wordlessly, she followed and stared at them, lips pinched, until the boys shifted back to four legs.

"You can't leave me here," the red-caped stranger protested. "Let me go!"

Zienna grabbed Papa's spear and marched outside again. Holding the weapon poised for use, she asked, "You do not want to stay up there?"

His eyes widened, and he clutched the net. "No, I'm fine. I will wait here."

Leaving the spear prominently by the front door, Zienna went inside to wrestle her siblings into good behavior and start the laundry. Before lighting the fire to heat the water, she lectured Nashoba about the dangers of climbing into chimneys. Though the little pup listened carefully, Zienna didn't know if she planned to obey or not, especially with the boys yapping mockingly in the background.

She had the same questionable success with her other two little sisters.

When she lectured the boys about traps and the respect due big sisters, they sagged on the floor and rolled their eyes, tongues hanging out. Finally, she gave up, poured the hot water into the laundry tub, and dumped in the first load of tunics.

A few hours later, she had all the clothes washed, but her hands were puckered from the water and cracked from the lye soap. Her siblings had actually tried to help, but they weren't strong enough to wring the clothes, and they tired of scrubbing after only a few minutes. Instead, they brought her new loads and dragged the baskets of wet clothes to the clothesline. The boys managed to get some hung up, but they weren't quite tall enough, and it took them a long time.

As she dumped the last barrel of dirty water and started hanging the last load to dry, Mama appeared in the distance, heading toward them from the village. The little girls, still in wolf shape, scampered to meet her, while the boys shifted and grabbed tunics from the driest batch before they ran to Mama.

"Mama, Mama, we caught a bad man," they babbled.

The stranger rocked the net and opened his mouth until Zienna collected the spear, then he pressed his head against his prison and waited, gaze fixed on Mama.

"What is going on?" Mama asked. "Zienna, what stories have you been telling the children?"

"No, Mama," Roukan protested. "Look!"

Mama turned and looked up, and the red-caped man waved his fingers through the net. Mama's mouth fell open, moving soundlessly like a fish. She snatched the spear from Zienna and marched toward the stranger.

Zienna folded her arms and smirked. That would teach the man not to invade their territory. Or rather, he wouldn't have to worry about learning boundaries when he was dead.

Mama stood on her tiptoes and slashed — and the net fell to the ground with the stranger intact.

Zienna gasped and reached for her siblings. Why had Mama freed the intruder? "But, Mama, he stalked me in the forest. And then he walked into the house! And he isn't wearing a safe-conduct pendant."

Carefully, the man got to his feet, not retrieving his knife from the dirt. "I didn't want to bother anyone who was working, but she was walking as if she knew the area. So, um, I followed her? I guess I arrived too early?"

Mama slammed the butt of the spear on the ground. "You mean you were too embarrassed to tell an adult you were lost. Where is your pendant? And I told you to meet me in town, not at my home!"

The man shrugged as pink crept up his face. "The string broke, and I lost it somewhere in the forest, so I thought it would be better to wait at your house and avoid alarming the villagers. I remembered you live on the far side of the village, and this is the only house here. I wasn't expecting your family to be home."

Mama groaned. "Idiot. Why did the Bulls send *you*?"

"I don't mind the forest or wolves." The man glanced at Zienna and turned as red as his cape. "Um, usually."

"And how did you get into my house?"

"The door was unlocked," the man whispered with an apologetic look at Zienna. "I thought either you would be here or it would be empty."

"Idiot," Mama repeated.

From the way she glared at them both, it was unclear if she meant the stranger or her daughter, and both of them winced.

"I must say," the man said, "your children are, um, very brave and, er, capable."

Zienna bared her teeth at him, and the man cringed.

"Ferocious, even," he muttered.

"And what do you expect?" Mama turned to Zienna. "I'll take him back with me to get a new pendant and meet with the elders. This is an important trade discussion. You — stay out of trouble, please." She glared at the younger children, then handed the spear to Zienna.

"That way," she said to the stranger, pointing toward town. After he started walking, shoulders hunched, she sighed and turned back, catching Zienna in a hug. "You were indeed brave and capable. Thank you for protecting your siblings from the threat you saw."

Zienna sighed. "The threat that wasn't even real."

Mama squeezed her tighter. "But if it had been, you would still all have been safe." She took three steps away, then called over her shoulder, "Lock the door this time. Prevention is better than ferociousness."

"Yes, Mama." Zienna scooped up two of her sisters and herded everyone else inside. "Boys, let's discuss your net." She looked at their sad faces and extended her arms for a hug. "And then I have a new joke to tell you."

I f you liked this story, you might like the traditional Earth fairytales:
Red Riding Hood
Little Golden Hood
Little Red Cap
The Wolf and the Seven Young Kids
The Goat and Her Three Kids
Peter and the Wolf

TRANSFORMED

1. SPRING

(CAPRID TERRITORY, DARRENDRA)

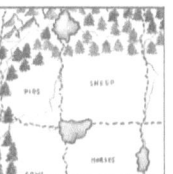

He wished to change his life.
The Legend of the Shifter

With the first hints of spring, Kokoro Dayandi Shekeda itched to be outside in the sunshine. Before Mama could assign him an indoor chore, he grabbed a basket and bolted for the exit.

"I'll take care of the marketing today," he called. The door slammed on her reply, and he hurried for the road.

"Get onions," Mama yelled.

Kokoro turned around and waved, and she pulled her head back inside the window.

As he reached the edge of the yard, Netra left her house next door. Kokoro changed his path to meet her.

"Good to see you." He clasped her arm in greeting and took the empty basket she carried. Born the same day, they had been best friends their whole lives.

She laughed. "Good to see you, too. Give me back my basket."

"I don't mind carrying it for you."

"You have your own basket to carry. I don't want to delay you." Despite the chiding words, she looped her arm around his.

"You won't, and don't make Mama think I need to hurry." He stretched into a longer stride, pulling her with him.

"You are an adult," she said mildly. "You don't have to listen to your mama."

He shrugged. Now seventeen years of age, they were barely adults, but convincing their parents to break a lifetime of habits was difficult.

Netra's sage-green eyes sparkled as she laughed again. The sunshine gleamed on her brown skin and sparked highlights in her dark hair, and she looked nothing like the dreary shadow his friends called her. If her parents would let her wear the usual colorful clothing instead of drab grays and browns, others would see how beautiful she was. Hmm. Maybe gray and brown were good colors for her. He didn't mind being the only one who noticed her loveliness.

Her lips parted, and pink crept up her cheeks, and he suddenly realized they had stopped walking and were standing in the middle of the road, nose to nose.

Kokoro straightened, cleared his throat, and turned to face the right direction. "So, anyway, I'd rather go to the market than stay inside scrubbing floors for Mama."

Netra sighed and stepped forward. "Your mama's not that bad. *My* parents..."

Kokoro winced. "Never mind. Your papa has a loud voice. I hear him anytime we leave a window open."

He patted her hand on his arm. He could move out whenever he wanted, with the excuse of building a house for his future bride, but Netra would have no escape until she married. And she had no suitors yet. No one but him was smart enough to see past her boring dress, and not even he was brave enough to face her parents. He expected her mama and papa to chase away all the young men until the last possible moment of her eighteenth birthday. And then the betrothal would still leave her at home for another year. Poor Netra.

They talked of easier things after that, laughing their way through their shopping and back home again. When Kokoro heard her parents arguing at full volume about their usual nonsense, he said a quick farewell and left her in her front yard. The last time he tried to intervene for Netra, he had only made things worse.

After making sure all the windows were closed and putting away the onions and other purchases, he dropped a kiss on Mama's cheek, gave Papa a hug, and cleaned his room and swept the entire floor without being asked.

"I finished my chores. May I go for a run now?"

"Be back by the evening meal," Papa said.

In his bedroom, Kokoro removed his tunic and shifted to goat form, ignoring the tan and white hairs that fell from his winter coat to litter the floor. Within minutes, he was outside in the chilly air and warm sunshine, staring up the mountain at the snow still covering the peak.

This wasn't the highest ridge in Darrendra, but it was almost the highest in Caprid territory, lucky for him. Most of the village nestled at the base, but his family and a few others lived halfway up, giving him a choice of directions to run. Today, he dug his hooves into the rock and bounded as straight up as the terrain allowed. When he reached the top, he charged down. Then he spiraled around the peak, bouncing from ledge to ledge.

After three circuits, he went home, sweaty and pleasantly tired. He banged the door open and pranced to his tiny bedroom to shift back to two legs.

"We need to talk," Mama called from the kitchen.

Kokoro sighed and pushed his arms through his tunic sleeves. When he left his room, he found her stirring soup, her pale hair tied back and her loose sleeves rolled up to expose her brown arms to the elbow.

"What, Mama?"

Her eyes, as blue as his, looked tired, but she moved as quickly as someone half her age. She smiled at him and stacked dishes on the counter.

"You have seventeen years now," she said. "We need to talk about your betrothal."

He groaned. "My birthday was only a few weeks ago. I have a year to decide. What's the hurry?"

Mama shrugged. "No hurry, but I thought maybe you already had someone you liked. I've noticed a certain girl watching you, and I could be wrong, but I think you watch back." She wiggled her eyebrows at him.

Kokoro ducked his chin and straightened his sleeves. "I don't know who you mean."

He did, but it was none of her concern. What good would it do, anyway?

Mama frowned, but her eyes crinkled with amusement. "Yes, you do."

"What if I want to *not worry* about marriage for the whole year?" Kokoro complained.

He would think about it, of course, but since Netra's parents wouldn't consider anyone for a year, what was the point in discussing it? Talking wouldn't fix anything.

Before Mama could reply, he rushed out the door. He would rather skip a meal than think about what he couldn't change.

As the weeks went on, Mama hinted more often and enthusiastically that he should pick a girl — any girl he liked — and start making plans. No, of course she wasn't trying to get rid of him; she just wanted him to be happy.

Kokoro ran more than ever to escape the nagging. He *was* happy. Wasn't he? It wouldn't hurt him to wait a year to win his beloved. Much.

At the top of the mountain one day, he stared south toward Equid territory. He was high enough to see their plain running for leagues of open space before it finally reached the southern forests. The lucky Horses could run for days without stopping. Mama's lectures would never catch up to him there.

He sighed and trotted down the mountain again.

Mama and Papa weren't home, so after shifting and dressing, he looked for Netra. He found her hiding in the forest, stifling her sobs not quite well enough.

Kokoro dropped beside her, leaning against the tree and gathering her into his arms. "What happened this time?"

Netra buried her face against his shoulder. "I didn't sweep up all the dirt."

He tightened his embrace while he took deep breaths. When he could speak without yelling, he said, "You should report them to the elders."

She mumbled into his shoulder. "For what? They don't hit me."

"They make you feel bad!"

She shrugged. "They're right; I did miss the corner."

"So?"

"They're my parents. They just want me to learn properly."

"Is that what you think?"

She shrugged.

"You're an adult now," Kokoro said.

"Not in their eyes."

"Who cares what they think? Move out."

"You know I can't. Custom says girls stay home until the wedding, and that means another two years, according to them. If they could, I'm sure they would keep me from marrying at all."

He swore under his breath, but not quietly enough, because Netra pinched him.

"Then agree to marry me right now," he said.

Netra sat up and smiled at him through her tears.

"That would save you from your parents," Kokoro added.

Netra frowned and jerked out of his arms. "I don't want you to save me."

"No, I meant, if we were betrothed, you could move out. You can have the house as soon as it is even partway finished, and *I'll* stay with *my* parents." He reached for her again, but she jumped to her feet.

Lip quivering and fists clenched, she flushed three shades of red. "Are you stupid? I said no." Before he could argue, she turned and ran away.

"I love you," Kokoro whispered to the empty forest.

But she didn't love him. If she had, she would have said yes. His stomach churned, and his chest felt hollow enough to collapse. He should have stuck to his original plan and waited until their year was almost over. Surely by then, he could convince her to love him.

He sat against the tree until he found enough energy to drag himself home.

The next day, Mama again asked about his plans for marriage.

"Leave me alone," Kokoro snarled.

Netra didn't want him, and he didn't want anyone else. He quickly shifted and bolted up the mountain for another run.

Once again, he paused at the top and surveyed the land below. At the sight of Netra's house next to his, he pressed a fist to his heart. He looked past the village, toward the endless Horse plains. If he went there, he could run for days. No soft eyes and sad face reminding him he wasn't loved, just the pounding thunder of his hooves on the grass.

Why couldn't he be a Horse?

Hail, Darravani the Omnifarious, he prayed in a rather irreverent tone, *can I be a Horse?*

To his surprise, a yellow carnation bloomed at his hooves in response to his joke. The Goddess of Earth spoke to her people through the language of flowers, though usually at one of her shrines where her shamans could help interpret complex messages.

But this one, though it appeared in the middle of nowhere, simply meant *No.*

Why had she even answered? It was only a joke. Every Darrendrakar had one other form and one only. No Goat would ever be a Horse. Kokoro sighed and headed home again.

He stopped by Netra's house, but she wouldn't come to the door, and her papa was so nasty that Kokoro fled. They could talk later.

But whenever he was home, she stayed inside her house. Was it her choice or her parents' will? Either way, she only emerged when he was off working with Papa, and Mama said she merely waved.

The next week, he climbed to the top of the mountain again, puffing from frustration as well as exertion.

"I would rather be a Horse," he huffed. "Not being able to talk to Netra is torture."

Even staying in Caprid territory would daily remind him of her. No, he needed to completely change his life. A yellow carnation popped up, waving its head emphatically.

"Well, why not?" Kokoro was becoming more attached to the silly idea, impossible though it was. If he was an entire territory away, maybe he could forget his crush on the girl who didn't even want him. She wasn't even talking to him anymore, and he missed his best friend almost more than he mourned for the sweetheart she would never be. He still didn't understand why trying to help her was so horrible. Would he really be a bad husband? And even if she hated the idea, they could have stayed friends.

A whole bouquet of flowers sprouted, and Kokoro danced backward to avoid stepping on them. Three of the blossoms immediately died, even though he hadn't touched them. He recognized the common dandelion and the little white stephanotis frequently used in the safe-conduct pendants given to travelers who needed to cross kindred borders, but he wasn't sure about most of the others.

After checking that he was alone, he shifted to two legs and carefully picked the flowers. He tied the stems together with a bit of braided grass, then shifted back to goat and took the bouquet in his mouth. This would be easier on two legs, but he couldn't walk into the village naked. Walking carefully instead of running headlong as usual, he made his way down the mountain to the shaman's house and laid the bouquet at her feet.

"What does this message mean?" he asked.

The shaman raised an eyebrow and rubbed her chin. "What did you ask Darravani?"

He shook his head, relieved he couldn't blush in goat shape.

"Did you kill these flowers?"

She sounded more curious than angry, so he shook his head. "They came that way."

The shaman grunted, then crouched to sort the flowers. "These three mean happiness, basically, or happiness at home. The three dead ones are related to travel or leaving. I'm guessing Darravani thinks you'll be happier at home than whatever plan you were considering." She sat back and examined him for a minute. "Were you thinking of running away?"

Kokoro shook his head quickly, then nodded slowly, then shrugged.

The shaman's mouth twitched. "It's normal to wonder what life would be like somewhere else, you know, but I don't recommend going through with it." She gathered the flowers into a tiny basket and let him take the handle in his mouth. "Come talk to me about it sometime, if you like."

Since he had no hands for the traditional arm clasp, Kokoro bent his front legs in a little bow before trotting home with his flowers.

He hid them in his room and forgot about them until the next time he was at the top of the mountain, looking toward Equid territory. Netra had again refused to see him with no explanation. Despite numerous attempts, they hadn't talked at all since she rejected his proposal. Even when the neighborhood bully, Aran, cornered her at the market, she turned away from Kokoro's attempted rescue. She must hate him to avoid him like this, and his heart was lodged near his hooves.

"It's not like I'd be abandoning you for another country," he begged Darravani. "The Horses are still your children."

A dandelion and dead stephanotis sprouted.

"I need a change." To go somewhere *else* to forget a certain beautiful girl who didn't want him. If she walked away from him once more, without even a word, his heart would forget how to beat.

This produced a new bouquet. Since the only flower he recognized was a crocus, Kokoro excitedly took them all down the mountain for the shaman to interpret.

When he dropped the plants in front of her, she squinted at them, then cursed. "You carried these here in your mouth? Idiot boy!" She jumped to her feet and dashed into her house, returning in moments with a foxglove plant. "Eat this. Right now!"

Kokoro choked down the flower as the shaman watched intently. After he swallowed the last of it, she sat again to look at his bouquet.

"All of these are warnings," she said. "Beware, danger, abuse not. And this oleander — are you paying attention? — is poisonous. Don't put it in your mouth again." She pursed her lips. "What exactly have you been asking Darravani? If she's willing to risk you poisoning yourself, idiot, it seems more serious than a little travel."

Kokoro mumbled something that didn't make sense even to himself. No way would he admit to anyone that Netra didn't love him.

The shaman rubbed her hands over her face. "If you won't talk to me, then you at least need to have better conversations with Darravani that won't end in your accidental death. Wait here."

She hopped up again and came back with a book, which she put into a drawstring bag. "We wrote this dictionary of flower meanings with descriptions and pictures and other useful information. I can make another for the apprentices." She tightened the drawstrings and held them for him to take in his teeth. "Please, come talk to me anytime, but don't put any more plants in your mouth unless you're sure they're safe. And if you decide you don't need my book, I want it back."

Kokoro bowed and went home. Once safe in his room, he hid the book under his pillow and rinsed his mouth several times. After chores, he would research every poisonous plant listed and memorize what they looked like.

For several days, he managed to ignore his sorrow, until Netra saw him in the yard and ran inside, slamming the door. Like the melting snow, his contentedness dissolved. He again climbed the mountain, this time with the book.

Kokoro knelt, bowing until his head rested in the sparse snow. As the cold mud soaked through his fur, he prayed to Darravani. "Please," he begged, voice cracking. "Please let me go somewhere else to forget."

A yellow carnation bloomed and died. In its place, three flowers slowly sprouted.

At the sight of the red carnation that everyone knew meant yes, Kokoro shouted in triumph before he remembered to check the other two in the book. The little yellow one was a coronilla and meant "success crown your wishes." The blue harebell meant both submission and grief, but Kokoro didn't care what Darravani thought about his idea as long as she agreed to it.

He shoved the book back into the bag and clattered down the mountain.

At the evening meal, he played with his food, then blurted, "I'm leaving the village."

Papa blinked. "But — why?"

"There is nothing here for me," Kokoro said.

That started a long argument from both parents, which Kokoro ignored while he smashed his meal flat.

"How long will you be gone?" Papa finally asked.

Kokoro twitched. "I'm never coming home."

Mama's brown skin turned ashen. After a long pause, she sighed. "You'll change your mind."

"Never," Kokoro swore.

Papa patted his shoulder. "If you don't, we'll come visit you. But you're welcome to return anytime."

"I'll let you know where to come," Kokoro said.

Now was not the time to tell them he was leaving the entire territory. He could surely find some border spot where they could meet.

Mama helped him pack, though she bit her lip the whole time. Papa ran down to the village to get a safe-conduct pendant for him, a white stephanotis blossom embedded in layers of clear resin.

In the morning, he slung his pack over his shoulders, hugged his parents, and left. At the road, he paused, then turned toward Netra's house. Cursing himself for being an idiot, he snuck around back and tapped on Netra's window.

When she saw him, she turned away, but he tapped again and pressed his hands together in entreaty. "Please," he mouthed.

Frowning, she opened the window. "I'm not ready to talk to you," she said.

"Then listen. I'm getting out of here. Darravani said she would make me into a Horse."

"That isn't possible."

Kokoro folded his arms. "Anything is possible for Darravani." Anything but making Netra love him. He wouldn't even ask, since her heart belonged to herself. "I just wanted to let you know so you don't think I abandoned you."

"Oh, Kokoro." She sighed. "That was never the problem. I hope you find what you are seeking." She softly closed the window and disappeared.

His heart cracked, and he staggered before he found his balance. One step after another, he walked down the mountain, through the village, and away from his old life. If he ran far enough, fast enough, maybe he could forget Netra.

He must forget.

2. SPRING & SUMMER

(EQUID AND FELID TERRITORIES, DARRENDRA)

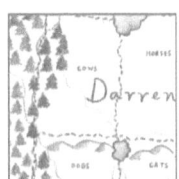

Still unsatisfied, he wished for a greater change.
The Legend of the Shifter

Kokoro walked for days, still as a Goat. Before he rolled in his blanket to sleep in the foothills at the very end of the mountains, he reminded Darravani of her promise. Tomorrow he would cross into Equid territory, and it was time to be a Horse.

In the morning, he shifted to graze for his morning meal, saving his supplies for later. In the nearby stream, his reflection was no longer a tan-and-white-spotted goat but a black-and-white-striped horse. He pranced and tossed his new mane. Amazing! He squinted at the burbling surface of the water. Actually, he was... a zebra?

He mentally shrugged. A horse was a Horse, and no one smart would complain about Darravani's sense of humor. Kokoro shifted back to pack his belongings, and in his two-legged form, he had the same brown skin as before, and the same light brown hair with pale streaks.

After his morning meal, he crossed the border, moving from Caprid-scented meadows to grass that smelled of Horses. Kokoro tucked his safe-conduct pendant into his pack, shifted to zebra, and ran south.

With plenty of spring plants to eat, he didn't even have to stop to cook food. Since he had nowhere in particular to go, it didn't matter what route he took. While he ran, he didn't notice the color of the grass, green as Ne — nothing; it was just grass under his feet. All day, he ran straight south for the sheer joy of the wind in his hair and the mind-numbing stride.

In the morning, he ran again. With no need to watch his footing, the endless drumbeat of his hooves was nearly mesmerizing, and he let his thoughts drift into a pleasant blur of nothing. This was a better life. Darravani was mistaken. He hadn't found happiness at home, but out here, it coursed through him with every step of forgetfulness. Kokoro pranced a dance step, then returned to an easy canter, ignoring the streams babbling like the happy laughter of N— nobody.

Day after day, he ran south in the warm spring weather. He trotted for hours without getting tired, enjoying the flat plain of soft grass. No more stone underfoot to bruise his hooves. No more ridges and rocks to slow his pace. No more balancing on narrow ledges that overlooked his house or — anyone else's.

From time to time, he encountered families or herds of other Horses. During his first encounter, he was almost caught as an imposter because Horses apparently used their parents' first names as family names, with the mama's name last and most important. Fortunately, one eager little foal introduced himself first and gave Kokoro a minute to calculate what his name ought to be. Kokoro Erardo Raisa. How peculiar. Netra would laugh when he told her.

No, he would never tell Netra anything again.

He flinched, pretended he thought he saw a snake to cover his reaction — no, just a stick — and chatted politely with the Horses. After a few minutes, he excused himself to run again. Just run. One, two, three, four. One, two, three, four. After too long, his thoughts smoothed into oblivion again.

After that, he was afraid he would make some other subtle cultural mistake, though he surprisingly understood the Horse dialect without difficulty. So he nodded politely as he passed Horses, but kept running, only occasionally diverting for a wordless game of catch-me with the foals.

Eventually, the uniformity of terrain and activity stopped being as mesmerizing, and his thoughts turned again to Netra. His neighbor, his best friend, his favorite person, his other half. But not his sweetheart, not even in his dreams anymore. She didn't want him.

He shook his mane and pranced until he dislodged the painful memories. Concentrate on running. One, two, three, four. Darravani had granted his wish, and he would make the most of the gift.

But the mindless abandon was hard to recover, and he ran faster and faster to distract himself. By the time spring turned into summer, he had run far enough south that the plains rose into rounded hills with thick forest beyond. To avoid slowing, he turned to run parallel to the hills.

When he stopped for a drink, a distant guard approached, spear loosely in hand. Though the warrior looked like any Darrendrakar in his two-legger form, Kokoro was too far into Equid territory for this to be anyone but a Horse.

His heart sped to a gallop. Somehow, the Horses had discovered he was an imposter. Should he run or fight? Shift or stay a zebra? Indecision kept him frozen.

As soon as he was within speaking distance, the warrior hollered, "That's the Felid border." He gestured at the hills, then readjusted his grip on his spear. "Make sure you stay on this side unless you have permission to cross. Keep well." And he left.

Kokoro exhaled noisily and let his head sag to his knees. Just a standard warning from a border guard, then. His disguise was holding.

He ran along the edge of the plains for several leagues, until he reached an area where the forest crept over the hills, nearly to the border. As he neared the trees, the smell of pine and cedar reached his nose, overwhelming the scents of grass and flowers that had been prevalent for weeks. Kokoro stopped running and closed his eyes to better enjoy the sweet odors. Until they hit his nose, he hadn't realized how much he missed his mountain. And his parents. And he still missed Netra. Running hadn't been enough of a distraction, no matter how hard he tried.

Memory sucked him in, summoning pine and cedar and Netra's bowed head as she cried behind a tree.

"RAWWWRRRR!"

At the ear-piercing scream, Kokoro jerked sideways. He stumbled and nearly fell, and by the time he got his feet back under him, the roaring had stopped.

Under the trees and in the branches, several large yellow Cats watched him in varied states of amusement. One rolled on the ground, purring a cat laugh.

Without thinking, Kokoro charged toward them. Just before crossing into the forest, he remembered where he was and swerved back.

The cougars laughed even harder.

Kokoro neighed loudly and turned away, flipping his tail in disdain. Stupid Cats. Scaring people wasn't funny. He turned and neighed again, and the cougars pointed beyond him.

In the distance, another border guard headed toward them. The Cats streaked into the forest. Two of them scampered up a tree and bounded from branch to branch and tree to tree, almost as quickly as their friends on the ground.

Kokoro watched open-mouthed until they disappeared into the distance. They weren't as fast as a Horse, naturally, but he'd never imagined they would be that quick and agile, and they climbed at least as well as they ran, if not better. And they made it look so easy.

"Did they hurt you?"

Kokoro turned to the guard. "What? No, just scared me a little."

"Did they cross the border?" The spear twitched in the guard's hands.

Kokoro shrugged. "They were still in the trees?"

"Hmph." The guard thumped the butt of his spear on the ground. "Too bad. One of these days, they will take a step too far, and then..." He wandered off, muttering to himself.

Kokoro trotted again, keeping one eye on the trees. No dumb Cat would scare him again.

At nightfall, he made camp. As he slept, he dreamed of growling cats, purring cats, cats climbing trees, cats jumping from branch to branch at almost full speed, cats chasing zebras and eating them. Cats clawing Netra.

He woke in a panicked sweat, kicking his legs under his blanket as he tried to save Netra from the lethal cats.

But no one was there. He was safe. *Steady, calm.* He took a deep breath, then another. What goat was afraid of a stinking cat? Goats could climb a mountain just as well, and could balance on a smaller ledge.

Oh. Goats could. Horses couldn't. He was a horse now. Homesickness shook him like an earthquake. Climbing was fun. He missed climbing, the higher the better. Though he didn't know how to climb trees.

He pulled the blanket over his head and rubbed his stinging eyes. Darravani had given him what he wanted, and he ought to remember that.

The cure for any sadness was to run. And Horses were better at running. So it was time to run. Dawn peeked above the horizon, and Kokoro rolled out of bed. He ate his morning meal, packed his bag, and shifted to four legs for another day of running.

Between the memory of Netra and the uneasy remnants of his dreams, he was anxious for most of the day. At trotting speed, his tail twitched. While cantering, he eyed the forest and wondered how far a tiger could jump if it started on a branch. Even at a gallop, he watched over his withers to see if a lion was following him.

And without being able to lose his thoughts while running, he thought constantly of Netra.

By the time he stopped at night, he was tired of it all.

"Hail, Darravani," he said. "I want to be a Cat."

Surely the effort of learning to climb trees would be enough to distract himself again. Obviously, a Horse was too close to being a Goat. He should have asked for a radically different form.

In the morning, he woke on a bed of flowers. He thought he recognized this combination, half alive and half dead, but he researched them all to be sure. Yes, he'd seen most of these before, and the new lily of the valley meant return of happiness, while the yellow rose was for friendship or forgiveness.

"Home is happiness. All is forgiven if you go home." He slammed the book shut. "Forgiven for what? I did nothing wrong, and I want to be a Cat."

Cats lived even farther from the Goats, far enough that he wouldn't even be able to see the mountains if he tried. Far enough, different enough, to forget Netra.

A new crop of flowers sprouted so rapidly they almost smacked him on the nose. He picked one of each and leafed through the book until he identified them all. Evening primrose was inconsistency, and rye grass was a changeable disposition. A pink larkspur meant fickleness.

Kokoro sniffed. No need for Darravani to insult him. He wasn't fickle, just searching for a better life.

At night, he again begged Darravani to change him to a Cat. When a crocus and oleander bloomed, he remembered the poison and didn't bite them like he was tempted. Though a yellow carnation also sprouted, he didn't need it to understand his goddess had denied him again.

Each day brought more memories of Netra, and loneliness thundered with every beat of his hooves. He must change, must become so different that he couldn't remember his heartache.

It took a week of constant wheedling to change Darravani's mind, but one night, he went to bed in a field of white heather with a red carnation in his hand. She had promised all his wishes would come true.

In the morning, he woke as a Cat and ran to the stream to see his new self. Instead of a tiger or leopard, or even a cheetah, the tufted ears and spotted pelt of a lynx greeted him in his reflection.

Huh. He stretched one foot and bared his claws. Still a Cat. He shrugged. Any kind of Cat was very different from being a Goat. Learning how to use his new shape should offer plenty of distractions.

But right now, he needed to get his bedroll and his new body across the border into Felid territory before the border guard caught him roaming around. Even his safe-conduct pendant could only do so much. He shifted to two-legger, just in case, and started walking.

A quick trip straight south led Kokoro into the forest before anyone saw him. As a Cat, he spent the first week exploring what his new body could do. He could still run fast, though not for long, but his jumping abilities were improved, and he could climb even better than he could as a goat.

And learning all the new skills was so fun, so busy, he didn't have any time to remember a certain girl back home. Yes, being a Cat was better than being a Horse or Goat. Finally, he had found happiness.

Day after day, week after week, he ran and walked and balanced on tree branches. But as time wore on and he grew more accustomed to his new body, he got bored. Then more bored. With boredom, his thoughts turned to his home and the girl he loved. Not even the whole new world of scents his nose detected could distract him.

To distract himself, he spied on Cat villages from high tree branches, too afraid of being discovered as an imposter to approach anyone. To his surprise, the predatory cats didn't seem at all like the stories he grew up hearing. They were as kind to each other as the Goats or Horses, as loving as Netra. They did, however, have some strange customs, like an entire village sharing the same surname derived from their location. He could never pass as a native, even if he called himself, oh, Montego or something else meaning mountain. The Cats would recognize a strange name, and if he used a real one, anyone from that village would know he was an imposter.

No, he was on his own. Alone and bored, his memories haunted him, nagging, painful. Some mornings, he lay awake for an hour, trying to decide if it was worth getting up. His parents' home was unbearable, but now his new life was no better. What would he have to do to forget that Netra didn't love him?

Kokoro stopped running as a lynx and merely trudged westward on two legs, continuing on because he had no better ideas. He wanted to see his parents. He missed his friends. Most of all, he longed for Netra.

Maybe he should listen to Darravani and go home. Even though Netra didn't love him, his parents did. He had other friends. He could meet other girls. Was this lonely life better than marrying a different girl?

But he didn't want anyone else. And at home, he would have to watch Netra marry someone else.

Pain struck him so hard he staggered. No, he couldn't go home.

By the time summer was cooling into autumn, he reached the border of Canid territory, marked with the scents of Dogs. He could travel north until he bumped into Equid territory again. He could go south and see the ocean for the first time. Or he could reverse and go back east.

He stared blindly eastward, pressing a fist against his aching heart.

"What are you doing here, stinking Cat?" someone growled.

Kokoro blinked and turned to search for the speaker. Under a bush, he finally saw a coyote, teeth bared and tail held low. He spoke in trade tongue, though with a heavy Canid accent.

"I was just walking," Kokoro said. "I did not realize I was at the border until I got here. I have not crossed." He backed up a step to make it clear.

"An unlikely story," the coyote said. "We do not want your kind here."

Kokoro laughed. The habitual wariness between the kindreds was even more ridiculous now. "My kind. You have no idea what my kind is."

The coyote narrowed his eyes. "I have a nose."

Kokoro laughed again. "You cannot believe everything you smell."

The coyote left his bush, stalking toward Kokoro with a stiff gait. "Go. Away." He growled, a low rumbling growl that lasted for an impressive time.

What a bully. Kokoro hated bullies. Aran used to pick on him and Netra until Kokoro got big enough to defend them both, but now he had left her to Aran's mercies. He sucked in a shuddering breath. It was her choice, not his.

But as a cat, he had sharp claws for defense, and a growl, too. He dropped his pack under a bush and stepped behind the leafy branches to strip and shift. When he circled back around the shrub, he took a deep breath and roared. To his surprise, instead of the impressive roar of a tiger or the hair-raising scream of the young cougars, his voice sounded like a squeaky hinge.

The coyote stopped pacing and stared at him.

Kokoro tried again, pushing more air through his lungs and into his growl. The squeaky hinge grew louder but no more impressive.

The coyote fell over, laughing and waving his paws in the air.

Red washed across Kokoro's vision, and before he thought twice, he pounced across the border and landed on the mocking coyote. He dug his claws into the red fur and clenched his toes. The coyote yelped and rolled, flipping Kokoro to the bottom. The lynx clawed harder as the coyote bit.

Kokoro squealed, and the coyote gnawed through his fur. Kokoro scratched and bit anything within range. The coyote growled and ripped with his less-impressive claws. His teeth, however, were very impressive, and Kokoro was soon bleeding as badly as the coyote. They rolled across the ground, still fighting. As they rolled, thorns and burrs stabbed them, tangling in their fur and adding to their wounds.

Despite Kokoro's impressive weaponry, he obviously had less fighting experience than the coyote, and in an embarrassingly short time, Kokoro had to surrender or risk death.

"I yield," he squeaked. "Please stop."

The coyote bit him again, then paused, mouth still closed on Kokoro's leg. "Mmmph." He spat out the leg and backed off. "I accept. Get out of my land and do not come back."

Kokoro stumbled across the border, crawled under the bush, and licked his wounds. The bite wounds on his back were difficult to reach, and the ones on his neck were impossible.

Meanwhile, the coyote wandered off. Once he was out of sight, Kokoro retrieved his pack and shifted so he could use his hands to clean his injuries with soap and water, then bandage them.

As painful as his wounds were, they still ached less than the memory of Netra rejecting his proposal.

However, since the rest of Darrendra was more dangerous than his home territory, he was asking Darravani for the wrong things. Rather than merely distracting himself, he needed a more powerful shape for protection. Dying in the jaws of a dog would help nothing.

"Darravani," he whimpered. "I want to be a Dog. A strong wolf with long teeth and a powerful jaw. Make me a wolf."

Oleander and crocus bloomed all around him.

"I don't care how dangerous it is," Kokoro wailed. "*This* is dangerous. Look at me!"

More flowers popped up, along with a seedling tree. He recognized the miniature pine, but he had to research its meaning and those of the other plants. Sweetbriar: I wound to heal. Chamomile: energy in adversity. Eastern chrysanthemum: cheerfulness under adversity. And the pine was hope in adversity.

Hmph. Adversity and wounding was the only accurate part of that message.

"I will have no hope or cheerfulness until I'm a Dog," he insisted. "And if you want me healed, make me powerful enough to defend myself."

The next crop of blossoms was the mix of dead and alive that was much too familiar.

"I don't want to go home," Kokoro said, "and I wasn't happy there."

A zinnia popped up under his nose. The book said it meant thoughts of absent friends.

Unfortunately, she was correct. He missed his family and friends like an amputated paw. But going home wouldn't solve his problems.

Unless he shifted into a ferocious dog and tore Netra's parents to shreds. For a moment, he enjoyed the imaginary scene. But as awful as they were, Netra would be heartbroken. Besides, she said she didn't want him to save her, and he would be executed as a murderer, so what would that help? No, he had made his choices, and he would have to live with them.

Tomorrow, he would turn south and head for the ocean. He had never seen it, after all. If he tried a little harder, he could numb his aching heart.

Kokoro closed his eyes and went to sleep. In his dreams, his ferocious Dog-self defended Netra. She fell in love with him, and they lived happily for the rest of their lives.

And then he woke and remembered Netra didn't love him.

3. AUTUMN & WINTER

(CANID & URSID
TERRITORIES, DARRENDRA)

Always, he yearned for something different.
The Legend of the Shifter

I n the warmth of the rising sun, Kokoro stretched, and the instant pain
reminded him of the claw marks and bites all down his body. Stupid
coyote. And stupid dreams.

Nothing he could do about either, so it was time to get moving.

All he had left to eat was a slice of stale bread, but as a Cat instead of a
Goat or Horse, he could hunt. Shifting took only seconds, as always, but
he shrank farther than expected. And his paws looked wrong. Lynx feet
were very furry and large, but his were now smaller, short-haired, and had
non-retractable claws. Behind him was a whip-like tail.

He was a dog!

What? Hadn't Darravani told him no? And he had only asked once
this time.

Unless she thought his dreams were continued requests. Couldn't the
goddess tell the difference? Or maybe she felt sorry he had been injured. In
a strong dog form, no one would pick on him again.

He peeked in the stream and deflated. He was no ferocious wolf, no
hunting dog. His new body was probably only knee-high to his two-legger

shape, and his teeth were no more impressive than his old lynx teeth. He had a sneaking suspicion "mutt" was the closest word for whatever he was.

Not funny, Darravani.

A pink larkspur bloomed under his paws.

"I am not fickle!" he shouted. "And this was your idea!"

A roar echoed in the distance. Several big, ferocious Cats dashed between the trees, coming straight for him.

Kokoro yelped and reached for his pack. No, no time. Hair standing on end, he ran for the border with the tigers and lions close on his heels.

Teeth snapped right behind his tail as he crossed. The Cats skidded to a halt when they reached the border scents, roaring and clawing the air. Kokoro ducked behind a bush, shivering. Look at those teeth and claws! He would be less than a mouthful if they had caught him. Why hadn't Darravani made him a dire wolf?

"And never come back," one finally yelled before they left.

To his surprise, he could still understand the dialect, though their accent didn't quite match the way he had spoken when he was a Cat. Was that from his lack of practice or a regional variant? Would he have betrayed himself with just his accent if he had ever talked to any Cats?

After an hour with no sign of the predators, Kokoro snuck across the border and retrieved his pack. Now that he was a Dog, he could go west again before heading for the ocean. He wanted to find that stupid coyote and beat him, but in this measly body, he wouldn't stand a chance. Maybe this was Darravani's way of making sure he couldn't get his revenge. Not fair. It also meant his dreams of protecting Netra were as dead as his hope for her love. How did Darravani think this was any better for him?

With no better options, Kokoro stepped out to explore the new territory.

His stomach growled. Exploration *after* a meal and bandages.

It took him several tries to catch a rabbit, thanks to his wounds. After caring for his injuries, Kokoro headed west, through territory not much different from the Felid lands. During the next few weeks, he walked and walked. Most of his wounds healed, but the two biggest bites continued to bother him. Resentment burned worse than the half-closed injuries. Had Darravani changed him only to punish him?

"Why, Darravani?" he asked.

A pink and white thorny rose sprouted.

Kokoro pulled out his book of flower meanings. Sweetbriar. I wound to heal.

Heal what? Being a Dog didn't heal anything.

He put away the book and walked on, fighting off memories of his best friend and beloved from which even his wounds could not distract him.

Long stretches of nowhere were broken by occasional Dog villages, and to save his healing body from the strain of hunting, he risked being identified as an intruder to trade small jobs for meals. The food tasted subtly wrong, with unfamiliar combinations and spices in the wrong proportions.

Their clothing, though obviously still Darrendran, was also not quite right, and the villagers gave his tunic the same squint-eyed looks. Apparently, Horse styles were close enough to Goat styles, but the Dogs were far enough from his home territory for the differences to be noticeable.

He might have been able to explain the clothing with a story of trading, but even though Darravani gifted him the language to match each new shape, his accent wasn't quite native. Like his clothing, it had been closer with the Horse dialect but was worse now. Whenever he first arrived at a village, the unbetrothed girls would smile and flirt while everyone else merely smiled. Then came the second glances at his clothes and the furrowed eyebrows as he spoke. After that, someone always gathered enough courage to ask him where he came from and where he was going.

Kokoro answered vaguely with a wave of his hand and distracting questions of his own. Though he gave only his first name until he discovered the Dog naming conventions (Papa's first name with a gender suffix, making him Erardsin), he never lasted more than a few days before the stares and questions and gossip urged him out of the village. He didn't blame the Dogs; they seemed a bit too odd to him, too, compared to Goats. Their eyes were different, and their hair was strange, and they even moved wrong, all in ways too subtle to pin down. Eventually, he started avoiding villages altogether unless he needed supplies, and then he kept his visits as short as possible.

Each week, Darravani grew plants for him that spoke of happiness or home or absent friends. It was enough to drive a Goat mad. Er, a Dog mad. She had given him this form. If she wanted him to go home, she should have changed him back into a Goat and given him a way to win Netra's love.

Besides, his eighteenth birthday was approaching, and if he went home, he would be betrothed to someone chosen by the village elders, since Netra didn't want him. Out here, no one knew how old he was or if he had a wife "back home." He pushed away the memory of Netra's sad eyes.

Unfortunately, his plan seemed to be failing. Instead of forgetting her as he traveled farther from home, he only thought of her more. The more he avoided the not-quite-right Dogs, the more he longed for the familiar places and people he had left behind.

Why had Darravani done this to him? Being a Dog was worse, not better.

Autumn turned cooler, and the tang of the chill air pressed memories of home on him until his chest ached. Mama would spend morning to night preserving the garden, while Papa sealed every crack in the walls and roof. If Kokoro were home, he would bounce between them, carrying and holding and finding. No, he was fine. It was normal to be a little homesick. He would get over it soon.

As soon as Netra stopped haunting his dreams.

Kokoro quickly discovered his new short hair didn't keep him warm, unlike the thick lynx fur. He had left his winter clothes home in expectation of the southern territories being warmer, and they were, but warmer wasn't actually warm anymore. Obviously, he should have done more research.

One morning he woke with frost coating his face. After brushing off the flakes of ice, he bundled himself in everything he owned and hurried to the closest town, half a day's journey. It took him hours to find someone willing to trade him an old coat and a night in a shed in exchange for garden chores.

After two days of harvesting and winterizing the garden while the owners watched him suspiciously, Kokoro took his warmer coat and a set of nearly worn-out boots with felt linings and slipped out of town to continue westward.

For a few days, he was warm enough, until the next cold snap hit. During the day, he stayed warm as long as he was walking, but at night, the cold crept in. His old Goat clothes would have been sufficient, but they were made for icebound winters.

Again, he considered spending the winter in a village, but when he stopped for supplies, he got as many stares and suspicious questions as always. In the market, he found a string of beads for Mama, and without thinking, he bought a second one. Idiot. He wasn't going home again, so how would he give it to Mama? And why buy one for Netra when he didn't even want to remember her?

Stuffing the useless beads into his pack, he headed out again. The endless forest was now broken up by a few hills, which made him miss his mountains even more.

"Happiness is at home," Darravani's flowers said each time they bloomed and died in the frost. Only the holly kept living.

"But I *wasn't* happy at home," Kokoro argued. "Not without Netra's love."

Unable to stay with the Dogs or to stop in the wilderness, he kept walking. Every morning, he turned south, but by midday, he had always wandered northwest. By the first real snowfall, he reached the western border of Canid territory, across from Ursid lands. Now he would have to turn south.

Darravani sprouted the "go home" bouquet in the middle of the snow, and Kokoro glared at the pretty flowers. Going home would solve nothing. Netra still didn't love him, and he couldn't forget her if he saw her every day. No, he could never go home. But he needed better equipment before he turned into a giant icicle.

Breath puffing in a frozen cloud, he paralleled the border for two days to the next village. After a week of chores and bartering, he had warmer winter clothes, a full pack of food, a warm tent, and a better fire kit.

Kokoro faced south toward the ocean, then irresistibly turned northward. Home was north. Netra was north. He couldn't go north, and yet he couldn't make himself walk south. East, then, back across all of Canid territory? With every snow-crunching step reminding him of home and Netra... His plan to distract himself wasn't working, and Darravani's constant reminders only made it harder.

"I think I want to be a Bear," he said, teeth chattering. "Bears sleep all winter. I want to sleep instead of remember."

Yes, sleep would bring the forgetting he craved. Kokoro pressed a hand to his chest where his heart lay as cold and still as the winter landscape, cracking like ice with the relentless step of memories.

A fluffy blossom sprouted, as white as the sprinkling of snow on the ground. Reluctantly, Kokoro removed his gloves to flip through his book. Meadowsweet: uselessness.

She always said no. At first. He set up a warm camp and a sheltered fire and started praying. "Please, let me be a Bear."

The entire clearing sprouted yellow carnations that lived only a few minutes before they froze.

"I won't accept no as an answer," Kokoro said. He gathered all the dead flowers and threw them on his fire. "I want to be a Bear."

If he couldn't distract himself, then the only way to forget was to sleep. And if he couldn't forget, his frozen heart would break in two.

For three days, he prayed. For three days, Darravani told him "no" and "go home" in a wide variety of ways, until he learned the flowers by heart. For three days, he burned her messages. She had changed him to a Dog when he hadn't really asked, so why wouldn't she let him be a Bear now that he knew what he really wanted?

Finally, a new batch of flowers sprouted while he cooked his evening meal. Kokoro already recognized the oleander as a warning. The snowball was aptly named for its appearance and meant "bound." The bay leaf meant "I change but in death."

Not a yes *or* a no. What did Darravani mean?

He was still pondering when his soup was ready and all during evening chores. As he lay down at night, he finally solved the puzzle.

"Oh, Darravani," he prayed, "Are you saying if I change again, this would be my last time? I would be a Bear until I die?"

A red carnation bloomed by his bedroll. Yes.

"But it's the only way."

Holly berries rolled through his tent door.

"I know," Kokoro groaned. "You think I would be happier at home."

He rolled over and covered his head with his blanket to block the cold air.

All night, he dreamed of home. Crisp air, bright apricot sky above the tall mountains, and four hooves bounding across rocks and hills and valleys. Mama and Papa, their cozy little house, and Netra next door, smiling at him. Then her mouth turned down, and her eyes filled with tears, and she told him no, and no again. Always no.

When he woke, his sigh half-filled his tent with a frozen cloud, and he wiped tear-crystals from his cheeks. As he stood to dress, he shivered violently.

The cold hurt less than this aching heart. He must forget Netra, no matter the cost.

"Darravani, I want to be a Bear. Or I will walk out and freeze, because I... I can't do this anymore."

A spray of yellow coronilla bloomed and froze. Success crown your wishes. Yes, she agreed!

Sudden pain drove him to his knees, twisting his guts into knots and burning through every muscle and tendon in his body. Kokoro groaned as he doubled over. The prior changes had been painless, but Darravani apparently had a point to make this time. It didn't matter; when he could finally forget his troubles, the agony would be worth it.

When the pain stopped, long minutes later, he gingerly patted his torso and limbs. He didn't look any different. Kokoro removed his night tunic, raced outside the tent, and shifted.

All he could see was a thick, hairy arm ending with six-inch claws on a massive paw. He bounded to the stream, smashing the ice to get a clear reflection of a big, ferocious bear with long teeth and impressive muscles. His white fur was thick enough he didn't even feel the cold that froze his breath.

"Thank you, Darravani," he called.

A blue harebell sprouted.

Well, that made two of them that were sad, then. But not for long, because soon he would be hibernating in peace. *Then* he would be happy.

He shifted back to two legs to load his belongings and lengthen his pack straps. Once back on four legs, he dashed quickly across the border into Ursid territory.

Every night, he found some kind of den and curled up to sleep, expecting to wake in spring. Instead, he dreamed of home. Mama and Papa. Laughing green eyes and a shy smile. Tall mountains and bounding from crag to crag. Home.

Every morning, he woke. Why couldn't he hibernate? What was he doing wrong?

Obviously, he didn't have a proper den for winter. As soon as he found one, he could stop running and sleep through his worries.

He missed running, actually. Real running. And climbing. Smaller bears could climb, or so rumor claimed, but he was much too big. He missed horns instead of claws. He missed being around other people. Bears might be solitary, but Goats were herd people.

Kokoro was no longer a Goat. He would never be a Goat again. And that's the way he wanted it.

And yet, day after day, when he woke from failed hibernation, he tried to go west but was pulled north as if he were a lodestone. The winter sank deeper into cold and ice and snow, and still he trundled northward, impervious to all weather and all sense, unable to sleep, unable to stop walking.

Home, his heart whispered, and he couldn't make it listen.

Home, his feet stomped, and he couldn't make them stop.

Home.

Why couldn't he sleep?

On his way through the forest, he found a forester staring at a fallen tree, hands on his hips. The tree blocked the entire path, and though the Bear had obviously tried to cut it, his small saw was a third of the trunk's diameter.

Kokoro stopped beside him and examined the tree. Most of the branches had already been cut flush, as had the top of the trunk as low as the saw could handle. The tree had broken halfway up, so the remaining chunk was only two or three yards long. Unfortunately, it had fallen between other trees and was wedged in place. Rolling it perpendicular to clear the path was impossible, though it could be dragged straight into the forest for a short distance.

The forester rubbed his chin. "I need to get the big saw and more help."

"What if we drag it into the forest?" Kokoro asked.

The Bear laughed. "All by ourselves?"

Kokoro shrugged. "I meant on four legs. We could rig a harness."

"Four legs during winter? Won't that trigger your hibernation?"

"I've been having trouble sleeping." Kokoro looked away, afraid he had already revealed himself as an imposter. Did Bears ever have insomnia?

The Bear squinted at him but held out his hand. "If you say so. Good to see you, stranger. I'm Molimo Kumaser."

While Kokoro clasped his arm, he frantically calculated his proper Bear name. Like the Dog's, they apparently used a gender suffix, but attached to their mama's name. "Kokoro Raisaser."

To keep Molimo from noticing anything else odd about him, he nodded at the tree. "So, shall we try it?"

Molimo shrugged. "Might as well. I can always get the saw later. I'll make a harness while you shift. How big should I make it?"

Kokoro shrugged. "Pretty big."

He walked behind a tree, stripped, and shifted as quickly as possible to avoid freezing.

When he padded back to the fallen tree, Molimo gaped, then started adjusting the rope harness. "Big indeed. And you have a wicked sense of humor. You almost had me believing you suffered from insomnia. An ice bear." He shook his head and chuckled. "Ice bears never hibernate."

Never? Kokoro almost collapsed in despair. What cruel trick was Darravani playing on him?

Molimo strapped the harness around Kokoro and tied the other end of the rope to the trunk. "If you can move it even a few feet, it will be good enough for now." He pushed. "Now!"

Stomping down his despair for the moment, Kokoro threw his weight into the rope. At first, the tree didn't move. Behind him, Molimo rocked the trunk from side to side until it shifted. Kokoro pulled, digging his claws into the frozen earth. One step at a time, he dragged the massive trunk until Molimo shouted again.

"Thank you," Molimo said, untying the harness. "Can I repay you in any way?"

"Do you have any extra food?" Kokoro asked absently, his mind still reeling from the news he would never hibernate.

"Now that I don't have to spend three days cutting up this tree, I can spare you some."

By the time Kokoro shifted and dressed, the Bear had a package wrapped for him.

"Thank you," Kokoro muttered.

For the rest of the day, he stumbled randomly through the forest. Never hibernate. Never forget. Always haunted by the memories of Netra saying she didn't love him, didn't want to marry him. Maybe he *should* let himself freeze.

At nightfall, he collapsed on the ground, still as a bear, and cried himself to sleep. In his dreams, Netra watched him with tearful sage-green eyes. "I don't want you," she said.

"I love you," he said, and she ran away.

The nightmare restarted, and again he watched her cry.

"I don't want you to save me," she said.

"I love you," he said as she ran away.

Again she wept, and his heart crumbled. "I don't want you to *save* me."

"I love you," he said, after she ran.

Kokoro woke with a jerk. Had she even heard him say he loved her?

But he had told her again when he left.

Had he?

No, he hadn't. He dropped his muzzle on his paws and groaned. She thought he only wanted to marry her to rescue her, not because he loved her.

He was an idiot. Darravani was right; his happiness lay at home.

But if Netra hadn't already picked someone else to marry, she'd be assigned a partner in spring, and it still wouldn't be him. At least a husband would take her away from her cruel parents. She would be happier, and only he would be miserable.

Unless she hadn't made a choice yet and he could get back in time to convince her he loved her. Hope sprouted in his heart like Darravani's blossoms, spreading like spring in the meadows.

"Please Darravani, change me back to Goat. I promise I'll never ask to leave home again."

A single bay leaf grew through the snow. "I change but in death."

His meadow of hope withered at the reminder. He would never change back until he died.

Netra was lost to him forever.

4. RETURN

(URSID TO CAPRID
TERRITORIES, DARRENDRA)

Where did true happiness lie?
The Legend of the Shifter

D arravani had said no more shifting, but she had always changed her mind before. Just before dawn, Kokoro struck camp and headed north as quickly as bear legs would take him. Every hour, he prayed, nagging and pleading and persuading.

No flowers bloomed in the snow, not even a denial of his request. Why wasn't she answering him? Had his goddess abandoned him? She wouldn't, would she? Surely she was merely annoyed at him and would eventually forgive him.

Clinging to useless hope, he kept going. The exertion of plowing through the snow kept Kokoro warm, especially with his thick fur, but he was always hungry. Despite his best efforts at hunting, he lost weight, and his stomach constantly growled as the weeks passed.

After midwinter, the days slowly grew longer again, but the cold deepened, and the snow reached to Kokoro's furry belly. Each step was a struggle, and he nearly wept in relief anytime he found an icy patch that allowed him to walk on top. The ice never lasted long enough, and soon he was buried in snow again. Still he walked and prayed, moving from first light until he collapsed with exhaustion at night.

Each morning, he woke to a longing sorrow more exhausting than the travel and more ravenous than his hunger.

"You were right, Darravani," he admitted for the thousandth time. "I had what I needed at home. I was stupid, and now I'm sorry. Please change me back to a Goat so I can convince Netra I love her."

No answer.

He'd been begging for over two months, and Darravani still hadn't given in. Kokoro turned east. What if she never changed her mind, and he was stuck as a Bear forever? Would he lose Netra *and* his home? Though his thick fur protected him from the winter weather, icy loneliness froze his heart.

Within a few furlongs, he stared at the treeless border between Bear and Cow. If he could get through Bovid territory, he had only a quick run through the corner of Suid before he was back to Caprid territory. But the Cows and Pigs would never let a Bear wander freely through their territories. Even if they did, the Sheep and Goats wouldn't allow a Bear to live with them.

Why hadn't he listened to his goddess? Being a horse or cat or dog or bear was fine for the Horses and Cats and Dogs and Bears, but he missed being a goat. Goats could run like a horse, climb mountains like a cat, jump better than a dog, and ignore the cold like a bear. Goats were perfect.

Worst of all, Netra would never want to marry a Bear. As a Goat, he would have still had a chance to prove his love.

"Please, Darravani, I beg you to change me back to Goat."

Nothing.

Kokoro flopped onto his belly and wailed. How could he get home like this? He dropped his head to the ground. If only he could disguise himself or look like everyone else.

Look like everyone else. He gasped. In his two-legger form, no one could tell his kindred. And his safe-conduct pendant gave him permission to cross borders as long as he didn't harm or scare anyone.

If he had to stay on two legs for the rest of his life to keep his kindred from knowing he was now a Bear, he would do it. He would do anything to go home. As for Netra, he hadn't quite figured out how to persuade her to marry him, but he would start by making sure she knew he loved her.

Kokoro hopped to his feet. This would take some preparation.

First, he spent a week hunting game. After skinning and gutting the carcasses, he chopped them into bite-size pieces and let them freeze solid, wrapped in the skins. As long as the weather stayed below freezing, the meat would stay good.

To make room for the meat, he thinned his belongings to the bare minimum. His pack held bedding, his fire kit, the minimum for hygiene, the frozen meat and the last of his food, a single pot and spoon, and one water bottle, with his tent strapped on the outside.

After shifting back to two-legger form, he dressed in all his clothing, summer and winter, and strapped his knife to his belt. He put his pack onto a small litter he had built, and pulled the rope harness over his shoulders. The beads on the pile of discarded belongings glittered in the sunlight. He could still take them for Mama and Netra. Two strands of beads weighed almost nothing but might improve his apologies, so he dropped them into his pocket and started walking.

Breaking through the snow was even harder on two legs, though his lighter weight allowed him to sometimes walk on top of the drifts, and pulling his pack was easier than carrying it. As long as the snow lasted, the trick would work. In the coming spring, the meat wouldn't stay frozen, anyway, and his pack would lighten in a two-edged blessing.

Kokoro crossed the border in the middle of the day, waving his safe-conduct pendant and spinning a tale of midwinter trade. After showing the beads to the Bull guard and lying about having more in his pack, he was allowed across but warned to behave himself.

He smiled as charmingly as his frozen lips could manage, then pulled his scarf across his face and trudged eastward. His bear shape could handle the cold without trouble, but his plan depended on not being identified as a Bear anymore.

Day after day, he plowed over or through the snow, walking east from dawn to dusk. His morning meal was meat and grains cooked overnight in banked coals, and in the evening, he ate a quick soup with more meat and a handful of dried vegetables. Neither meal was ever big enough to keep his stomach from growling, yet he skipped the midday meal to avoid stopping. The meager diet was enough to keep him alive and moving, barely. His thoughts of the beautiful girl next door grew to include elaborate meals, steaming and delicious, served at the familiar table with all his favorite people sitting around it. He didn't know if the tempting aromas from her house had been her cooking or her mama's, but if she didn't know how to cook, *his* mama could teach her.

His store of meat ran out as the weather finally warmed to just above freezing. Spring was coming, and so was his birthday and the deadline for choosing his wife.

"Please," he begged Darravani, as he had every day for months, "please change me back to Goat. You were right about what I need. See, I'm going home. Please change me back."

No answer, even though she had bloomed flowers in the snow before.

By now, he was halfway across Bovid territory and could see mountains ahead of him. As the snow slowly melted, he walked faster. After only a couple of weeks, he abandoned the litter in the mud. In two more weeks, he traded his heavy coat for a jacket and more food at a Cow village, supplementing his meals with early spring greens. The extra energy and the warmer weather sped his walk, though the steady march of the season warned him time was running out.

If he was late, he would lose Netra forever, whether or not Darravani yielded.

Spring was in full force by the time he reached the Suid border. He repeated his trader routine, claiming to be a Bull this time, and showed his safe-conduct pendant. Once out of sight of the border guard, Kokoro broke into a run. It took him only two days to skirt the lake and cross into Caprid territory.

At the next village, he traded his blankets, tent, and warm clothes for more food and a lighter pair of boots. Every hour, he ran as long as he could, then dropped to a walk for the rest of the hour. After a few minutes of rest and a bite of food, he ran again. Each night, he rolled into his cloak in utter exhaustion.

"When I said I wanted to run, Darravani, this wasn't what I had in mind," he murmured one night through his yawns. Though he had run all day as a Horse, he hadn't pushed himself as hard. But he had to get home.

Each morning, he prayed for a return to Goathood as he ate his morning meal, then continued his pleas with every thud of his boots. Despite the profusion of blossoms now sprinkled in the grass, they were all normal, in-season flowers spread across the entire area. No messages for him.

Finally, he saw his home mountain far to the north. He was almost there. He still had a chance.

But the merchant at the last village who traded him food in exchange for his pot and several hours of chopping wood, told him Kokoro and Netra's birthday was only a week away. He was almost out of time, and he still had a long way to go.

He turned north into the hills, thankful for the longer days in which to run, the lighter load to carry, and the travel food he didn't have to cook. Most of all, he was grateful for the mountain that daily grew larger in front of him, appearing and disappearing over and behind the hills that grew ever taller as he got closer.

Running grew harder in the rough terrain, but Kokoro refused to quit. By the time he had two days left, home was beyond only three more hills. He must find Netra before the council assigned both of them to marry people they didn't choose. If she hadn't already chosen someone else.

"I'm almost home, Darravani," he panted. "Please change me back."

No answer. Netra might marry him if he begged, but she wouldn't marry a Bear. Kokoro kept running.

On the last day, he reached the foot of his mountain and charged full speed up the slope, waving at neighbors but not stopping to talk to anyone. If he wasn't already too late, he had no time to lose. He dashed through the village, heading for the path to home. Just this once, he wished he lived farther down the mountainside.

As he passed the council clearing, he glanced sideways and screeched to a halt. A small crowd stood in the clearing or sat on logs to wait their turn to declare their choice for betrothals or be assigned one. The village elders were already there, and so were his parents and a few more families with children the same age. And Aran, the local bully, was talking to Netra with a sneer on his face while her parents nodded and smiled.

He was too late. Netra was already betrothed. He had lost her forever.

Kokoro leaned against a tree, knees shaking with exhaustion and despair. If only he had made it here yesterday.

But instead of Aran leading Netra around the fire, he sat with his parents and winked at her. Netra took a step back and wrapped her arms around herself.

Kokoro sucked in a breath. Was it not final yet?

No, the council members were still greeting each other. He had a minute, maybe.

Kokoro dashed from tree to tree, staying out of sight. Once he could reach Netra's elbow, he pulled her behind a large tree, holding a finger to his lips.

She smothered a gasp, then whispered fiercely, "Where have you been? We were worried about you. You look so thin. Are you well?"

"Tell you later," he gasped. "Are you betrothed yet?"

His stomach cramped, and he swallowed hard to keep from being sick. He still hadn't recovered his breath from running, and her answer might keep him from ever breathing again.

She glared. "You've been gone for almost a *year*. We didn't know if you were alive or dead, and that's all you want to know?"

He grabbed her hands. "Are you?"

"No!" Netra pulled her hands free. "But I will be in a few minutes. I think the council made their decision before they came."

She tilted her head toward Aran, who was grinning at Netra's parents.

Kokoro clenched his fists. Aran would be no better than Netra's parents, and she'd never be happy. Neither would he.

"Will you marry me instead?" he begged.

Netra sighed. "I'm not looking for pity. I want you to be happy."

Kokoro sucked in a breath. "But you're the only woman who would make me happy. I love you."

She blinked, and a single tear slid down her cheek.

"I know you don't want me to save you," he said, "but I do want to make you happy. And you aren't happy with your parents, and you certainly won't be happy with Aran. Please marry me? But before you say yes, I should tell you I'm no longer a Goat, not even a Horse. I'm a Bear, and I'm stuck as one."

Netra's eyes widened, and her mouth dropped open.

"Let's get started," he heard from the other side of the tree. "We will begin with the betrothal of Netra to—"

Kokoro jerked around the tree, pulling Netra with him. "To me," he shouted.

Everyone in the clearing turned to stare. The village elders frowned, and his parents gasped. He mouthed "please" at Netra.

"She belongs to me," Aran protested.

"She belongs to herself," Kokoro said, "but I wish to marry her. If she will take me."

His rival turned red and drew his knife. Aran's parents grabbed his arms, and everyone started shouting and arguing. Kokoro folded his arms and glared at the bully.

"Be quiet, everyone," the headwoman said. "Settle down."

Nobody listened, and now four people held back Aran.

The shaman shouted, "Quiet!"

The noise stumbled to a halt, and the shaman gestured emphatically to the headwoman.

"Netra," their leader asked, "do you have a preference?" When Aran started to speak, she held up her hand. "Netra?"

Kokoro squeezed Netra's fingers and tried to put all his love and pleading into one look. Her parents frowned and pointed at Aran, who puffed out his chest.

Lip quivering, Netra turned her face from her parents and pulled her hand free from Kokoro. Looking only at the headwoman and the shaman, she wrapped her arms around herself. "May I speak to you privately?"

"No," her papa protested. "We need to help you with the decision." He nodded toward his chosen candidate again.

"She is a grown woman," the shaman said.

She led Netra and the headwoman aside while the other village elders physically blocked Netra's parents and everyone else from following.

The conversation took a very long time, and Kokoro began to sweat. He couldn't hear anything, and all he could see was an occasional arm waving past a tree trunk. Netra was telling them she wanted him, wasn't she? What if she wasn't? She couldn't possibly prefer Aran!

Maybe the elders wouldn't agree since Kokoro had left for almost a year. Stupid! Why was he so stupid? He should have stayed and proved himself to be reliable and worthy. He should have stayed to convince Netra he loved her.

And they still kept talking. What was taking so long? Aran looked pleased at first, then gradually developed a wrinkle between his eyebrows while his parents patted his arms. Every few minutes, Netra's parents tried to get past the elders with persuasion or force.

Eventually, the three returned, and with Netra behind the leaders, the headwoman spoke. "We have determined that, with the agreement of the other elders, Netra will marry Kokoro."

The elders looked puzzled, but they shrugged and nodded.

Kokoro exhaled in relief and sagged against the tree before his shaking knees could dump him in the dirt.

Before he could step forward, Netra's parents and Aran protested at the top of their lungs.

"Furthermore," the headwoman shouted. When the noise settled to a dull roar, she continued. "During the betrothal year, Netra will live with the shaman. She has no more claim on her parents, nor they on her. Kokoro will pay the bride price to the shaman for her care."

Netra's parents charged the women, shouting again. The village elders, eyes wide, once again blocked their way. Kokoro nodded sharply. If he had known the elders could separate the family, he would have suggested it years ago.

"I am appalled at what I learned today," the shaman said. "The council will discuss further details in private. All of you but the elders, Netra, and Kokoro and his parents are dismissed."

When no one moved, the headwoman pulled herself to her full height. "Get out of my sight in the next minute, or face the consequences. We'll settle the rest of you later today."

With frequent glances behind them, the crowd scattered. The elders crowded around the headwoman, babbling questions.

Kokoro held out his arms, and Netra dodged the elders to run to him. He wrapped his arms around her and leaned down, nose to nose.

"So, this is a yes?" he asked.

She blushed and nodded. "Not that I believe a word of your story," she whispered, "but I love you, too."

A million dandelions of happiness sprouted in his heart. Oh, yes, he definitely should have said something earlier. He pulled her closer, regretting a year of lost opportunities and anxious not to lose another second. Just before their lips touched, someone tapped him on the shoulder, and Netra pulled away.

Kokoro straightened reluctantly. "What now?"

"We want to formalize this betrothal immediately," the shaman said, "so no one can protest it later. The council and your parents will be enough witnesses." She motioned toward the fire in the middle of the clearing.

Kokoro took Netra's hand and walked around the fire three times. Even the leaping flames couldn't match the warmth of joy in his heart. At the end, he gathered her in his arms and leaned in for the best kiss ever.

One year later, Kokoro slammed the door of his new house and hurried toward the council clearing, tugging on his green tunic with one hand while he clutched Netra's bouquet in the other. The symbols marking his heritage were painted on his face, and all other requirements had been met earlier. All that was left was the actual wedding ceremony, and he couldn't wait another minute.

He raced down the mountain path at full speed and reached the clearing not even out of breath, courtesy of staying in two-legger shape for the whole year. Even Netra urging him to prove his story had not persuaded him to risk exile for being a Bear. He would stay on two legs forever rather than lose her.

At least his time away had taught him a few useful things. The elders had given him permission to start a new apprenticeship as a trader, and two legs was better for that. In fact, they were excited for his new occupation, since he knew *five* languages, though he lied about learning them the normal way in his travels rather than through magic. Even his not-quite-right accent wouldn't matter when he wasn't trying to pass as a native.

His parents arrived at the same time he did, and they waited a few anxious minutes for Netra to come, escorted by the shaman. Her green dress made her eyes even brighter, and he stared, blind to everything but her, until Papa elbowed his ribs.

"Here." Kokoro shoved the flowers at her and fumbled for her hand.

Netra admired the blossoms with a chuckle at the dandelions, which were rarely used at weddings.

"But I am happy," Kokoro whispered, touching one of the sunny yellow blooms.

"So am I," she said, and then it was time.

The ceremony passed in a blur, and before he knew it, he was shutting his door with his new bride inside his home.

The next morning, he woke to a small scream. He fell off the bed, scrambling for footing, and discovered Netra staring at him.

"Sorry," she said. "I guess I'm not used to waking with someone in my bed. And please don't sleep on the sheets when you're like that." She yawned. "I knew your story wasn't true."

Kokoro took a step forward, and his hooves clattered on the wooden floor.

His hooves?

He looked down and discovered he was in his goat form. Not Bear, but Goat! Darravani had changed him back after all. Last night as a wedding gift? Sometime in the past year when he hadn't tried shifting? But why, when she had told him no?

And outside the window, his front lawn was covered in white. He shifted to two legs, grabbed his tunic, and bolted for the door. Netra followed behind him, still in her night tunic.

"What happened to the grass?" she asked.

White flowers bloomed so thickly the green barely showed. Lily of the valley for return of happiness, white heather for wishes come true, and against the fence, pink and white sweetbriar bushes.

Thank you, Darravani, Kokoro prayed, as he put his arms around Netra. *I* am *healed.*

I f you liked this story, you might like the traditional Earth fairytales:
    The Stonecutter
The Fisherman and his Wife
The Story of the Ambitious Mice
The Husband of the Rat's Daughter

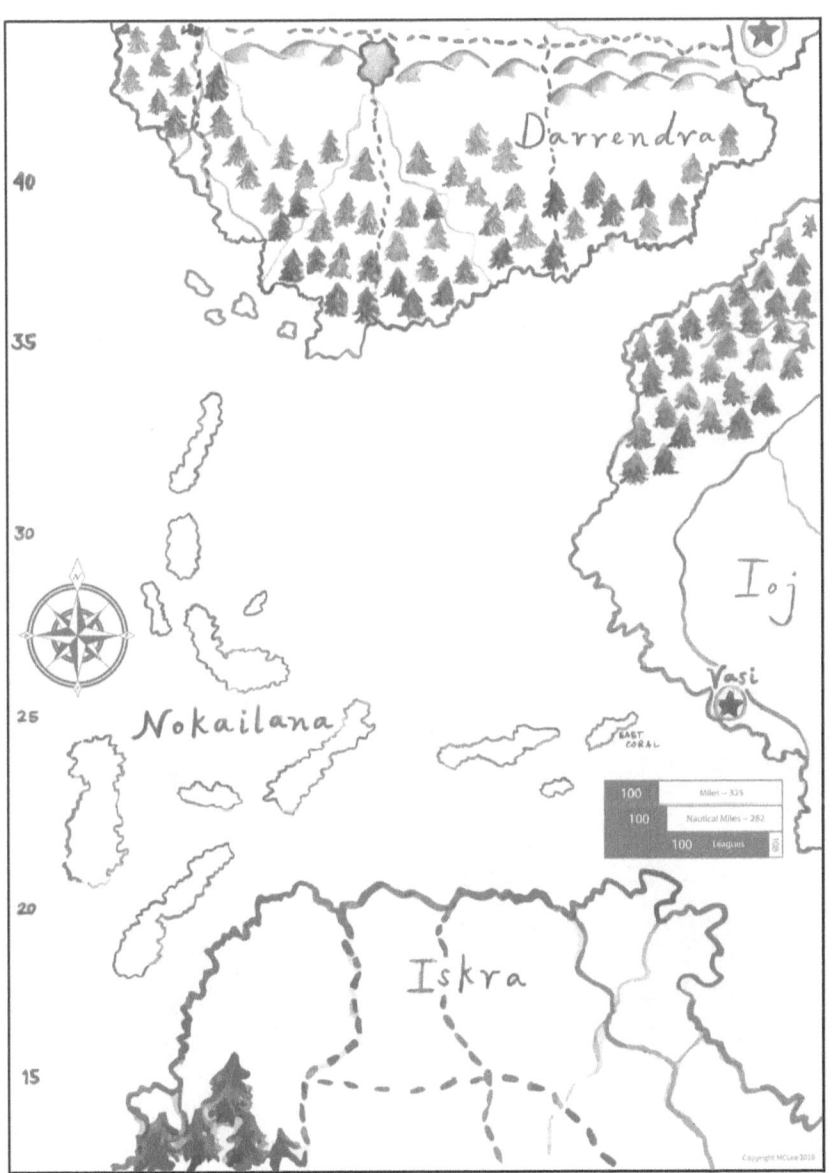

IMPOSSIBLE

1. PROPOSAL
(AINONANI, NOKAILANA)

She asked him to prove his love.
The Legend of the Frog

Kamala dug her bare webbed toes into the warm sand and rolled her shoulders. After a delicious meal on the beach, a nice game of catch was the perfect way to end the day. She cranked her arm backward and hurled the ball. It sailed between her boyfriend's outstretched hands and landed in the ocean.

"Manami," she groaned. "Again?"

He shrugged and splashed through the shallow waves to retrieve the floating wooden ball. "I don't know why you think I'll suddenly be good at this." He awkwardly threw the ball underhanded in her general direction.

She lunged sideways, smashing into the beach but catching the bright yellow ball. Scrambling to her feet, she brushed sand off her ocean suit and her face, paying special attention to the gills on her neck.

"Practice is good for you," she scolded. "If you practice enough, maybe you'll start catching the ball. Or throwing it in a straight line."

Her dad used to spend hours playing catch with her. He died when she was little, but she still remembered his smile and encouraging words. Every time she threw the ball, she thought of him.

But when she tossed it again, Manami flinched, letting the ball drop beside his feet.

"Manamikamoku," she scolded. "You didn't even try."

"Kamalalokelani," he mocked. "You're right." He sat on the sand and flopped back, resting his head on his linked hands. "Why don't we take a break? I have a question for you, anyway."

His saffron-yellow braids were coming loose, but his eyes, the exact lavender of the ocean, sparkled as he looked at her.

After sitting beside him, she tossed the ball from hand to hand. "What question?"

"Well, um... I was thinking..."

Kamala rolled her eyes. "As usual."

He cleared his throat. "About us."

"Oh, well, that's a change." She rolled onto her belly and fluttered her eyelashes at him.

To her surprise, he blushed.

"I'm serious," he complained.

"Why?"

"Why am I thinking about us?"

She laughed. "No, why are you being serious?"

Manami groaned. "Could *you* be serious, please?"

Kamala scooted over and put her head on his shoulder. Throwing an arm across him, she smiled. "Maybe."

He pulled an arm out from under his head and wrapped it around her. "I love you."

"Mm-hm." He smelled of salt water and sunshine, and she buried her nose in his neck and inhaled. "I love you, too."

"I never want to be with anyone else."

"Mmm. You're my favorite person." She tickled his ear with one of her braids, appreciating the contrast of the palm-green to his golden skin.

The setting sun cast blue rays across the apricot sky, turning the sand pale blue and the ocean a deep purple. From where they lay, she could see both the ocean and the island flowers that grew rampant before merging into the community gardens.

After a minute, Manami cleared his throat. "So I think we should get married."

Kamala froze, then laughed. "I get it. First you tell me to be serious, and then you pull out the joke. That's very sneaky."

She tickled his sides, but he grabbed her hands.

"No, I *am* serious," he said. "Will you marry me?"

She jerked her hands free and sat up. "You can't be serious!"

"Why not? You said you love me."

"I haven't even reached seven thousand days yet! And neither have you. We're both too young."

"No, we aren't," he argued. "We're both adults. And we've been together ever since we *became* adults. Did you want to end our relationship?"

"No, of course not!"

"Then why not marry?"

"Nokai don't get married!"

Manami folded his arms. "Sometimes we do."

"How many married Nokai do you know?"

He ducked his head and counted on his fingers, lips shaping the names of their family and neighbors on the island. "About forty couples," he finally said. "Forty is a lot."

"Forty. And how many people are in our clan?"

He ran his hands through his hair, further disarranging his braids. "I don't know. A thousand or so?"

She shrugged. "Sounds about right. And about a quarter are children. So eighty married adults out of seven hundred. That's not a lot. And you know why."

He took her hand and gazed into her eyes. "But darling, I don't care that marriage is permanent. We won't ever want a divorce. Nothing will go wrong. I want to be with you forever."

Kamala stroked his cheek. "Forever is a very long time. What if we change our mind in a few years?"

Manami puffed out his cheeks. "What can I do to convince you I'll never change my mind?"

"Impossible," she said.

He frowned.

"Fine," she said. "Prove you can do the impossible by doing the impossible. Find me a thousand fathoms of farmland beneath the sea and over the sand," she said. "Grow me a crop on it to show you can provide for me. Then reap it with a ram's horn and tie it with rope made from heather. If you can do that, you'll prove you're a true love of mine."

He shook his head. "What about just a kiss?"

"And what does that prove?" She crossed her arms. "You kiss me all the time."

He shrugged. "I love you all the time. And what if I asked you to do something impossible to prove *your* love?"

"I'm not the one who wants to get married."

But he kept talking. "What if I asked you to make a shirt for me, to show my mom you can take care of *me*?"

"That's not impossible at all," she scoffed. "I don't like sewing, but I know how."

Manami scooted backward and crossed his arms. "What if I asked you to make a shirt without using a needle or leaving a seam? What if I asked you to spin the thread with wool from a golden sheep?"

"Now you're getting silly." Kamala reached for him, but he scooted backward again.

"You asked me to do the impossible," he said. "Fair is fair. What if I asked you to wash the shirt in the unfinished well that has no spring water and is sheltered from the rain? What if I asked you to dry the shirt with a thorn?"

"Forget it." Kamala threw her hands into the air and jumped to her feet. "Let's just play." She grabbed the ball and tossed it into the air.

Manami glanced toward the ocean. Their underwater village was out of sight, but she could barely see the blue lights from the atolla jellyfish that had been netted into position for the festival tonight. The atolla blinked on and off at random intervals, marking their alarm at the passage of other Nokai through the water.

"Don't you want to go to the festival?" he asked, still frowning.

"Not really. If you don't want to play, I'll go home."

Sulkily, he climbed to his feet and walked away, hands extended. But he missed the catch again and had to chase the ball.

"I'd rather go to the festival." He leaned back and threw the ball harder than usual, but no straighter. It curved to the side and lurched down the beach.

Kamala waved her arm at the ball in frustration, but Manami just shrugged.

"You wanted to play; you go get it."

After glaring at him, she stomped along the shore. In the twilight, the yellow ball was invisible on the sand, but she kept walking. When she reached its landing place, little indentations and furrows marked its bouncing, rolling path.

After a few fathoms, the path ended at a small hole.

Kamala laughed. "How can he miss me but drop it exactly in a hole?"

She stuck her fingers into the hole, which was much deeper than she expected, but couldn't feel the ball. Fine, then. There was more than one way to kill a shark. She dug the sand to enlarge the hole, but the tunnel went on and on, and no matter how much sand she moved, she couldn't find her ball.

"How long will you dig?" Manami asked.

She looked up and discovered him watching her, brows wrinkled.

"Until I get my ball back! Look what you did!"

"I didn't do it on purpose!"

The sun dipped below the horizon. Now the only light was the refraction of the blinking atolla in the ocean. Hidden in the darkness, Kamala wiped away tears. It was only a ball, but it was the only gift she had left from her dad. A sniffle escaped.

Manami's hand touched her shoulder. "Come here." He pulled her to her feet and wrapped his arms around her. "I'm sorry. I'll figure out how to get it back in the morning."

"How will you do that?" She stifled another sob.

"Right now, I have no idea. But I'll look at it in the morning, when I can actually see it." He rubbed her back. "I know how important the ball is to you, and I'd do anything to make you happy. Please don't cry. I promise I'll fix it. Let's go home and sleep."

"I'm not leaving," Kamala protested. "What if something fills in the hole and I can never find it again?"

His sigh ruffled her hair. "We can sleep on the beach. You stay here, and I'll go find our things."

She nodded, bumping her chin against his collarbone, and he rubbed her back again before disappearing into the dark. Careful not to step in her excavation, she sat next to the hole. The sand was still warm, and the ocean waves whispered hypnotically. Stars appeared one by one and then by the dozens and hundreds, and she leaned back to trace the constellations.

If she couldn't get back her ball, would her memories of her dad fade like the stars in daylight?

Eventually, Manami returned. The food basket thumped near her head, and his warm body settled next to her, not quite touching. He carefully draped a blanket over her, then lay down with a sigh.

"I'm sorry," he repeated.

Kamala wiped more tears on the blanket. "I know you are."

He touched her lightly on the arm, then withdrew.

With a choked sob, she rolled over and hugged him. "I love you." Burying her face in his shoulder, she cried herself to sleep.

In the middle of the night, she half-woke to the sound of whispers.

"Please, Makanavailea," Manami prayed to their goddess, "please help me rescue Kamala's ball. Whatever it takes."

Kamala mumbled and wiggled closer.

"Shh, go back to sleep," he whispered, stroking her back until she did.

When Kamala woke, the sun was already above the trees. As she blinked, the beach gradually swam into focus. In front of her face was the hole where she had lost her ball. Sadness pricked at her again, and she sat up to rub her eyes.

A frog croaked, and when she lowered her hands, a tiny, bright yellow frog stared at her with bulging eyes.

"Poison frog," she shrieked, dumping the contents of the food basket and flipping it upside-down over the amphibian. "Manami, help me get rid of it!"

She turned to shake him awake, but the sand was empty except for her ball.

"My ball! How did you get it back?" Kamala cradled it to her chest, then scanned the beach for her boyfriend.

Nothing. Though she saw a few Nokai, none of them had his saffron hair. But her ball was here, so he must have retrieved it somehow.

Somehow... She remembered his prayer to Makana in the middle of the night. He told their goddess he would do whatever it took to rescue her ball. And here it was, but he was gone. Unless...

She stared at the basket in horror. Makana had turned him into a tiny frog to retrieve her ball from the hole! The frog was the same color as his hair, proof of the transformation.

"Oh, why did you do it?" she wailed. "Change back now!"

Kamala tapped the basket, and the frog croaked.

Still a frog. Oh, this was terrible! She already knew he loved her. That had never been the problem. They had never *had* a problem until his marriage proposal and now... this. No matter how much she treasured her ball, it wasn't worth losing him. And she had never seriously meant he had to prove his love.

Kamala chewed on her fingernail and whimpered. How long would he stay a frog?

She leaned down and whispered through the side of the basket. "I love you. Please change."

Gribbit.

Kamala dropped her head on the sand and wept. Still a frog. No loving smile, no warm voice, no strong arms embracing her. He couldn't even talk to her.

Maybe it would wear off in a while. Until then, how could she keep him safe? What would she feed him? How could she keep him damp without letting him swim away? And now that she needed Manami's endless thinking, he couldn't tell her how to solve her problems.

Open one clam at a time. First, keep him safe. Somehow, without touching him and poisoning herself.

The basket would do. No, it was loosely woven and wouldn't hold water. His skin would dry out.

Plug the holes.

Plug them with what?

Kamala whimpered. Fine, the first step was to keep the frog from getting lost while she figured out the rest. Careful not to tip it up, she turned the basket back and forth, grinding the edges into the sand. She left her ball by the basket and ran inland.

"Plug the holes," she chanted. "How do I plug the holes?"

As she darted through the flowers, her bare foot landed in a mud puddle. "Ugh. Ick." She shook her toes, and the thick mud plopped back into the water.

"Wait, mud is perfect! No, it will leak through the holes." She hummed a high, distressed note and turned in a circle. "Moss *and* mud!"

She picked several big leaves and laid them on the ground, then filled two with thick mud and one with moss. After stacking them, she carried the entire pile back to the basket.

Kamala arranged the leaves in a circle around her, then reached for the basket. "Don't run away," she chanted. "Don't run away."

Quickly, she flipped over the basket and started packing the weave with mud, thickened with moss, always keeping one eye on the frog.

Once all the holes were filled, she set the basket near the frog. "Come on, jump in."

The frog ignored the basket.

Kamala sighed and flipped the basket upside-down over the frog again. She closed her eyes to think, then rummaged through the pile of discarded food and dishes to find both cups, a plate, and a fruit rind.

She walked back to the flowers and put the fruit rind on the plate, nestled under the blossoms. Then she went to the mud puddle and filled a cup with water. Though muddy, it was fresh instead of salty.

Back by the plate, she sat and waited, not moving a thumb-length. Soon, insects swarmed the rind, and birds came to eat the insects. Quietly, she slipped the other cup over the rind, trapping the insects. One small bird protested, flying to her shoulder to chirp at her.

"Sorry," she whispered.

The bird squawked again, then chased an ant across her shirt. Once the tasty nibble was in its beak, it jumped down the front of her shirt and snuggled in for a nap.

"Oh, no," Kamala groaned. She nudged the bird, but it merely grumbled and wiggled farther into its makeshift nest.

Well, it would wake soon enough.

She carefully carried the plate of insects and cup of water back to the basket. Turning it right-side up, she emptied the water and the insects, rind and all, into the basket. With a gribbit, the frog jumped in.

Slowly, she draped a napkin over the top of the basket and tied it with hair ribbons.

There. Now Manami would be safe until he changed back. And when would that be?

Kamala nibbled on a fingernail, then spat out mud. Ick.

Maybe he couldn't change back by himself. Maybe he needed help.

If Makana had turned him into a frog to let him prove how much he loved Kamala, then maybe she needed to prove she loved him, too. Impossible though they were, maybe she had to accomplish the tasks he requested in order to break the enchantment. She had to at least try.

2. TRUE LOVE

(AINONANI, NOKAILANA)

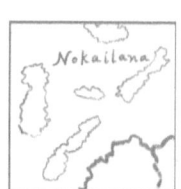

She performed impossible tasks to try to change him back.
The Legend of the Frog

W here does one start in attempting the impossible?
Kamala closed her eyes and tried to think. Manami would have an idea. He always did. She had no idea if he could think now or if he had the mind of a frog. But even if he could still think, he couldn't talk or help her.

What had he asked for? She could barely remember. Something about a shirt. Ah, yes, a shirt made without seam or needle. How was she supposed to do that?

Wait, he wanted the thread spun from a golden sheep first. And after the shirt was finished, she had to wash it in a well filled without rain or spring water, and dry it with a thorn.

Tears pricked at the back of her eyes. It was all impossible.

The frog croaked in the basket, and Kamala gulped back her sobs. Impossible or not, she had to do it.

Lava before obsidian. First, she must consult with a tailor.

She wrapped the dishes and leftover food in her blanket, gathered the basket with the frog, and headed inland. Crisis or no, she still had weeding to do. Nothing other than serious illness ever excused anyone from community chores, and she could talk while she worked.

Fortunately, she found one of the clan's tailors already working and claimed an unweeded row next to him. Striking up a conversation, she started with casual comments on the weather and the state of the gardens, and then gradually added questions about his work. While he talked about his latest projects, she slipped in her vital questions.

"I'm so clumsy, I always stab myself with the needle. Is there any way to make a shirt without one?" Kamala held her breath and bit her lip, turning her face away to hide her intense interest. If anyone discovered Manami turned himself into a frog to save her ball, they'd laugh her right off the island.

"Hmm. You could felt one, I suppose. Or crochet it. Crochet hooks aren't at all sharp." He laughed. "In fact, you can crochet with just your fingers, though it's harder and usually ends up quite uneven."

"That's fascinating," Kamala said. "Please, tell me how both of those work."

When he finished his explanation, she was sure felting wouldn't work. If she used the frog as a model, it wouldn't fit Manami when he changed back. And it would require touching the poison frog. No, she would have to settle for crochet, which at least sounded possible.

Please, Makana, let it be possible.

"If I brought wool, could you teach me to spin?" she asked. "And crochet?"

He leaned back on his heels and smiled at her. "Certainly, I'd be pleased. Let me know when you're ready."

Heart aching with hope, she rushed through her weeding while the bird somehow kept sleeping in her shirt. Though it was awkward, she didn't want to wake the poor creature yet. Once she dumped the weeds into the compost, she gathered her basket and headed for the other side of the island. The Nokai generally used plant fibers for cloth, but she knew one who was experimenting with sheep. He'd been assigned a tiny plot of land in a grassy area away from the gardens. All she needed to do was buy the wool from his most golden sheep.

But when she asked him, he stared at her as if she were crazy.

"*Gold* sheep? Sheep come in white, or sometimes black. Nobody has a *gold* sheep." He stopped and rubbed his chin, and a sly smile crept across his face. "No, I have one golden ram. You can have his wool if you can get it yourself. I'll even give it to you for free. But he's a sly beast, and I don't want you hurt. Can you prove you're strong enough to handle him?"

Kamala thought frantically. "What if we both throw a stone into the air and see whose goes farthest?"

"I suppose that might do," the shepherd said.

He picked up a stone and threw it quite far. While he watched to see where it landed, Kamala scooped her hand inside her bodice and grabbed the bird.

"My turn," she said, and before he could see what she held, she threw the bird into the air. Waking abruptly, it flew away and disappeared.

"Was that... a stone?" the shepherd asked.

She widened her eyes innocently. "Of course it was. But if it isn't enough to convince you, I can squeeze water from another."

Without waiting for a reply, she bent toward the ground. As she picked up a rock, she dipped her hand inside the blanket and grabbed a leftover bit of cheese. Holding both hands around them to hide what she was doing, she squeezed the soft cheese until whey dripped. While keeping the cheese in one hand, she opened the other to expose the rock.

"Is that strong enough?"

The shepherd skeptically examined her from head to foot, then shrugged and opened the gate to his pasture. "Go ahead, then."

Kamala tucked her basket and blanket out of the way and crept through the gate, which slammed shut behind her before the shepherd latched it. His flock was small, just four ewes, a couple of lambs, and a single ram hiding at the back. His fleece was indeed a dark golden color, but when she tried to approach, he lowered his horns and charged at her.

Squealing, she ran for the fence and leaped over.

The ram wandered back to his grazing. No, she was definitely not strong enough to deal with *that* sheep.

She crept around the outside of the fence, spying on the ram and skirting thorny bushes as she got closer. Despite their long thorns, they had pretty yellow blossoms.

No, those weren't flowers, those were tufts of yellow wool caught in the thorns!

Kamala ran back for a napkin, then sat on the fence and waited. Whenever the ram wandered farther away, she jumped down and grabbed as much wool as possible before he charged at her. Retreating to the fence, she waited again. By sunset, she had an armload of golden wool. Though her fingers were dotted with thorn pricks, it was worth it!

Since she couldn't take the frog into the salty ocean to her home, she slept on the beach again. In the morning, she took her salvaged wool and found the tailor working in the warm sunlight.

"I'm ready to spin," she said.

He fingered the wool and frowned. "But this wool is spoiled. It has canary stain, an infection. It will never make good thread. Come feel the waxy texture of it."

Kamala burst into tears. "Won't it wash out?"

"No."

She collapsed on the ground and wailed harder.

"Stop it," the tailor begged. "Stop crying. Oh, fine, let's see what we can do with a thick yarn."

Kamala sat up, sniffling, and pressed her hands to her mouth.

"But it will be terrible," he warned.

She clamped her lips together. "I don't care."

First, he made her wash the entire pile of wool in a strong soap to kill the infection, then spread it to dry.

"Come back tomorrow," he said, turning back to his work.

She returned to the beach, found one of the many hammocks always lying around, and hung it in the closest trees. If she must sleep away from home for several days, she might as well be comfortable.

In the morning, she weeded quickly and showed up ready to finish her thread, but it seemed gathering the wool would not be the hardest part. Kamala spent the next thirty days, all day long, combing wool, spinning thread, plying thread into yarn. The waxy golden wool pulled at her fingers and snagged into lumps as she worked.

While she spun, she thought of Manami and prayed for his safe transformation. This had to work. Every day she checked on the frog and caught more insects for him, but he still remained a frog. Her true love was gone, and all she had were too many yesterdays holding memories in time.

Whenever her friends or family asked where her sweetheart was, she laughed and lied about him being busy elsewhere. A sailing voyage. A long exploration swim with friends. A job on the next island.

If only her lies were true. She missed Manami. He was clumsy and always thought too much, but he was eternally sweet and kind.

When she finally finished spinning, she had a rough, ugly yarn, but it was indeed a golden color.

Then the tailor taught her how to crochet with her fingers, since the lumpy yarn was too irregular for a hook. Her first attempts were terrible, and she had to unravel them several times before she finally had enough practice.

And still the frog remained a small, bright yellow amphibian.

All together, it took her another twelve long days to crochet the shirt, working in the round from the hem and following the tailor's instructions to avoid seams.

When she finished, she nearly wept in relief at the nearness of his cure. Then she held it up and nearly wept in despair. It was an ugly shirt and looked like no kind of magic.

But she wasn't finished yet. Manami had given her more requirements. His curse would last until she fulfilled them all.

One bucketful at a time, she carried ocean water to the dry, unfinished well until it held enough to wash the ugly shirt. Then she carried the sopping heap of wool back to the shepherd's pasture and hung it on the thorn bushes to dry.

But when she draped the dry shirt over the basket the next day, the frog merely croaked.

Yet again, Kamala bawled. But this time, she stopped and picked herself up. Crying hadn't helped yet. If one plan didn't work, she would find another. She must have Manami back as himself.

If his impossible shirt wouldn't break the enchantment, then maybe she needed a magic potion.

It was time for another talk with an expert.

Kamala hurried to the healer's little house by the herb gardens and volunteered to help in return for basic lessons. Without mentioning magic, it took days to glean the information she needed, but she finally pieced together herbs that might work.

Sage increased strength, and thyme enhanced courage. Rosemary stood for love and parsley for comfort. If she mixed all four and bathed the frog in the combination, maybe that would break the spell.

And if it didn't work?

She choked back the nagging tears that tried to choke her.

Then she didn't know what else to try, and her love would be a frog forever.

Kamala gathered her chosen herbs and brewed them into a tea. After it cooled, she carefully poured it into the frog's basket. He croaked and fidgeted, hopping around as if bothered by the herbs, but he stayed a frog.

She splashed the herbal water over him, thinking he might need more exposure. Still a frog.

Had she failed, then?

No, she couldn't accept failure. Though Manami's love had imposed impossible tasks, it must not be more than his heart asked. There must be a solution somewhere. Kamala closed her eyes and replayed their conversation on the beach.

Before he had demanded that ridiculous shirt, he had asked for something else.

Marry me.

Kamala shook her head. She could *not* marry a frog. No, what had he said after that?

What about just a kiss?

Ew. Kiss a frog? How disgusting!

Kiss a *poison* frog? That could kill her!

And yet, she had tried everything else.

Did she want Manami back, or didn't she?

He had been gone for weeks and weeks, and she missed him so much. They had always been together, and she hadn't realized how much she expected him to be there until he was gone. She couldn't even look at another boy.

She would even marry him, if he would change back, but she could not, would not marry a frog. He couldn't even talk to her like this!

Then she only had one choice left — kiss the frog and hope Manami changed back, or be lonely forever.

And if the poison killed her, she wouldn't be lonely anymore. Manami was worth the risk.

Kamala scribbled a note to her mom, in case her plan didn't work, then settled herself under a tree with the basket in her lap. Slowly, she removed the napkin and stared inside.

The saffron-yellow frog looked at her. *Gribbit.*

Kamala swallowed hard and raised the basket to eye level. "I'll give you one last chance to change back now."

She stared at the frog. The frog stared back.

Gribbit.

Kamala took a deep breath and closed her eyes. She puckered her lips and leaned forward, praying harder than she ever had before. *Please, Makana, return Manami to me the way he was before.*

Gribbit.

She braced herself to touch the deadly, slimy skin. Closer and closer. Any second now. How much would it hurt?

The basket jerked out of her hands, but her lips landed.

Familiar arms embraced her, and warm hands pulled her closer. The lips kissing her were definitely *not* amphibian. It had worked!

Kamala opened her eyes and pulled away from the kiss. Her sweetheart knelt before her, back to normal.

"Manami," she gasped, then threw her arms around his neck and returned to the kiss.

When they both finally let go, she leaned her head on his shoulder, soaking in his presence.

"At least the kiss worked," she said.

A silent chuckle shook him. "I enjoyed it."

"I mean, to break the enchantment."

"What enchantment?"

Kamala sighed. "You don't remember being a frog. I suppose I shouldn't be surprised."

"I wasn't a frog."

She shook her head. "Total memory loss."

"*That* frog?" Manami pointed, jiggling her shoulder until she sat up to look. "The frog I knocked away before you touched it and poisoned yourself? What were you doing with it, anyway?"

In the bushes, a bright yellow frog watched them.

Gribbit.

Kamala stared from the frog to Manami and back again until the frog hopped away.

"I found the frog sleeping by my ball the morning after you lost it. I thought you had asked Makana to turn you into a frog to fetch my ball."

Manami laughed, slapping his knee and doubling over. "Turn into a frog? I just poured water down the hole until the ball floated up."

"But — but — if you weren't the frog, where were you? You were gone so long!"

"You asked me to make you a farm beneath the sea and over the sand. So I did. Did you know some seaweed is farmed on nets hung where low tide will expose them to air?"

He reached to the side and presented her with a bundle of black seaweed, tied with a braided rope of tiny flower stalks. "I had to wait for the karengo harvest to prove I did it. I even managed a rope of heather, though I'm afraid it doesn't work very well."

Kamala stared at the bundle in shock, mouth hanging open.

Manami kept talking. "As you requested, I harvested the crop with a ram's horn. It worked better than I thought, since an iron rake would rust. I'll have to go back every dozen days or so for the next harvest, but you can come with me. I'm tired of being separated from you."

Kamala sucked in a breath and let it out again. "You did all this for me?"

"You said that's what you wanted. I would do anything for you." He wrapped his arms around her and tucked her head under his chin.

"Why didn't you tell me where you were going?"

He shrugged. "I thought you'd guess I was doing what you asked."

"Well, I didn't! And you asked me to do impossible things!"

"Did I?"

She sucked in another shuddering breath and jumped to her feet. "You asked me to spin thread from a golden sheep!"

He shrugged. "It was just a joke."

"You told me to make you a shirt without needle or seams!"

He reached toward her. "You don't need to."

"You told me to wash it in a dry well and dry it with a thorn."

He pursed his lips. "I was upset."

Kamala stomped around the tree to retrieve the shirt and dropped it in his lap. "Well, I did it! All of it!"

Manami held up the lumpy, yellow-splotched shirt. "Um, do I have to wear this?"

She flopped to the ground and leaned her head on his knee. "No. It's ugly, isn't it?"

He cleared his throat. "But you did all this for me? It does seem impossible."

"I know." She sighed. "But I figured it out. And if I can do one impossible thing, I suppose I can do another."

He stroked her back. "What impossible thing are you planning next?" A hint of laughter colored his voice.

"Marriage," she mumbled.

His hand froze.

"Unless you don't want someone dumb enough to think you turned into a frog," she muttered to his knee. "Or you have some other ridiculous task you want me to do."

Manami grasped her arms and pulled her upright, then into his lap. "I love you," he said. "All I ever wanted was a kiss and a wife."

"We can have the wedding tonight," she said, "but we don't have to wait for the kiss."

Kamala wrapped her arms around his neck and tilted her face up. He leaned down, and their lips met in a decidedly un-froggish kiss.

If you liked this story, you might like the traditional Earth fairytales:
The Frog
The Frog Prince
The Well of the World's End
Scarborough Fair
Cupid and Psyche
Valiant Little Tailor

TWELVE

1. SISTERS
(KAHALE, NOKAILANA)

Every morning, the sisters were worn out despite being locked in their rooms all night.
The Legend of the Trapped Sisters

While his sisters were still yawning, Tuakahakina grabbed an extra helping of fish. Who wanted to sleep when breakfast was ready? Besides, if he didn't grab it now, it might float away. Though the shutters were closed during mealtimes to reduce the current, the water always had *some* movement.

"Tua," Mom said, "leave some for your sisters."

He mumbled a protest through his mouthful. When Mom shook her head, he covered his mouth with a webbed hand to avoid another scolding.

"Girls," Mom said, "why are you so tired? Didn't you sleep well?"

Mahi, the oldest and Mom's copy with poppy-red hair, leaned her cheek on her fist and poked at her breakfast. "Guess not?"

At the mature age of more than sixty-six hundred days, she still lived at home. Too lazy to cook her own food. Even her gills fluttered lazily.

"Can we go back to bed?" Nohea asked.

She was only three hundred and fifty days younger than Mahi and just as lazy except when it came to the elaborate hairstyles she twisted into her salmon-pink braids.

Mom sighed. "*May* we. And no."

"But Mom," Uilani and Mililani chorused, as usual.

The twins wore matching disappointment on their identical faces, though Mililani hadn't yet re-dyed her shell-pink hair to match Uilani's darker rose. The two of them would probably move out when they reached their six-thousandth day, and Tua couldn't wait.

Akoni merely yawned and shoved her plate aside so she could rest her head on her arms. Her unbraided hair floated around her in the water, a cloud of pink the same shade as the coral necklace Mom imported from East Coral Island. Tua snuck a slice of fruit from Akoni's plate when Mom wasn't watching.

"I don't know." Mom frowned and held the back of her hand to Mahi's forehead. "Maybe I should get Leimomi."

Tua cackled. Mother Leimomi's potions tasted awful. That would teach his sisters to go to bed on time!

Mahi shoved Mom's hand away. "We don't need a healer! I'm going back to sleep."

She pushed off the hammock bench and swam slowly down through the hatch to the bedrooms on the bottom floor. The other four girls drifted after her, though Akoni grabbed her plate as she left.

Mom shook her head. "Some days, I don't know what to do with your sisters."

Widening his eyes innocently, Tua said, "Make them leave. Then I can have a bedroom instead of sleeping in the corner."

"Tua—" Mom laughed. "I'm sure they'll get tired of me soon enough. Now, braid your hair and go up top to weed. Tell the supervisor I'll make sure your sisters go later, hot sun or not."

Stupid weeding. Stupid sisters. Grumbling half-heartedly, Tua braided his dark purple hair and swam out of the house. Perching on the domed roof for a moment, he surveyed the area. His neighbors were already out, though he didn't see any of his near-sisters leaving their houses down the street. Why was he the only one in the family that had to do his chores on time? Was it just because all his sisters were older? Not fair.

He muttered to himself through the whole swim to the island, but shut his mouth when he surfaced. The only thing worse than weeding was *more* weeding as a punishment for complaining. Instead, he dug his webbed toes into the sand until he reached the fertile dirt. After ambling slowly to the garden, he weeded his assigned rows without comment, then disappeared for a nice, long swim.

When he got home, his sisters were finally awake again, but Mom had left for work. Once the girls grudgingly went to their own chores, Tua swam into one bedroom, then the other, trying to decide which one he'd rather have. Not that it mattered; even if his four oldest sisters moved out, he was sure Akoni would use the advantage of her extra seven hundred days to take whichever bedroom she wanted.

In the corner of the younger girls' room, something glittered in the sunlight, something heavy enough to not float in the currents sweeping through the window grilles that blocked sharks. Tua swam closer and kicked at the mess of clothes that almost covered the gleam. Nohea's favorite shirt fluttered in the water, uncovering — a gold ring?

Where in Makana's wide ocean did his sisters find gold?

He kicked the shirt back over the ring and swam away for a long think. They were up to something, and he would discover what.

Just before supper, Tua watched his sisters return from weeding with his near-sisters. From his perch on the roof, they looked like a flower garden of red, pink, purple, and orange. In fact, their father, Pekelo, sometimes called them his flowers. The ones with red and pink hair were Tua's own sisters. The three purple were the oldest, daughters of Kahoni, while the orange belonged to Leimomi. Eleven girls, all older than him. What had Tua ever done to be cursed with so many sisters?

Akoni teased Tua about not really belonging to the family since he had a different dad. Which was ridiculous, since according to Nokai custom, the family included all five parents and twelve siblings, and he was welcome in any of their homes. But because he was only a near-brother to half of them — and the youngest of all — they wouldn't let him play with them. As if he wanted to play with a bunch of *girls*.

But he did want to know where they found gold.

Tua flattened himself against the roof, anchoring his fingers and toes in the tile to avoid floating up, and peered over the dome. His sisters still looked tired, and his near-sisters had equally dark circles under their eyes. After huddling together for a few minutes, they split up to go home. The Purples lived together, taking advantage of their adult status to stay without their mom or dad. The Oranges were too young to live alone, starting at Akoni's age and ending fewer than two hundred days older than Tua. And yet they were convinced they were *so* much more mature than he was. He stuck out his tongue as they swam inside Leimomi's house.

"What are you doing, codfish?" someone said.

Tua jerked, floating away from the roof as he let go. When he rolled in the water, he discovered Nohea hovering above him. Somehow, he had missed seeing when she slipped away from the group.

"Nothing," he protested, paddling backwards.

She followed with crossed arms, propelling herself only with her webbed feet. "Were you spying on us?"

"No." He tried to smile the way Mahi did when she was fooling Mom, but he must not have done it right.

Nohea snorted. "Stay away from us, shark breath."

"Why would I want to go anywhere near you *girls*?" he taunted, then dove over the side of the roof and swam inside the house before she could answer. By the time she followed, he was safely next to Mom, innocently helping her set the table.

Nohea whispered something to the other four sisters, who all glared at Tua. After supper, they disappeared together into the older girls' room, and that was the last he saw of them all day.

For the next two mornings, Tua's sisters again looked half-asleep. Mom insisted on a visit from Leimomi. The pineapple-haired healer examined all five, then made them drink something nasty.

"I can't find anything wrong with them," Mother Leimomi said, "but my daughters have the same fatigue. The potion will give them a little more energy, at least."

Tua hovered in the background, hiding his grin. His sisters didn't look like they thought more energy was a fair trade for the taste Akoni was still trying to scrape off her tongue.

Mom grimaced. "Is it a new epidemic of some kind?"

Mother shrugged. "I haven't heard of anyone else with the symptoms, but I'll ask around." She gave Mom an extra bottle of the tonic and left.

His sisters stayed in their room all day, foiling Tua's plans to follow them.

When Leimomi came back, she reported no other patients except her own daughters and the Purples, who had escaped notice because they lived alone. None of them would discuss the matter, and all of them denied anything unusual happening during the night.

Tua narrowed his eyes as he tread water in the next room and eavesdropped with the intensity of a hunting shark. All of his sisters were tired, but nobody else. That sounded a lot more like mischief than illness. What *could* they be doing? And the parents seemingly agreed, since the conversation on the other side of the wall had moved to the possibility of the girls sneaking out.

"Do you think they are?" Mother asked.

"I suppose we could test it," Mom said. "If we lock them in and they don't notice, then they aren't. And if they complain, then we know."

"I suppose so." Mother sighed. "At least the younger ones. I don't know what to do about the Purples."

Tua covered a chuckle at her use of his nickname for them.

"Kahoni might have some ideas," Mom said. "Pekelo will be useless."

"Always was useless at the hard parts," Mother grumbled.

When they started listing Pekelo's faults, Tua slipped away to find something more interesting to do. He followed his sisters to the Purples' house, where the Oranges were already waiting, but Uilani caught him and sent him away.

At home, Tua entertained himself by helping Dad install new locks on the outside of the bedroom hatches.

The next day, the girls were again worn out. Tua's sisters wouldn't wake for breakfast, but Leimomi still couldn't find anything wrong with them except fatigue. Yet again, they claimed they had slept all night and didn't know why they were exhausted.

Mom shut the bedroom hatches, leaving the sisters napping. "What can they possibly do to make them so tired? And without me hearing anything!"

"They didn't sneak past me," Tua promised.

"No, darling, I didn't think they did. The hatches stayed locked. If only I knew what they were doing..."

"If I find out, could I have my own room as a reward?" Tua joked.

Mom's eyebrows rose. "I suppose that would be fair enough. We will make it work."

"Really?" Tua flipped a somersault and bumped into the wall. His own room! He had to discover what his sisters were doing! "Will you tell them to let me sleep in their room tonight? So I can see what they do?"

"I suppose we could. If you behave."

"I promise. Wahoo!" Tua rolled in the water again, stopping only when Mom grabbed his feet. Since his sisters were still asleep, he hurried up top to finish his chores early.

On his way home, he investigated his near-sisters. Leimomi confirmed the Oranges were as exhausted as the Pinks and with as little cause. When Tua swam by the Purples' house, he peeked through a broken shutter and saw them curled in their hammocks, fast asleep.

All day long, he tried to act normal while keeping an eye on his sisters. They tolerated him until bedtime, then tried to shut the hatch in his face.

"Mom says I get to sleep in here," Tua protested.

"No way!" Akoni squealed. "Get out!"

"Let me in," he protested, pulling on the hatch.

She and the twins yanked down, nearly smashing his toes as the hatch slammed shut. In the next room, Mahi and Nohea closed their hatch.

Alerted by the noise, Mom swam in. "Let him in, girls. If something is happening to you while you sleep, we need to know."

"Nothing happens while we sleep," Uilani whined. "We don't want a stinky boy in here."

Tua folded his arms. "I don't stink."

"Tua." Mom pursed her lips at him. "Girls, open the hatch and let him in, or I'll take it off."

"But, Mom..." Mililani wailed.

"Now."

After a minute of frantic muttering inside the room, Akoni opened the hatch so abruptly it hit Tua's knees.

"Ow," he howled.

Akoni ignored him, and Mililani swam up through the hatch, nearly kicking him in the face.

Uilani pointed to a corner of the room. "Stay there and don't talk to us."

After a long time, Mililani returned with Tua's hammock and a small crate of fruit juice. His sisters strung his bed in "his" corner while Mom locked the hatch from above. After that, they pointedly ignored him. Tua settled in, watching as the girls fussed with their braids and cleaned their room. He carefully didn't look at the corner where he'd found the ring. Eventually, they ran out of things to do and lay in their hammocks.

"How about that juice?" Akoni suggested.

"I'll get it." Mililani rolled from her hammock and dashed to the crate in the corner. She pulled out four bottles and tossed one to Tua. "Here, turtle. You can have one, too."

His sisters sucked the juice, watching Tua like a shark in seal territory. Suspicious of their generosity, he subtly inspected the juice. Was it a different color than theirs?

"Hurry and drink it," Akoni said. "I want to go to bed, and I don't need your disgusting sucking noises keeping me awake."

She drained her bottle and dropped it in the crate, as did the twins. All three stared at Tua. He poked a hole in the seal and put the juice to his mouth, covering the hole with his tongue to keep the liquid inside.

"Mmm," he said, then rolled over in his hammock to face the wall.

His tongue tingled as if the juice was acidic, but it tasted sickly sweet. His sisters wouldn't poison him, would they? No, but he wouldn't be surprised if they had stolen some of Mother Leimomi's knock-out potion. And, of course, they wouldn't mind using it on him to keep him out of the way. They *must* be up to mischief.

Hunching his shoulders to hide what he was doing, Tua grabbed a shirt from the floor that had been missed in the unusual cleanup and pressed the cloth to the bottle. While he continued to make sucking noises, the juice slowly absorbed into the shirt. When the bottle was mostly empty, he yawned and let the bottle roll from his fingers. As he closed his eyes to feign sleep, the currents shifted in the room, and silence fell. Someone covered the jar of luminescence, and the room fell dark, lit only by the moonlight filtering through the water.

His tongue still prickled, and fatigue crept over him. With the hand next to the wall, Tua pinched himself to stay awake. Still the room was silent. Had he been wrong about them? But then why the sleeping potion?

"He's asleep," someone whispered. "Hurry."

The currents shifted again, and something rasped quietly. Tua cracked open one eye to see how they would open the hatch. But the ceiling was empty in the moonlight. Carefully, ever so slowly, he let his head roll a bit to the side, eyes closed. The currents stilled. When the water finally moved again, Tua cracked an eye again.

Three shadowy figures lifted the shark grate from the window and leaned it against the wall. One by one, they wiggled through the small window, helped by two more shadows. Tua held his breath and waited. A head poked back inside to stare at him, then withdrew, settling the grate loosely into the window. The shadows swam away.

He rolled off the hammock and floated above the floor to the wall, then slid up the wall until he could peek out the window. Wait until Mom heard they were sneaking out. Tua grinned. They'd be in so much trouble they'd be grandparents by the time they were free.

The five shadows from his house were joined by more as they swam through town toward the island. But they swam deeper instead of heading for land. Where were they going?

Tua removed the grate, slithered through the window, and followed at a distance. Though only the tiny twin moons shone tonight, they cast enough light to follow the large clump of swimming shadows. If they had split up to swim alone, they might have been too hard to see. If he was quiet and didn't get too close, they wouldn't see him, either.

And then the girls vanished.

Tua tread to a stop and peered through the dark water. No sisters. They hadn't surfaced, so where did they go?

He swam closer, trying not to disturb the currents too much. By the time he reached the roots of the island, he still hadn't found where his sisters went.

Then a giggle reached his ears. A faint light sprang up, so faint he would have mistaken it for moonlight if he hadn't seen it come on.

Very slowly, Tua crept along the island base, pulling himself hand over hand instead of swimming.

More giggles floated in the waves. The light vanished, but Tua followed the sound. Suddenly, his hand fell through the plants and landed on empty water instead of rock. He found another handhold and pulled himself sideways until he could peer through the seaweed and into the hole. Light flickered *inside* the island.

It wasn't just a hole, but a tunnel! Why didn't anyone know a tunnel ran inside their island?

And his sisters were inside.

Tua swam through the entrance and headed for the light.

2. CAVE
(KAHALE, NOKAILANA)

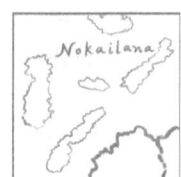

In the cave, they found a fortune.
The Legend of the Trapped Sisters

As Tua swam slowly forward into the tunnel, the giggles continued, accompanied by a metallic clink. The light flickered ahead, too dim for him to see anything around him. He kept his arms outstretched to ward off walls, propelling himself with his feet. In the darkness, the journey seemed to take forever, but it was probably only a few minutes before he reached the end of the tunnel and could see the glowing jar instead of just its light. It sat on a shelf in the middle of an entire cave, above his sisters, who were... playing with gold?

Tua gaped and stopped swimming. Nohea wore gold earrings as big as her hand, and Mahi was stacking coins as she counted them. Akoni and the Orange twins, Kini and Hanini, rolled in the uncounted coins until Mahi kicked them. Mililani and Uilani gathered jewelry with Kamaka, the youngest Purple, laying their finds across an empty shelf. Lanakila and Ipolani, the older Purples, searched through buckets and boxes for jewels. Pomaikai, the Orange who was the same age as Akoni, floated on her back while humming off-tune. All eleven of his sisters and near-sisters were here.

Tua's mind raced with questions. How much gold? Where did it come from? What did they plan to do with it?

"If I could spin gold thread from these," Mahi pondered dreamily, "I could weave cloth-of-gold and make a fortune."

Ipolani chuckled. "It's already a fortune with no work. Why bother?"

Slowly, Tua's shock faded, and he noticed more details. Though there was a lot of gold, it wasn't the mountain it had first seemed. The loose coins were probably the contents of only a chest or two, and not all were gold. The Purples had no more than a double-handful of jewels in their pile. There was a fair amount of jewelry, but some of it was abalone or bone or a less precious metal.

He edged into the cave and picked up a gold coin from a shelf near the entrance. The foreign imprint was too blocky for Iojic. Iskrit, maybe? Or Darrendran? What did Darrendran writing look like?

"Hey." Pomaikai stopped humming and paddled upright. "What is Tua doing here?"

Tua jerked backward into the tunnel, but it was too late.

"Tua!" his sisters howled, and then they were upon him, grabbing ankles and hands and hair. They dragged him into the cave and pinned him against the wall.

"You followed us?" Mahi asked. "You little sneak."

Uilani nudged her twin. "You grabbed the wrong potion," she hissed.

"I did not," Mililani said.

"I didn't drink it," Tua croaked. "I'm not stupid."

"You're stupid if you think you can tell the parents about this." Akoni made a fist in front of his face.

"You're stupid," Tua said, then grunted when his sisters pushed him harder against the wall. "This isn't your stuff. What if the owner comes back?"

Ipolani crossed her arms. "They never have before. And if they do, we'll pretend we found the cave tonight instead of a few days ago. Oops, so sorry, we'll go now." She smirked with the superiority of her adult years.

Tua rolled his eyes. "Nohea is wearing their earrings. You obviously didn't just arrive."

Nohea stuck out her tongue and yanked the earrings free.

"He's right, you know," Lanakila said. "We've been here long enough. Tonight is the last night."

The younger girls groaned and protested, but Lanakila held up both hands. "Sisters, enough. Enjoy yourselves for a little longer, then put everything away. Tua, go home."

"And keep your mouth shut," Mahi threatened. "Since we won't come back here — and I'll remember this is your fault — you don't need to tell any of the parents."

Kini and Hanini bumped Tua against the rock again, until he nodded vigorously. He would think about whether to actually keep their secret, but it was stupid to disagree when he was outnumbered. His sisters dragged him to the tunnel and shoved him out, then stretched across the entrance to the cave to block it.

With no choice, Tua turned and swam away. He reached the ocean before he realized he still had the gold coin in his hand. Turning to toss it back in the tunnel, he paused. Without some sort of proof, would Mom believe his story? He tucked the coin into his pocket and swam for home. By next week, he'd have his own room.

The window was still open, but Tua slipped inside the front door and went to bed in his usual spot in the corner. Sleeping near his sisters didn't sound safe at all until their irritation cooled.

In the morning, he woke later than usual and looked for Mom and Dad, but found only a note. "Left early to deal with a work emergency. Back in a couple of days."

Tua rubbed the gold coin, glaring at the bedroom hatches. Fine, then. He could talk to the other parents first. No sound came from his sisters, so he'd go while they were still sleeping. He yawned. Now he understood why they slept all day. His hammock beckoned him, but first he needed to report. If he gave his sisters the chance to ruin his story, he might not get his own room for months — or years!

Quickly and quietly, he snuck out the door and swam for Mother Leimomi's house. Father was as useless as everyone said, and Mother Kahoni had little influence over the Purples anymore.

He pounded on the door, but nobody answered.

After a few minutes, a neighbor came over. "She left to deal with a healing emergency," he said. "Someone got attacked by a shark. She told me to send her daughters to either of their mothers' houses if they wake before she gets back. Do you want me to help you wake the girls?"

Tua groaned. "Wouldn't help. Thanks for the info. When she comes home, please ask her to speak to me."

The neighbor nodded and kicked himself into the main current. Tua turned and headed for Kahoni's house. Influence or no, at least she was an adult.

But Kahoni was also not at home. Since she lived alone and her daughters were grown, she hadn't left a message with a neighbor. Tua growled in frustration. It wasn't the first time his mom and dad had left for a couple of days, but one or both of his mothers had always been around. What a lousy coincidence. He would have to try his father.

Since he was not currently in a relationship, Pekelo lived alone when not on a trip as a ship's carpenter. Tua wound his way through the kelp fields to find the little hut outside of town. He didn't have to knock on the door, since it was already open, swaying gently in the current. After looking for obvious sharks or jellyfish, Tua swam inside. The glowing plankton jar hung dark from the ceiling, so Father hadn't put it in the sunlight to charge. The current from the open door had swept the contents of the house into a mess on the floor.

Nobody was in sight on the first level, so Tua swam to the lower story. The bedroom was closed up, but a crooked shutter let in just enough light for him to find the occupied hammock. Old food floated in the current, so it was good the shutters kept out marine life. Something in the water made Tua's gills burn.

He grabbed Father's shoulder and shook hard, desperate to hurry from the contaminated space. Pekelo didn't move. Tua shook again, and Father groaned, rolling to his side and cradling a bottle.

Ugh, he'd been drinking again. That explained the caustic water. Tua pushed upward for the hatch. Father would sleep all day and be useless tomorrow. The best Tua could do now was escape the poison. He exited the house quickly, shutting the door behind him, then swam around to straighten the shutter. Nobody else would want the alcohol floating through the town.

Tua floated back toward his house. At least Pekelo wasn't *his* dad. Should he wait for one of the other parents to return, or should he confront his sisters himself?

If all eleven ganged up on him, he had no chance. Waiting was smarter. But he would watch the girls and give a full report to the parents. They would be in so much trouble! He smirked a little. His own room *and* the only one with freedom to play. Life would be so sweet.

And now that he knew how they were escaping, he could stop them. At home, he collected a hammer and nails from Dad's tools, then headed for the bedrooms. They wouldn't get out if he nailed the shutters closed, and removing the nails would be noisy enough to alert him. When Mom and Dad got home, they might have a better idea, but at least his sisters wouldn't sneak out before then.

But when he unlocked the hatch and peeked in, the younger girls' room was empty. No, not empty. A small shark swam idly through the room.

Shark! Tua slammed the hatch shut and locked it without checking what kind of shark. Stupid; he hadn't replaced the window grate last night. If the hatch hadn't been closed, the shark could have roamed the whole house. Maybe he would omit this from his report to Mom and Dad...

So when his sisters got home and discovered a shark in their room, they must have all piled into the other bedroom. These shutters could wait until the shark wandered out, and now he only had to nail one window shut without being stopped.

He unlocked the other hatch and dropped through. As he headed for the window in a quiet rush, the other flaw in his plan became obvious. With five girls against him once they woke, how would he finish nailing the shutters? If only the shutters were on the outside, but of course, privacy required them on the inside.

Tua lunged against the window, reaching for the shutter — and the grate fell out. Why hadn't they put the windows back together when they got home? Another shark could have nosed this grate aside and eaten all of them. Even though they were annoying, that wasn't the way he wanted to get his own room.

He grabbed the grate and fumbled it into place, wincing at the clang as he banged the bars against the frame. But no one woke to stop him. He threw a glance over his shoulder and froze.

In the light streaming through the window, the room was obviously empty. No shark, but also no girls.

Of course. They must have seen the shark and slept upstairs, afraid sharks had gotten in both rooms. Girls were skittish fish.

Tua grinned as he hammered the shutters closed. At least their fear gave him the opportunity to fix the window without interference. Now all he had to do was make sure he fixed the other when the shark left, before his sisters could reclaim the room.

Mom and Dad would be so surprised and pleased.

He swam up and locked the hatch, not that it would keep the girls confined if they had slept upstairs. He could wake them to gloat, but the longer he let them sleep, the less time he'd have to spend keeping them from pulling the shutters free before the parents returned. If he waited until just before weeding time, maybe he could hurry them from the house before they noticed.

Brilliant. He was absolutely brilliant. His sisters were no match for him.

Grinning, Tua swam to the kitchen and filled a plate. With no one awake, he could also eat as much as he liked. This was a perfect day.

After stuffing his belly, he swam to the roof and found a perch where he could spy on all the exits as well as the houses of the Oranges and Purples. No measly girls would sneak past him.

And they didn't. He watched for hours, and they never emerged from any of the houses. Finally, he couldn't delay their chores any longer, and he swam back inside to wake his sisters.

But the house was empty, no matter how many times he searched every room.

He couldn't possibly have missed them.

Or had he? Had they somehow snuck past him and already headed out? They probably hoped he'd be late and get in trouble.

Tua shot outside, slammed the door, and kicked furiously for the island. He could still make it in time.

He was the last to arrive before punishments were disbursed. Marching smugly to his assigned garden row, he looked for his sisters so he could gloat.

They weren't there. Neither were any of his near-sisters.

Tua knelt and absently pulled weeds, mind whirling. Where were they? Not at home. Not at chores. Not with Mother Leimomi and the Oranges.

They must have slept at the Purples' house last night. He grimaced, feeling stupid. They'd still get in trouble when the parents got home, but they had successfully avoided him. Unless they were avoiding the shark in their room? And the Oranges were staying with them because their mom was gone. So they could probably convince the parents that they were being responsible and avoid extra punishment. How unfair.

He finished his weeding and rushed back home. The shark had finally left, so he repaired and nailed shut the window, then hurried to the Purples to tell his sisters it was safe to come back home. Safe until he talked to Mom, anyway, but he wouldn't mention that.

The Purples' house was also empty.

Panic rising like a tidal wave, Tua checked everywhere and asked everyone. His sisters were gone. No one had seen them since yesterday. He stopped in the middle of town and tread water, desperately trying to think.

They had promised last night was the final trip, and rotten girls though they were, they had always kept their promises before. But they hadn't come home.

Had sharks eaten them on the way? All eleven of them?

Swimming faster than ever, he headed for the root of the island, scanning the water for any evidence of shark attacks. His stomach churned, and he suddenly regretted his large breakfast.

All the way back, he saw nothing, but he couldn't decide if that was good news or bad. Would sharks leave any remains? He reached the island without incident and began circling it, searching for the cave. Halfway around the island, he knew he must have passed it and turned around. It should be easier to find it in daylight, and yet somehow, he had missed it. Slowly, he swam back, searching every ell of the underwater mountain for the opening.

Still nothing.

Had the cave collapsed? Tua clutched his aching stomach and tried to remember last night. He had come the same route this morning, yes. He had pulled himself across the rock using the plants as handholds to avoid stirring up currents. Then he had found the cave when he put his hand into empty space. Wait! He had shoved *through* the plants to the opening. There must be seaweed hiding the cave!

Relieved, he backed up to his starting point and tried again, hand over hand as before, eyes closed. Time crawled as slowly as a starfish, but finally his hand found the opening. Tua opened his eyes and pushed through the seaweed. For the entire length of the tunnel, he prepared a lecture for his sisters for worrying him.

Nearly to the end of the tunnel, the girls' light silhouetted a kraken that stirred and reached for him.

Tua flipped a somersault and fled.

3. TRAPPED
(KAHALE, NOKAILANA)

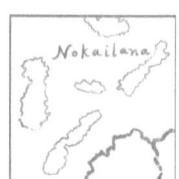

But they could not get free.
The Legend of the Trapped Sisters

Tua plowed out of the tunnel and careened around the corner. Why was a kraken in the cave? Had it smelled him? Would it follow?

He flattened himself against the mountain. Were his sisters still in there? Were they *dead*?

His gills fluttered too quickly, and he leaned his head against the rock and let his tears dissolve in the ocean. How would he tell the parents? This was his fault. He had left his sisters behind and let them die. If he had broken his promise and tattled last night, they would still be alive.

His sobs floated gently in the current, and he pressed his hand over his mouth to smother the sound. Still the cries continued, increasing to a wail that suddenly stopped.

Wait, someone else was crying. Someone was alive!

Tua held his breath, desperately listening to nothing but the ordinary underwater sounds.

It had only been his imagination. Or wishful dreams. He sucked in a shuddering breath and squared his shoulders. Time to go home and face the storm.

Another sob floated above him, and he jerked his gaze upward. Hardly daring to hope, Tua crept up the wall of seaweed. The sound died again, and he stopped to listen.

There, still above. He climbed again, stopping every time the sobs disappeared.

Finally, the direction changed to somewhere on the left. Slowly, he repeated the process sideways. When the sound suddenly came from the right, he froze. Nothing was here but various types of seaweed clinging to the mountain, but the sound had to come from somewhere. He started pulling seaweed from the rock, looking for the source. After clearing an ell in all directions, he found a small hole that echoed with sobs. Girlish sobs, as he well knew from a house full of sisters.

Tua rested his forehead on the rock. Someone was still alive. His heart pounded with hope, but his stomach still churned. What if they hadn't all survived?

The hole was narrow and too shadowed to see details. The broad shoulders he inherited from Dad would never fit through.

When he thought he could keep his voice steady, he leaned into the hole. "Sisters, are you well?"

The sobs broke off mid-sound, but no one replied. What if his sisters had died and some random stranger had been trapped by the kraken? Surely that wasn't very likely.

"Are you there?" Tua pled.

"Tua?" someone gasped, voice distorted by the distance and rock.

"Quiet," someone else ordered. "What if this is a trick of the pirates?"

"I faked sleep last night," Tua said, relief bubbling like the island's hot springs. "I call all of you by your hair color. I read Mililani's journal, and she likes—"

"Stop!" Mililani screeched. "You rotten toad! When we get out, I'll kill you!"

Tua doubled over in hysterical laughter. Some of his sisters were still alive, at least, and that was worth Mililani's fury. Of course the kraken hadn't eaten all of them; it was only a fathom-long specimen.

The memory of its long tentacles were enough to make him stop laughing. Eaten or not, the monster could still kill his sisters.

He yelled down the hole again. "Are you all there? Are you well?"

"All here. Mostly well. Where are you?" The voice grew louder and softer. The girls must be searching for where his voice came in.

"Higher than the entrance and a bit left. My left," he clarified. He kept talking, explaining about the kraken to give them time to search.

"There's light coming through a hole here," Lanakila said, close enough for him to easily recognize the oldest Purple's voice.

"I cleared off the seaweed," Tua said. "I think it's wide enough for you to escape." He remembered the shapely figures of his older sisters and winced. "Some of you, anyway."

"Well done. But I can't... get through... Come here, Hanini."

The Orange twins were the smallest, and Hanini was a little skinnier than Kini. If anyone could make it, she could. Tua held his breath and stared uselessly into the dark hole.

The noise deteriorated into chaos, then his youngest near-sister's fingers emerged from the hole, stretching for open water.

"Uh," Hanini groaned.

Tua swam forward and grabbed her fingers. She clutched at him for a minute, then her arm moved backward.

"The hole narrows too much in the middle," she panted, "but it goes all the way out. I touched him." She broke down into noisy tears.

Tua fought the urge to do the same.

"Tua," Lanakila said, "go get the parents."

"I can't," Tua said. "I already tried. Everyone but Father is gone, and he's drunk."

Below him, his sisters argued.

Finally, Lanakila came back. "You were right, little brother. We should have left earlier. Listen fast. This cave belongs to pirates, and they came back last night. They can't afford to let us go to tell their secrets, so they say we have to join them. We told them no, and they said they would leave us here until we get hungry enough to agree. That's when they left the kraken. They control it verbally, but we can't guess the correct orders to make it leave. Go find help from the neighbors. Someone. Anyone!"

"Are the pirates from another island?" Tua asked. "What are they doing here?"

"Who cares?" Nohea protested. "Go get help!"

"Wait!" Lanakila said. "He's right."

"I am?" Tua couldn't remember the last time any of his sisters admitted he was right about anything.

"About what?" Kini said.

"We don't know where the pirates are from," Lanakila said. "They stayed in the shadows of the tunnel, but if we had seen them, we might have recognized them from our very own clan. If Tua asks random people for help, he might accidentally ask one of the pirates."

Tua gulped. If he told a pirate he knew about their treasure cave, none of them would survive!

"Then the only people we can trust are our parents," Kamaka said, despair filling the middle Purple's voice.

Someone started crying again.

"Is anyone coming right now?" Lanakila asked.

"I don't see anyone," Tua said.

"Then we have time to think. When are the parents coming back?"

"Mom and Dad in a couple of days; Leimomi whenever the medical emergency is over. Your mom didn't leave a note."

Lanakila grumbled something Tua didn't catch.

"Tua," Uilani said, "can you bring us food? If the pirates can't starve us into submission, we'll have more time."

"Yes, food," Akoni begged. "I want my breakfast."

"All the meals," Pomaikai added. Besides being Akoni's age, the oldest Orange shared a love of plentiful food.

"Anything else?" Tua asked.

"That's enough for now," Lanakila said. "Be careful. Don't talk to anyone, and don't get caught."

"I'll be back." He spun away, then stopped. The hole gaped open behind him, and the pirates might see it when they returned. They'd know someone had been spying. This was his only way to talk to his sisters, and he couldn't afford to lose it. Besides, the pirates might punish them.

Tua swam a few fathoms and pulled seaweed, roots and all, from scattered places on the mountain, careful not to take too many from the same area. He chose the longest, fluffiest kinds he could find, then transplanted them above the hole so they hung down over it. The narrow tunnel wasn't as well hidden as originally, but it wasn't obvious, either. Unless someone was looking for it, they weren't likely to find it. It would have to do.

He rushed home, cursing the distance that had seemed so short last night. Tua threw food into a sack, then added one of the small hand nets. If any fish made it past the kraken or through the speaking tunnel, his sisters would have another source of food. He considered adding some kitchen knives, but they had their own serrated belt knives. He added a couple of charged plankton lamps instead, since the one they had would run down soon, then threw in shades for when the pirates came back.

What else would be useful? Water flowed around them in abundance. Light, food, weapons, communication... The family had no money for ransom, and they couldn't bribe the pirates with their own gold. Their gold! He hurried to the younger girls' bedroom. He threw their clothes around the room until he found the gold ring. If the pirates hadn't seen it was gone yet, maybe they could return it unnoticed.

Yet again, he swam for the underwater mountainside. The ocean was as warm as always, but a chill ran down his back. His sisters were prisoners and their parents were gone. If he didn't save them soon, it would be too late, but how could he defeat a kraken and a crew of pirates by himself?

Later, worry about that later. For now, food. He tucked the bag closer to his side and kicked harder for a little extra speed, not that it would matter. With his sisters trapped, they were forced to wait for him.

As he approached his destination, he heard voices. Mostly male voices coming from below him. Tua swam a little higher and faster, diving for the first big patch of seaweed growing down the mountain. Fortunately, he had worn a seaweed-printed ocean suit this morning, and he blended in. Even his dark purple hair would look like shadows. When the voices continued exactly as before, he peeked out carefully.

Nobody was in sight, but they must be close to be so loud. By the tunnel entrance, most likely. If he could sneak to the upper hole, maybe he could eavesdrop.

Slowly sliding from leafy patch to leafy patch, Tua pulled himself up and around to the speaking tunnel. Here, alas, the only large bunch of seaweed was over the hole itself, so he jammed his legs and torso into the narrow tunnel and tucked his head behind the plants.

Sound filtered to his ears sporadically, and he strained to hear.

"We already told you no," Lanakila shouted. Then her voice dropped to a murmur before rising again. "We will never change our minds about joining you, but maybe we can offer a different bargain?"

A male voice said, "I doubt you have anything else we want."

"A trade agreement?"

"We take what we want."

"A new ship?" Ipolani suggested.

"We have a good ship," the pirate said. "And if we didn't, we would take one."

"I can make cloth of gold," Mahi said in a choked voice.

"You can spin straw into gold?" the pirate exclaimed. "Now *that's* an amazing birth gift from Makana. It's like magic."

Many male voices babbled excitedly.

Tua rolled his eyes. How stupid were they? Nobody had magic to spin straw into gold. Makanavailea did give gifts to all the new babies, but they were small, practical talents. Perfect pitch, or an amazing memory, or hand-eye coordination. Even never getting seasick or being a good gardener. His talent was finding crabs, and Mahi could spin strong thread from almost any source, but she couldn't change one thing into another.

"Not *straw* into gold," Mahi said, "*cloth* of gold. Melting your coins, spinning the thread, weaving *cloth* of... gold..."

But the pirates weren't listening to her. Even when the other girls joined her in shouting the correction, the pirates kept talking about how much straw they could bring to Mahi.

"You can't do this," Akoni wailed. "Wait until our parents come home."

The pirates fell silent, then murmured to each other. Several girls started crying, and Tua clenched his fists. He was the only one allowed to make his sisters cry.

"We can fix that problem," the pirate finally said. "Unless you give us a note to take to them saying you ran away and are never coming back, we'll kill your parents. Sooner or later, we'll discover who they are."

Tua sucked in a breath so hard he choked on the water and had to smother his coughs.

"Well," the pirate said, "what do you say? Will you give us a letter for your parents?"

"Let us think about it." Lanakila's voice shook.

The pirate laughed. "Think as long as you like. You can't escape and will get no food until you agree. We will check on you tomorrow to see if you are ready to cooperate."

Tua hunched into the tunnel as much as he could, flattening his head and arms against the rock so the seaweed would cover him better. Gradually, swimmers came into view below him. From the distance, they looked like ordinary Nokai in ordinary ocean suits. One carried a harpoon, but the others had nothing but their belt knives. If he hadn't heard them threatening his sisters, he would have thought they were any group of friends out for the day with protection against sharks. Unfortunately, they were too far away for him to see their faces.

They swam lazily, and Tua's skin crawled with impatience. One, two, three... Thirty-nine, forty! How were he and his sisters supposed to defeat forty pirates? When they were finally out of sight, he pulled his legs from the hole and crammed in his head.

"Sisters," he hissed. "They're gone now. Are you well?"

"Did they see you?" Mahi asked.

"No, I hid. I'm not stupid."

"I didn't mean — I'm sorry; I worry about you out there alone."

"At least I'm out here and not in there. Are you ready to catch the bag?"

"Don't drop it," Hanini said. "It might get stuck in the middle. I'll come get the stuff."

While he waited, Tua pulled the first light from the bag. If she thought the bag might not fit, it was better to hand everything through separately. When Hanini's hand emerged, he handed her the light and waited for her to pull it down and come back. One at a time, he passed her each item.

"Last one," he said when he hooked the net over her fingers. "So you can catch fish."

Hanini vanished back inside, and after a minute, Mahi's voice came back. "Did you hear what they said?"

"Yes, most of it, I think. What were you thinking to offer the cloth-of-gold? You want to be *less* valuable, not more."

Mahi growled. "I know, I know. I just thought — I guess I didn't think."

"You wouldn't think well if you were hungry and scared," Nohea added.

Tua wasn't hungry, but his hair still stood on end, and his mind raced endlessly, caught in a whirlpool of doubt and fear and longing for his parents.

"Then start eating," he said, "so we can decide how to get you out of there."

He started talking, throwing out random ideas. His sisters apparently took turns eating, since one or two were always ready with an answer for him. Usually, they pointed out a huge flaw that ruined his idea. In normal circumstances, they would drive him crazy with their fault-finding, but right now, they couldn't afford to fail with a broken plan.

After discarding ideas to chisel the speaking tunnel bigger (the rock was too hard), kill the kraken (how?), and bribe the pirates (already tried and failed), they were left with only two options.

One, find the code word to call off the kraken. His sisters promised to try guessing, but everyone knew the chances of finding the right word by chance were as slim as a flounder. They could try to overhear it, but if they hadn't heard it yet, it didn't seem likely they would hear it in the future.

Two, wait for the parents to get back. But would Tua have enough time to warn them about the pirates before the enemy found them?

"If you wait for Mom and your Dad on the dock," Mililani said, "you might catch them before they get home."

"I'll try," Tua said dubiously. He swam away, feeling more alone than ever. If he failed, his sisters would eventually have no choice but to accept the pirates' deal.

If only one of his parents were available to help! Even Pekelo would be slightly better than nobody, but when Tua checked on the way to the surface, his father was still passed out drunk. Or drunk again.

As the sun sank lower, staining the apricot sky with streaks of purple and blue, Tua sat on the dock and watched the ships come and go. None of them were Mom and Dad's, but he kept watching for the red and purple sails. Blue, green, yellow, pink. Red! No, those were red and blue. He slumped, resting his elbow on his knee and his chin in his hand while he kept scanning the ocean.

Not only were the sails colorful, but some Nokai painted their boats just as brightly. Some even decorated them more. A tiny fishing boat was painted to look like an entire shark, and he suspected the merchant ship with a coral reef along its side came from the east end of Nokailana. One ship was decorated with flowers, but most of them showed some kind of ocean scene, like a kraken wiggling around the bow.

Kraken! Like the monster holding his sisters prisoner? Was this the pirates' ship? Tua jumped to his feet and shaded his eyes. What was its name? He nearly cursed when the shark boat swung in front of the kraken, blocking his view with its sails. The kraken ship turned slowly, heading away from the island. In another minute, it would face entirely the wrong direction.

"No, no, no," Tua pled, racing down the dock for a better view.

The shark boat pulled for the dock, and for an instant, Tua could read the name on the side of the kraken ship. Ekewaka. Though he couldn't report it to the authorities without proof, he could tell Mom and Dad when they returned.

And what if it *wasn't* the pirates' boat? What if it was just a coincidence? Maybe the pirates were actually on the flower ship, or the one with painted crabs climbing over it. This was hopeless.

Tua tipped himself off the dock and plummeted through the water. When he drifted to a stop, he turned and swam for home through the darkening water. Maybe his parents would return tomorrow.

But in the morning, Tua was still alone. Keeping the pretense that nothing was wrong in case some of his nosy neighbors were among the pirates, Tua reported for weeding early in the morning, eating on his way. Mind spinning with worry, he absently crawled along the row, tossing weeds over his shoulder. Though he was silent, the other workers chatted, filling the air with a murmur of conversation that washed over him like the ocean current.

"I didn't sleep all night. The baby is teething again."

"He is the *cutest!*"

"I've been training my pet again."

"How many times do I have to tell you that's not a weed?"

"... so that's when I told her to get lost."

Tua froze. Had someone mentioned training animals, or had he misheard? Kraken were animals, even if they were stupid ones. And dangerous. Lousy pets, really, except for stupid pirates who wanted a mindless guard. Tua listened harder. Babies, sweethearts, scoldings. No, not what he wanted! Slowly, he moved forward, turning his head from side to side.

"Sure, he's making great progress. He already learned to chase a ball."

There! Tua leaned forward, straining his ears and pulling every single weed, even the tiniest sprouts.

"Oh, it's not that hard," the man continued. "All pets should learn some basic commands."

Tua turned his head away a little more, both to point his ear at the voice and to hide his face. He wished he dared see who was talking, but if the man noticed him listening and was a pirate, they would surely capture him too. Then his sisters would be doomed. And since none of them had seen any faces, *anyone* could be a pirate.

"Come, drop it, stay, back up," the voice said. "Once they've learned those, you can evaluate if they're smart enough to learn more."

Tua held his breath, but the man switched to a story about his fishing trip. But maybe he had said enough. If there were standard commands, then maybe they would work on the kraken. Tua raced through the rest of his chores and dove underwater. As he approached the cave, he slowed, watching for anyone else in the area.

Once he was sure he was unobserved, he swam to the speaking tunnel and listened. Below him, his sisters were singing a common dance tune, so the pirates must not be around.

"Sisters," he called down the tunnel.

The music stopped. "Tua?"

"Yes. What are you doing down there?"

"Just dancing."

"Why in Makana's wide ocean are you dancing? What if the pirates hear you?"

"Because it's boring waiting for you," Akoni shouted.

"It doesn't matter," Kamaka said. "I don't think they care what we do as long as their monster is still guarding us."

"They prefer to keep us," Lanakila said. "Hurting us is only their backup plan."

"What took you so long?" Nohea demanded.

Tua made a face. "If you don't like the way I do things, I can go home."

A chorus of voices shouted, "No."

"I'll try to make the kraken leave," Tua said. "Just in case it doesn't work, stay away from the entrance."

"Tua, don't be stupid—"

Ignoring them, he swam lower, hovering just inside the entrance tunnel.

"Drop it," he quavered, then cleared his throat and tried again. "Drop it!"

The kraken swam closer. Was it working? It stopped a fathom away from Tua and watched him.

Maybe a different word would work better, since the beast had nothing to drop. Maybe he *was* stupid.

"Back up," Tua commanded.

The kraken reached a tentacle toward him.

Tua squeaked and backed up. "Go home!"

The monster opened its beak and swam forward, tentacles reaching for him.

Tua flipped a somersault and swam farther, then paused. If he could get the kraken to follow him, could his sisters escape?

Heart pounding and gills pumping with fear, he swam toward the kraken.

"Go home," he croaked.

When the creature reached for him again, he retreated very slowly. The kraken followed, and Tua backed up again. All the way to the entrance, the kraken swam after him, but when he left the tunnel, the monster retreated to its post by the cave.

4. RIDDLES
(KAHALE, NOKAILANA)

He must guess the monster's name to free them.
The Legend of the Trapped Sisters

T ua returned to the speaking tunnel and leaned into the hole. "It
didn't work, and neither did luring it away."

"It was worth a try," Mahi called up. "But never mind; we have a
different idea. Can you borrow tools from Dad so we can make this tunnel
big enough for us to escape?"

"I thought you said that wouldn't work."

"What do we have to lose?"

"I'll be right back." He swam away, then hurried back. "Do you need
more food?"

"Not yet. We caught a few fish."

As Tua swam off again, another dance tune floated quietly from the
speaking tunnel. Dancing, bah!

He hurried to Pekelo's house and knocked on the door. No answer,
but when he tried the latch, it opened. Tua swam to the lower level, but
his father was gone. If he had taken his tools on a job, the girls were out of
luck. But when Tua checked the upper level, the tools were scattered on
the floor. Pekelo was probably drinking again.

Fine, Tua could do it himself. He wrapped a couple of hammers and chisels in a carry-net and strapped them to his back, then swam to the cave. If nothing else, he could tell Mom he got plenty of exercise while she was gone.

At the small tunnel, he passed a hammer and chisel inside and used the other set to attack his end. Though hard, the rock gradually crumbled under his repeated blows, and little by little, the hole grew larger. From the delighted sounds coming from the inside, his sisters were having equal success.

For hours, they chiseled at both ends. The girls took turns, and as Tua shook his aching arms, he envied the help. But he didn't stop longer than it took to eat a quick snack at supper time, and the tunnel grew wider and wider. When he reached through, the narrow part was only a hand-length thick. With a bit of luck, they could finish tonight and slip away in the darkness.

He set the chisel against the next section of rock and hammered, but it skittered across the rock without chipping it. Ugh, he was getting too tired. Tua carefully reset the chisel and banged. Again, the tool slipped across the rock instead of biting in. He leaned in and stared at the rock, then picked a different spot and tried again. That worked, but the next bit was also too hard.

"Mangy sea turtles," Uilani cursed a few feet away. "Ow! It won't break."

"Let me try," Ipolani said.

Tua kept working, tapping his way around the entire tunnel. Though he broke off a few more pieces, the entire layer was hard, and he soon gave up.

The frustrated banging on the other side also stopped.

"Tua?" Ipolani's voice wavered. "I don't think we can break any more on our end. How are you doing?"

He took a deep breath to steady his voice before he replied. "It's too hard over here, too. But don't worry, I'll find another way."

"Tomorrow," Lanakila said.

"But—" Tua protested.

"Tomorrow. We're all tired, and we don't want to make a stupid mistake. We'll be fine until tomorrow."

Tua gathered his tools. "Fine. Keep the hammer and chisel. I'll come back tomorrow."

Riddles | 181

"With food?" Akoni begged.

"With food," Tua promised, rubbing his stinging eyes. "And maybe some of the parents will come home."

S leeping alone in the house was no longer fun, and Tua tossed and turned all night. In the morning, he sniffed his shirt, decided it was good for at least another day or two, and reported early for weeding, hoping for another clue. Halfway through his row, almost ready to despair of finding the animal trainer again, he finally heard the correct voice.

This time, the man was talking about using the animal's name for attention. That made sense, but Tua didn't *know* the kraken's name. Still, it was more information than he had before, and worth trying guesses. If nothing else, they could make a list. Eleven of them with nothing to do ought to think of a lot of names.

When he finished his chore, he hurried home, past his still-empty Mothers' houses, and packed more food for his sisters. Feeding all eleven of them was emptying his cupboards faster than he liked, and Mom might be upset when she got home. But it was worth it. And what would he do if he couldn't free his sisters and their parents didn't come home soon enough? His chest tightened, and he curled around the bag of food. Annoying as his sisters were, he still loved them. No, he had to succeed, or at least stall until their parents arrived.

The now-familiar trip to the underwater cave passed quickly, and nobody was around when he arrived. He slipped the food through the speaking tunnel and explained the newest information he had heard.

"Did any of you hear what the pirates called the kraken?" he finished hopefully.

"No," Nohea said. "They always lowered their voices to talk to each other and the kraken."

Tua groaned. "Well, try to listen if they come back. In the meantime, call the kraken lots of names and see if it responds to any of them."

"Hey, Alani," Pomaikai shouted below him. "Kahoni! Laka! Manami!"

The others joined her until a flurry of names floated in the current.

"One at a time," Ipolani reminded them. "And give it time to respond."

While the chaos below continued, Lanakila pushed herself into the enlarged tunnel, all the way to the hard stone blocking the middle.

"This is hopeless," she said quietly. "Maybe I should tell the pirates I'll go with them if they let the others go. Or bargain for a child for them if they let me go after."

"Don't be ridiculous," Tua yelled. Lanakila hissed, and he closed his eyes, damming the flood of fear and anger until he could whisper again. "It won't work. They still can't let any of you go to spoil their secrets, and why would they surrender the other ten? No, escape is the only way."

"I don't see how we can escape," Lanakila protested. "I'm sure that's why they left the kraken standing guard instead of a pirate. Eleven of us could overpower one of them, and if they left enough to hold us all back, someone would notice their absence."

"At least the kraken is stupid," Tua said. "Keep trying names. One step at a time."

His oldest sister reached through the tunnel and grasped his fingers tightly, then sank to join the others.

"Girls," she said, "let's do this methodically."

Tua swam away. While they tried names, he would check on Pekelo again. Worthless as he was, he was better than nobody. If only Mom and Dad would return, or one of the mothers. He imagined the red-and-purple-sailed ship coasting into the harbor and anchoring at the dock above him. Maybe it would tie up next to the shark ship, or the one with blue fish and red crabs, or the kraken one. No, not the kraken one, just in case it really belonged to the pirates.

He stopped swimming and floated in the warm ocean, excitement running through his veins like a cool current. What if it *did* belong to the pirates? What if the ship's name also belonged to the kraken painted across the hull?

They wouldn't be that obvious, would they?

Tua raced back for the cave, checking for any eavesdroppers as he swam. Rather than go to the speaking tunnel, he swam directly to the main entrance. His sisters were still shouting names at the kraken from inside.

"Sisters," he called. "Hush!"

"Don't tell me to hush," Akoni bellowed.

"Please," he begged. "Be quiet for a minute."

Ferocious arguing on the inside finally died to silence. Poised at the outside of the tunnel and peering at the kraken, ready to flee if his guess went badly, Tua took a deep breath.

"E—" His voice squeaked, and he tried again. "Ekewaka!"

The kraken immediately turned to face him, tentacles gently waving.

Yes! He was right!

"Ekewaka, stop."

The kraken kept watching him.

"Ekewaka, sit."

The kraken backed against the wall, but when Tua stuck his head inside the tunnel, it moved toward him.

"Ekewaka, home."

Again, the kraken did nothing.

Argh! So close, and yet it still wasn't working. There must be some command to make the kraken give up, but what was it?

Before he could try another word, he noticed a swimmer heading his way. Bolting upward, he headed for the speaking tunnel and crammed himself in. Now, at least, the wider tunnel allowed him to get his entire body inside, feet on the hard rock in the middle. He peered through the seaweed hanging over the hole, watching until the aquastrian left. But traffic was picking up as late risers finally woke, and more Nokai appeared before he could return to the kraken.

Tua reversed his position to whisper through the speaking tunnel. Once he had someone's attention, he said, "Its name is Ekewaka. Keep trying different commands. I have to go before I get caught."

"Be careful, brother," Mililani said. "We'll see you later."

"Later," Tua promised.

When it looked clear, he swam quickly into the closest travel lane, then slowed to look inconspicuous.

For the rest of the day, he waited on the dock, watching for red and purple sails, but Mom and Dad didn't come home.

The next day, Tua considered skipping weeding, but the punishment chores would take time from helping his sisters. Besides, he didn't have any better ideas about the kraken yet, anyway. After checking for Mom's ship at the dock, he dragged himself to the community garden and discovered weeding was on hold while they harvested the current crop of vegetables. Though more physically tiring, harvesting was also less boring, and he grabbed a wheelbarrow and a shovel with relief.

Within a few minutes, his barrow was full, and he raced it through the crowd to the storehouse, careening to a stop at the back of the short line. The wait was explained when a woman showed up to call off the dog protecting the entrance.

"Laka, leave it," the woman ordered. When the dog obediently trotted to the side and lay down, the woman passed him a treat.

Tua closed his gaping mouth with a snap and trundled forward in a daze. He hadn't tried that command, nor had he rewarded the kraken. Would either work?

He almost abandoned his wheelbarrow to try immediately, but forced himself to return to the garden for another load, and a third. Finally, the vegetables were gathered, and Tua bolted for the ocean.

First, he needed a treat for the kraken. Fish? No, crabs. He could always find crabs, thanks to his birth gift from Makana. After grabbing a basket, net, and bait from home, he swam to his favorite crab-catching spot, which was fortunately unoccupied. He closed his eyes and listened until he could hear the crustaceans. Or feel them, maybe, since his family always claimed they couldn't hear anything.

Tua arranged the net flat at a likely spot and dropped a chunk of fish in the middle, then he strung out the line and hid himself behind a rock outcropping. Quietly, he waited, eyes closed to listen better. Soon, the tip-tap of crab claws on rock whispered in his ears. Not yet. Wait... The tapping stopped, and Tua yanked the line up and in, closing the net and pulling it toward him.

Inside the net, a little blue crab clawed at the mesh. One down. Tua pried out the crustacean and dropped it into his basket, then reset the net and bait. An hour later, his bait was gone, but he had a basketful of tiny crustaceans. Hopefully, they were enough, at least to see if his plan would work.

He tied the basket to his back with the net and set off for the underwater cave. The swim took forever, and stopping to make sure the area was clear was torture, but finally he reached the entrance tunnel.

Tua wedged himself near the mouth of the cave and untied the basket. Carefully, he grabbed a crab's hind legs and pulled it free.

"Ekewaka," he called, rolling the crab into the tunnel.

Something crunched in the darkness.

"Ekewaka," Tua called again, sending another sacrifice into the dark.

Another crunch, and then the kraken appeared halfway into the tunnel, where the light outlined it.

With shaking hands, Tua retrieved another crab and held it out at his side. "Ekewaka, leave it!"

The kraken watched him for a moment, and his heart sank. Then it swam forward, exiting the tunnel and lazily swimming to one side. Its tentacles reached toward Tua, and he quickly threw. With one quick snatch, the kraken caught the snack and stuffed it into its beak. Instead of returning to the tunnel, it waited.

Tua dashed into the entrance and shouted, "Sisters! Come here. Hurry!"

He backed up to watch the kraken, which didn't move.

After a minute, Lanakila poked her head from the tunnel, turning to examine the kraken.

"Hurry," Tua begged.

"Yes," Lanakila said, but she disappeared back into the tunnel.

Tua smothered a scream, and when the kraken twitched, he threw it another crab. "Ekewaka, stay." That seemed to work, too.

In a moment, Lanakila reappeared, towing Kini and Hanini behind her.

"How long can you hold it?" she asked as the three of them passed him.

"I don't know," Tua whimpered. "Are the others coming?"

But already, they were appearing in the tunnel, watching the kraken with wide eyes. Ipolani dragged Pomaikai, one hand over her mouth. Kamaka escorted Akoni, who shook like seaweed in a current. Good, they were practical, with the older girls taking care of the younger ones. All that were left were the rest of Pinks, the sisters from his own house.

The kraken stirred, and Tua tossed another crab. "Ekewaka, stay."

Past him, his sisters swam madly toward home. But where were the Pinks? His crab basket was already half empty.

The kraken crunched the crab like nuts, and someone yelped. Inside the tunnel, faint figures appeared.

"Hurry," Tua said. "Get out here."

The last of his sisters jerkily approached the edge of the tunnel. Mahi towed Nohea, while Mililani covered her mouth and Uilani pushed from behind. Nohea swatted and pulled at her sisters in panic, squealing through the makeshift gag, and cringing from the monster.

"Quiet," Tua hissed. "Don't startle the kraken." He threw another crab. "Ekewaka, stay."

Nohea whimpered but stopped struggling and closed her eyes, letting the other three tow her. Once in the open, all four separated, swimming for home as fast as they could kick.

Tua tossed another crab to Ekewaka to keep him from following his sisters, then another and another, until the girls were out of sight. He only had two crabs left, and he still needed to get to safety. If the kraken didn't follow him before, it probably wouldn't now, but he what if he was wrong?

"Ekewaka, stay," he repeated.

He threw both crabs inside the tunnel, pushed off from the mountain, and fled. The ocean water flowed over his gills like warm love, but it didn't warm the panic freezing his heart. Faster, swim faster.

He needed a plan. His sisters were safe, so how could he get to safety faster? Get out of the water!

Tua kicked for the surface. Soon, he emerged near the beach, breathless and aching from the racing speed. He dashed onto the sand, then peered down into the clear water. No kraken. Were they safe then?

From the kraken, maybe, but not from the pirates. When they got back, they might go looking for his sisters again, to keep their secrets. He had to protect them, but he still didn't know who to trust. Any of the Nokai in his clan could be in league with the pirates, and he had no way to tell who was honorable.

Tua flopped onto the sand, staring across the water. Something hard pressed into his hip, but he ignored it. Sails drifted across the bay, striped and spotted and splashed with color. The only ship with white sails stood out like a tuna in a koi pond.

Tua bolted upright. White sails weren't Noki! He squinted for a better look. The sails had no trim indicating which country was approved for trade, so the ship wasn't Darrendran. The flag wasn't colorful enough for the Iojif, so that left Iskrin. And the Iskrins would certainly not want pirates operating in the area.

If he could convince them he knew what he was talking about.

The ring! He slapped the lump in his pocket, then shoved his hand inside for the gold ring from the girls' bedroom. In the chaos and worry, he had never remembered to return it to the cave. Now it could prove his story.

And how would he tell the Iskrins? He didn't speak Iskrit or trade tongue, and letting them ask a random Nokai for translation seemed risky. Flopping back on the sand, he threw his arm across his eyes. Why did everything have to be so hard?

Maybe he had no choice but to pray to Makanavailea and leave it in her hands. Casually, he strolled inland and borrowed ink and a pen, then scribbled a summary on a broad leaf, including instructions to the cave. He rolled the leaf around the ring and shoved the whole thing into his pocket, then returned to the beach and swam toward the foreign ship.

Though not actually docked, it wasn't moving fast, either. Probably waiting for a chance at a mooring station. Tua found a fishing net hanging over the side and scaled it far enough to throw his leaf package over the bulwark, then dove back into the ocean.

If that didn't work, then... then the parents would have to find a better idea!

Planning to sleep for hours, Tua wearily swam home. To his surprise, Mom was there, feeding the Pinks a hearty meal. He threw his arms around her and squeezed, relief spreading through his veins like octopus ink in water. Laughing, she set another plate on the table and touched his cheek.

"You look as tired as your sisters today," Mom said.

Tua slumped into his hammock-seat and reached for his fork. "Yeah, but wait until I tell you what I discovered. The girls found a pirate hideout and have played with their treasure every night. That's why they've been so tired."

Mom jerked back, then laughed. "Really?"

Nohea rolled her eyes. "Sure, Mom. We rolled in gold coins in an underwater cavern and didn't bring a bit of it home."

Mahi snickered. "I'm sure they wanted me to spin straw into gold for them."

"Sure, Mom," Mililani and Uilani said in chorus, eyes wide and chins resting on their hands.

"They have a kraken for a guard," Mililani said.

"And they trapped us for days," Uilani said, "trying to starve us into obedience."

Akoni nodded vigorously. "And they wanted to keep all eleven of us forever." She winked very broadly, then held a finger to her lips.

Mom chuckled. "You have good imaginations."

"But it's true," Tua wailed. "And I rescued them." He crossed his arms and slumped in his hammock.

"Sure, Mom," Mahi said. "All by himself, Tua rescued us from forty pirates and a kraken." She pursed her lips and shook her head a little, eyebrows raised high.

Tua glared at his sisters. They had been eager for the parents to rescue them, but now that they were safe, they were making him look like a liar to avoid punishment. They always ruined everything!

When Mom turned to grab the next course, Akoni stuck out her tongue at Tua.

The rest of the meal was spent in silence while his sisters gloated.

When Mom passed around dessert, Tua stabbed it with his fork. "It doesn't matter. I'd rather have my sisters safe than have my own room."

The girls stared at him, and he shrugged. "I've slept in the corner for years. What difference does it make?"

Mahi cleared her throat. "We've been thinking, Mom, and Nohea and I are ready to move out. The Purples said we could share their house, and then Tua can have our room." She smiled at Tua and mouthed, "Thank you."

"Yes!" Tua pumped his fist. "Tonight?"

"I suppose."

Gleefully, Tua gulped his dessert. The sooner he finished, the sooner he could help pack.

They had nearly finished eating when Dad swam in.

"You're just in time," Mom said, adding another plate. "What took you so long?"

The girls lined up to kiss Lono's cheek before heading down to their bedrooms.

"If you can believe it," Dad said, "I got hauled in to translate for the Iskrin ship. They got an anonymous note claiming there were pirates in the area."

Mililani froze, lips against his cheek.

"Pirates?" Mom laughed. "There seem to be a lot of those stories lately."

Mililani bolted for the hatch, which was suddenly clogged by five sisters trying to escape at once.

"No story," Dad said. "When we followed the directions, we found the hideout, still full of loot. The authorities are setting a trap for the pirates right now. When they come back, we'll catch them. The note even gave the name of their ship, so there's no escape."

Mom raised an eyebrow at Tua, who crossed his arms behind his head and leaned back, grinning.

"Girls!" Mom called, and the five of them froze. "I suddenly want to hear more about this imaginary story Tua made up."

Nohea groaned. "We'll move out tomorrow, Tua. I think we'll be too busy today."

They dragged themselves back to the parents, floating in disappointed lumps around the table.

Cackling in triumph, Tua descended through the hatch and strapped himself into his hammock for a well-deserved nap. Tomorrow he would have his own room!

I f you like this story, you might like the traditional Earth fairytales:
The Twelve Dancing Princesses
Kate Crackernuts
Ali Baba and the Forty Thieves
Rumplestiltskin

FEARLESS

1. QUEST
(SERAFI AND HERESA DISTRICTS, ISKRA)

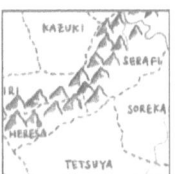

He wished to learn how to shudder.
The Legend of the Boy Who Sought Fear

Tanvir Sahira hurried home for dinner, such as it was. After washing off most of the coal dust at their small well, he burst into the house, still wiping his face on his scarf. As he moved to close the door, he stumbled over the bucket. Within seconds, the dirt floor swallowed the spilled goat's milk.

"Tanvir!" Mother sank onto her stool and clutched her head. "Now all we have for dinner is bread."

"I'm sorry." He shrugged.

Without Father to teach him, his mining skills were poor and his pay scant. Every day, he went to work hungry and came home hungry and slept hungry. Years had passed since he had a full belly.

"Oh, Tanvir. I'm afraid we'll starve one of these days." Mother wiped her eyes with her faded burgundy sleeve. "Ever since your father died..."

He flopped on his blanket in the corner. "Afraid? What does that mean?"

Mother laughed. "You know. Worried, nervous, scared, anxious."

He shook his head. He had heard people use the words, but nobody had ever explained them to him. Everyone just seemed to know what they meant.

She blinked. "When you shudder." Mother shivered.

Tanvir hopped off his blanket and wrapped it around her shoulders. "Here, I do not need it."

"No, I'm not cold," Mother protested. She handed back the blanket and stared at him, brows furrowed. "Are you never afraid?"

He shrugged again. "I do not understand what you mean, so I cannot say."

"Oh, Tanvir." She sighed. "Well, I am afraid of many things. I cannot change most of them, but I can keep you from starving or dying in a mine accident like your father. Tomorrow, you must go into the world and earn your own food."

He grinned. The mine was monotonous, and an adventure sounded like much more fun.

"As you please, Mother." He pursed his lips. "Perhaps I can learn to shudder, if you think it so important."

Mother laughed. "I do not think that will help."

"But I want to learn." He winked at her.

"I envy your optimism," she said. "You have always been so cheerful."

He hopped to his feet and kissed her cheek. "Are you ready for dinner? Should I get the bread?"

"If you will draw water from the well, I will slice the bread."

Tanvir rushed out the door. Even a plain loaf was a blessing when sometimes they had nothing, and Mother made *delicious* bread.

Dinner ended quickly, and washing the dishes took no time. After feeding the goat and watering the small garden that was still not ready to harvest, they rolled up in their blankets on the floor. Tanvir spent some time rehearsing his plans before he went to sleep.

As soon as he finished his prayers in the morning, he brushed coal dust from his worn robe and wrapped his scarf around his head. It had been Father's scarf, and Mother had washed and mended it for so many years that the persimmon had faded to pink and nearly disappeared under many patches. Mother packed a basket with his blanket, clean but mended stockings, and the last loaf.

From the doorway, he could see the flour barrel was empty, so he reached for the bread to remove it. "What will you eat, Mother?"

She moved the basket out of reach and patted his cheek. "Goat's milk. And by next week, the early greens in the garden will be big enough. Now, go find yourself a good life, Tanvir."

"I will send for you," he promised. "I will take care of everything. And I will learn what fear is."

She shook her head. "Perhaps you will."

After kissing her cheek, he took the basket and left. The spring weather was pleasant, and the white sun shone in the apricot sky without a cloud to dim the brilliance. As he walked down the mountain, he peered in every direction. If Mother did not want him to be a coal miner, then he must leave Serafi, for he had no other skills and his home mountains had few jobs.

East led only to more Serafi mountains until the ocean. North was either the Tukiko district or the Kazuki, but both were across the mountains, a foolish path for a man alone, with no equipment and no warm clothing. And he knew nothing about healing or spices, anyway.

To the south were the fertile lands of the Soreka and Chiharu. He had no interest in making perfume, but endless fields and orchards of fruit sounded tempting indeed. An unskilled laborer could pick fruit in Soreka, but could he earn enough to send his wages home to Mother after he fed himself?

The mountains continued westward, but coal mining gave way to gems and precious metals. Perhaps his skills would be similar enough to be useful there, and working with jewels and gold and silver must pay more than digging coal. Then he could send for Mother.

An almost perfect plan. Tanvir tucked his basket more securely under his arm and whistled his way down the slope. Now all he needed was to learn how to shudder.

His bread was gone within two days, so Tanvir gathered edible plants as he traveled. He stopped each afternoon and set rabbit snares, since he was not in a hurry but was constantly hungry. Though he passed an occasional caravan, mostly he walked in solitude, which gave him plenty of time to dream of finding a good job and sending money home to Mother.

A week later, he camped for the night, rolling up in his blanket in the shelter of a bush. Before he fell asleep, another family approached. Their belts and scarves were steel blue and white, so Tanvir must be close to the Heresa border, if he had not crossed already. The parents let their little children play nearby while they set up camp, murmuring softly in the twilight.

Tanvir kept his blanket pulled to his chin. His parents used to talk like that, holding hands and snuggling close. Smiling. Then Father died, and Mother stopped smiling. Grief tightened his chest, and he closed his eyes to fend off tears.

When he opened his eyes, one of the children was peering into his face. Though the child's steel blue robe was worn, it was neatly mended and as clean as possible for a traveler. The neckline was embroidered with white runes that said protection, blessing, thanks, and then disappeared around the back of the robe.

"Bright stars," Tanvir whispered.

"Tar," the little one echoed, leaning to pat his face. Then he or she — it was impossible to tell at that age — waddled away.

Two of the older children screamed and jumped on each other, hitting and kicking, and the parents hurried to separate them. While they tried to settle the quarrel, the infant wandered farther, crouching to examine flowers or bugs or pebbles.

The wailing siblings kept flailing at each other, and Tanvir unwrapped himself from his blanket. Soon, the little one would be out of sight, but the parents were occupied.

The infant disappeared around a curve in the road. Tanvir grabbed his staff and followed. If the child would not tolerate being carried, then he could herd him — her? — back like a lamb. He expected to catch up quickly, but by the time he turned the bend, the child had disappeared.

Which way? He slowly rotated and finally glimpsed steel blue past a group of shrubs. He hurried after the blue, thanking Resef for the custom of putting children in the brightest clan color. The gap the child had gone through was too small for an adult, and Tanvir had to detour. As he rounded the shrubs and saw the little one bending to smell a flower, something growled.

Tanvir scanned the area, tightening his grip on his staff. From behind a tumbled pile of boulders, a half-grown mountain lion crept toward the child.

Tanvir ran forward, and the lion pounced.

Instead of landing on the baby, the beast met the end of Tanvir's staff. It skidded sideways and howled. Tanvir stepped in front of the child and swung again and again.

At each impact, the lion flinched and roared, slashing its claws toward Tanvir's face. The infant fell and started crying, but Tanvir could not spare more than a glance behind him.

Finally, the lion bounded away, bleeding from a gash above his eye.

Tanvir leaned on his staff to catch his breath until he was sure the beast was not coming back, then knelt, hands extended.

"Hey, little one," he crooned. "Did the kitty scratch you?"

The infant came to him with bleeding hands, still wailing. Gently dabbing at the tiny palms with the cleanest part of his sleeve, Tanvir examined them carefully. Though scratched, they seemed to be injured from the fall rather than the lion, and the forehead bruise was probably from the same cause.

He gathered the infant close and hummed a lullaby. Just as the wails calmed into teary hiccups, the frantic parents ran around the shrubs.

"What are you doing with my baby?" the mother screamed. "What was all that noise?"

Tanvir held out the infant. "I'm sorry about his injuries. I could not pick him up while I was fighting the lion."

"Her," the father corrected, grabbing his daughter. "What lion?"

Tanvir waved toward the mountain. "It ran that way."

"Kitty," the little girl sobbed, presenting her hands for her mother to kiss. "Bad kitty."

"Oh, thank you," the mother said to him. "You must have been so frightened."

"Should I have been?" Tanvir frowned. How was he to learn fear if he did not even know when it was appropriate? "Tell me, what does being frightened feel like?"

The mother stared at him, mouth open.

"Thank you for saving our daughter," the father said. "How can we repay you?"

"I need employment."

"I'm sorry," the man said. "We ourselves are looking for work. Is there nothing else?"

"Can you teach me to shudder?"

"To shudder? Why?"

"I want to learn what fear is."

The father furrowed his brow and shook his head. "If a lion did not scare you, I do not know what would."

"Oh." Tanvir sighed. "Then no, I need no payment."

They made their way back to camp, and Tanvir watched the family until they all fell asleep.

In the morning, the mother fed him breakfast and packed another meal for him, then they left in opposite directions. Though it seemed unfair that he would have two meals today while Mother drank only goat's milk, the only way to help her was to find a job. With a full stomach, walking was easier, and the day was warm and pleasant. Tanvir whistled merrily as he tramped through the foothills. If only he could find fear, he could accomplish both of his goals.

He saved the second meal for bedtime and slept well.

During the next week, he occasionally passed travelers or journeyed with them for a while, but mostly, he walked by himself. By now, nearly everyone he saw wore steel blue and white trim on their tan robes, and at the next major crossroad, he turned north to head into the mountains. Somewhere, he had to find a mine that needed a worker.

The people he passed on this road walked quickly, looking over their shoulders and gripping weapons. When Tanvir greeted them, they said little beyond, "Bright day." At night, everyone camped barely in sight of one another, weapons laid at their sides.

The next day, he turned onto a road heading straight into the mountains, a good possibility for leading to a mine. The other travelers continued on the bigger road, so Tanvir walked alone. By the end of the day, the ground was very rocky, and he kept walking longer than usual in search of a level campsite.

Blue crept through the apricot sky, darkening to purple, but barely before true night fell, Tanvir found the perfect camping spot. Someone had cleared the rocks from an area, placing the stones in a circle around a lone tree. In the near-darkness, he could barely see long shadows hanging from a branch. Perhaps it was a way to keep supplies away from wild animals. Sadly, he had no need for it himself, since his food was gone and his basket would not hang well without handles.

He lay on the cleared ground, and not a single stone poked his shoulders or hips. Yes, this was perfect. Within minutes, he was asleep.

In the middle of the night, a chill wind woke him, despite his blanket. Wrapping the cloth tighter did no good. Shivering, he rose and cut the driest branches he could reach. The spring grass, unfortunately, was too green for tinder, and he searched for an alternative.

The wind blew harder, and above his head, something rustled and bumped together. Ah, perhaps one of the hanging things would burn well. The owner would surely forgive him for taking enough to start a fire. If nothing else, perhaps he could use a bit of rope.

Working by feel, Tanvir climbed the tree and squirmed along the branch. Once seated securely, he reached down and grabbed the closest rope. The hanging bundle was heavy, and he struggled to raise it even a few inches. He might need to cut the rope and let it fall, but that was poor care of a stranger's belongings when all he needed was a bit of tinder. But finally, he pulled up the rope enough to grab the bundle at the end. To his surprise, some fabric came free immediately. Well then, good enough. He tucked it into his belt and returned to the ground.

After cutting a bit of fabric from the strip and fraying it to loose threads, he surrounded it carefully with dry branches and struck his firestarter. Within a few minutes, he had fed the spark into a small fire, just enough to warm his hands and feet. In the wavering firelight, the shadows swayed as the wind blew. Cloth rustled, and the shadows grew arms and feet and too-large heads.

Tanvir squinted overhead and saw bare feet. Seven pairs of feet hanging below seven dirty tan robes.

Not bundles hung for safety, after all. They were most likely bandits, which explained the way his fellow travelers clutched their weapons, but they were harmless now.

Should he change campsites to respect the dead? No, not for bandits who deserved their fate. He wrapped his blanket around himself and went back to sleep.

In the morning, he considered burying the bodies, but they had obviously been left as a warning for other bandits and thus should stay where they were. He debated returning his tinder fabric, a headscarf with an unusual striped pattern in the sapphire and auburn of the Itziri clan. Tanvir tugged on it. Still new enough to be sturdy and whole. Its owner no longer needed it, so he might as well keep it.

B y late the next day, the path reached into the mountains, but he still had not found a mine. Then the path faded to nothing in the evening, and Tanvir got lost looking for the stream he could hear babbling temptingly near. After fighting his way through a hedge of thorn bushes, he stopped to wind the striped scarf around a bleeding scratch on his arm. He should go back and find another road to try, but which way was back? Night was falling, and he could no longer see more than a stone's throw from him.

A light flickered on the mountainside. Firelight! Someone must be nearby, and people meant warmth and food. Tanvir headed for the light.

By the time he finally tracked down the fire, the stars were gleaming, and he was very tired. His breath puffed into clouds, and his hands and feet ached with cold. The instant he walked into the clearing, everyone sitting around the fire jumped to their feet. Tanvir promptly took one of the vacated seats on a log and stretched his feet and hands toward the flames.

"Ah, I was nearly frozen. Thank you for sharing."

He smiled at the strangers, who were a motley lot of various clans, consistent only in their dirty faces, sturdy boots, and staffs. Their faces were gaunt and their clothing as mismatched and ill-fitting as if it had originally come from different people altogether. Even their numerous weapons did not match. Some carried bows, some had swords, some far too many knives, and a few wielded more exotic weapons that Tanvir had never seen. They spread out and drew their weapons.

That did not seem welcoming at all. What about hospitality for guests? Tanvir examined the group again. Perhaps the seven men he camped with last night had been their companions, and he should not expect hospitality.

A tall man drew a sharpening stone along his dagger. No, not welcoming at all, but he was too cold and tired to continue in the dark. Perhaps they could be distracted.

"What a good idea," Tanvir said. "Do you mind sharpening mine, too?" He pulled his knife and handed it to the man, who took it with a puzzled look.

One of the men sat across the fire and slapped his knees. "No armed force dares venture here. Even the animals avoid our camp. Who are you to come so boldly?"

Though his scarf was nearly too dirty to distinguish the color, it was probably the bright, pale green of the Kazuki clan. His robe was a darker brown than the usual tan, which confirmed Tanvir's guess.

"Bright stars," he said. "My name is Tanvir. My mother sent me to find my place in the world, and I am in search of fear."

All the men roared with laughter.

"Fear is where we are," the man across the fire said.

"I only wanted a little warmth," Tanvir said, "but I would be happy to learn fear as well."

He pushed his feet closer to the fire. The men stopped laughing and gaped at him.

"*We* are fear," the Kazuki man said. "Give us all your money." He smiled sweetly, as if it were a completely reasonable request.

"I know no fear and have no money, alas for both." Tanvir shrugged.

The man's smile faded. "Then you must pay in blood."

Tanvir blinked. He certainly would not pay in his own blood. Perhaps they needed a reminder of what doom waited for bandits.

"I do not see how that benefits you, but if you wish." He whipped off the scarf tied around his injury and tossed it across the fire. "There is your blood."

"That belongs to—" one man blurted before their Kazuki leader waved him silent.

"Where did you get this scarf?" the leader asked.

So, Tanvir was right about them being comrades of the hanged bandits.

"Oh, last night I slept under seven men in high beds," he said. "I needed a bit of tinder, sad to say. But now I have returned it to his friends in exchange for warm feet, and so I see it is indeed a fair deal."

The leader covered his eyes and shook his head, then burst into laughter. "A fair deal, indeed. And in exchange for bringing us word of our missing men, would you care to play a game with us?"

He folded the striped scarf and beckoned two of his men, then whispered in their ears. Grinning widely, they scampered away, returning quickly with a bare, dry skull. They stood nine short logs on end in a triangular pattern and took turns rolling the skull at them. The man who knocked down the most logs crowed in triumph.

"And so," the leader asked Tanvir, "would you like to play?"

Tanvir eyed the game. He and Father used to play something similar, with rocks as uneven as the skull. "Oh, certainly. What are the stakes?"

The Kazuki grinned. "Your head if you lose; a noble steed if you win."

Tanvir beat Father often enough, though for lower stakes. More importantly, every bandit placed a hand on a weapon, indicating their stalwart determination for a new player. If he said no, they would surely kill him, but if he played, he at least had a chance. Though he hated to disrespect the dead, at least the skull was old and dry. Better the dry skull than his occupied one.

He rolled up his sleeves. "I could use a ride. Do you go first, or do I?"

The leader held out his hand for the skull. Eyeing the logs, he rolled. Eight logs fell over.

"Well done," Tanvir cheered. "My turn."

He took the skull and walked the ground between the starting line and the logs, examining every bump and obstacle. Finally satisfied, he returned and faced the logs.

The strangers gathered around him and leaned in. Tanvir held the skull in front of him, aligning it with the logs. He swung the skull forward, and the men sucked in their breath. He swung it back again, and they sighed. He swung it forward and let go.

The skull rolled slantwise, not quite toward the logs, and the men cheered.

Then it hit the bump on the ground Tanvir had aimed for. It abruptly changed direction, shooting in the air toward the logs. The men gasped. The skull landed in the middle of the logs, scattering them in all directions. The last log teetered, then fell.

"Nine," Tanvir said. "I win. Good, I was looking forward to sparing my feet tomorrow."

The men groaned and whipped toward their leader with angry faces, patting their weapons.

The Kazuki slapped his thigh and laughed. "Well done! You have earned your reward. Indeed, we will also feed you and let you sleep by the fire tonight."

Tanvir rubbed his hands together. "Better and better! I thank you for your hospitality."

He bowed, and the leader bowed in return.

Soon, belly full and feet warm, Tanvir rolled into his blanket by the fire and fretted over his continued problem. If even bandits could not teach him fear, then where would he find it? Eventually, he gave up and went to sleep.

2. SERVICE
(HERESA AND SERAFI DISTRICTS, ISKRA)

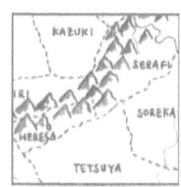

But no matter where he looked, he could not find fear.
The Legend of the Boy Who Sought Fear

W hen Tanvir woke in the morning, the camp was empty. His sharpened knife sat on a log, and an old, swaybacked donkey was tied next to a pile of grass.

"Noble steed." Tanvir laughed. No matter; a donkey would spare his feet as much as a horse, and would be easier to feed.

Since he had no food for breakfast, it took him only a few minutes to break camp and be on his way. He soon discovered how uncomfortable it was to ride the donkey and hopped off. When his feet hurt, he would rest for a while.

And that made the pattern of his travel for the next week, until he finally found a road that led to a mine.

Resef was smiling on him, for the gold mine was indeed looking for new workers in the less-skilled section for which Tanvir was perfectly qualified. His donkey was put to work pulling carts of ore or supplies.

His new life was nearly perfect. The pay was better, since the product was more valuable. Tanvir ate three times a day, though the food was simple, and slept in a warm company hut with several other unmarried workers. Between the food and the hard labor, he grew as strong as anyone in his team.

Unlike his old mine, this one expected the workers to learn and improve and move up the ranks. Once a week, the company introduced new skills, testing for talent in other areas. After two months, Tanvir was approved for a promotion and sent a little money home to Mother.

Then army recruiters came to the mine. Gossip ran rampant through the camp. The clan of Tetsuya was attacking. No, Tetsuya had kidnapped the Heresan chieftain's daughter. No, the daughter had run away and been captured by Tetsuya.

Finally, the true story emerged. The daughter of the Heresan chieftain had fallen in love with a prominent member of the Tetsuya clan. All was going well until the Tetsuya demanded a huge dowry, which the Heresa refused to pay. The suitor refused to forgo the dowry, and the girl refused to desert her suitor. In fact, she ran *to* her intended husband and insisted the dowry follow. Tetsuya had raised an army to take the gold and gems they claimed now belonged to them.

In response, Heresa was gathering an army to defeat the Tetsuya, retrieve the girl, and end the betrothal. The wages promised were greater than the mine offered, and Tanvir immediately signed up, donkey and all.

The evening before they were to leave was wet and stormy. While packing for the trip, Tanvir discovered his donkey was gone, leaving behind only a broken rope. If he could not find it, he would have to travel on foot, carrying his now more substantial belongings. He grabbed the rope, a lantern, and his staff and marched after the hoof prints in the mud.

Even when night fell, he stubbornly continued. Though he might have to march with the army, he did not want to carry his pack. That donkey was his, and he would keep it!

Soon, he rounded a corner and found the donkey. Unfortunately, it was quite dead and being eaten by a scrawny mountain lion.

"You thief!" Tanvir yelled.

He whacked the lion on the head, stunning it, then rained blows and curses on the beast until it could hardly stand. As it wobbled on its paws, Tanvir noticed a long scar above its eye, exactly in the place he had injured the lion that tried to eat the little girl months earlier.

"I need a mount," Tanvir said, "and since you ate the one I had, you must replace it. I am lucky, perhaps, since you are younger and faster and stronger than my poor donkey."

He tied the rope around the lion's neck and dragged it back toward the mine, step by step. Once home, he hobbled it and tied it securely, then threw himself on the ground nearby and went to sleep, exhausted by the effort to retrieve his new mount.

In the morning, he woke to a screaming commotion. Rubbing his eyes and stretching, he asked, "What is wrong now?"

"There is a lion by you!" someone yelled. "Roll toward us carefully, and we will shoot it with arrows!"

Tanvir jumped to his feet in front of the lion. "Do not shoot my steed! I need him for the army."

An army captain edged through the crowd. "Your *steed*?" His voice broke. "You intend to ride this beast?"

"Why not? He ate my donkey and owes me service."

"But — a lion?"

Tanvir removed the hobbles and climbed onto the lion's back, keeping a firm grip on the rope around its neck. "Indeed, and why not ride a weapon as well as carry one?"

The captain spluttered, then threw his hands into the air. As the mining supervisors shooed the workers toward breakfast, the army assembled to leave. After a solid thump to remind the lion to behave, Tanvir rode at the rear to avoid startling the horses and infantry.

To his surprise, the Tetsuyan army had made a lot of progress while the Heresa had been gathering, and it took only one day of marching before they could see the opposing masses spread at the foot of the mountain.

Both armies took up their positions, facing each other across an expanse of rocks and shrubs.

"I hate this," the soldier closest to Tanvir muttered.

"Are you afraid?" jeered another, whose spear shook in his hand.

"No!" the first one denied, half-drawing his sword and dropping it back into its sheath.

"Are *you* afraid?" Tanvir asked the second man. "Can you teach me?"

Both soldiers glared at him and turned their backs.

Tanvir stroked his lion's shoulder. "Ah, well, no luck there."

Horns blew, and the front ranks of both armies rushed at each other. The lion under Tanvir flinched and shuffled his paws.

More horns blew, and the second ranks advanced. The lion roared and slashed his front claws in the air.

"Whoa, boy," Tanvir said, but it was too late to calm his mount.

The lion bolted toward the clashing armies. Tanvir held on to its neck with both hands as soldiers scattered from his path. He yanked on the rope collar, but it made no difference. He could not turn the lion to one side or the other.

"I will skin you alive," he shouted at the lion. "I will wring your neck. I will break every bone in your body!"

"Yes!" the soldiers behind him yelled. "Kill the Tetsuya!" They gathered behind him and charged the enemy.

Desperate to dismount from the bounding lion before its erratic movements made him vomit, Tanvir grasped a large shrub to stop himself, but it uprooted in his hands. Waving the bushy shrub, he bellowed at the lion beneath him.

The Heresan soldiers cheered and ran faster. "Kill all the Tetsuya!"

Ahead of them, the clashing armies paused, turning to look at Tanvir and the racing soldiers, who stirred up a cloud of dust as they ran, footsteps like thunder.

"Save us," the Heresa cried. "Here comes their champion, riding a lion and using a whole tree for a club! And behind him comes a whirlwind of destruction!"

Indeed, the sunlight glinted off steel amid the dust, like a sandstorm carrying weapons. The Heresa parted to let Tanvir and his followers through, and the Tetsuyan soldiers scattered in a cacophony of horn calls.

The lion shied so strongly that Tanvir flew over his head and landed right on the Tetsuyan captain. Rolling to his feet, he waved his shrub at the fleeing lion. "Wait until I get my hands on you!"

The captain dropped his weapons, scrambled to his feet, and raced away.

"Come on," Tanvir shouted. "After him!"

He ran after his lion, and the Heresan soldiers followed, waving their weapons and shouting threats at the fleeing army.

By the time Tanvir gave up on finding his lion again and returned to the camp with sore feet, the fighting had ended. The Tetsuya chieftain and the two lovers sheepishly approached to discuss a truce with the help of one of the eight council priests who judged all Iskra. By the time the clans finished arguing, they had agreed on a compromise that pleased no one. The Heresa gave a larger dowry than they liked; the Tetsuya received a smaller one than they hoped. The council priest declared inter-clan marriages would no longer be allowed if the dowry would impoverish either clan or cost clan secrets.

And Tanvir, as the man who heroically ended the conflict, was awarded a sackful of gold at a banquet held in his honor. As he listened to the speeches praising his fearlessness, he leaned his chin on his fist and sighed. No matter how hard he tried, he could not seem to find fear. All around him, his companions whispered of how they shuddered at the sight of the army facing them, or how fear chilled their veins when the lion roared.

But Tanvir had feared nothing and still could not shudder. 'Twas not fair. Now he had enough gold to take care of Mother for the rest of her life, but he had failed to accomplish all his goals. What would she think of him being so incapable of learning what everyone else thought so simple?

He morosely declined a fourth helping of spiced scorpion, and when the speeches ended, he excused himself. He spent the night staring at his tent ceiling, then dragged himself out of bed in the morning. After packing his bags, he collected breakfast, suffered through more congratulations, and started walking home.

Though he dawdled, the journey took only a few weeks. Every traveler he passed had new stories about the ferocious hero of the battle of Heresa and Tetsuya, though fortunately nobody recognized Tanvir. Every time someone talked about how fearless the hero was, Tanvir winced. Truly, he had not learned to shudder, and Mother would be so disappointed in him. If she had not heard the rumors, he would not tell her himself.

As he traveled, he desperately looked for fear, but it never crossed his path. All too soon, he reached the closest city to home. The streets were so full of people, he could barely squeeze between them.

"Why is everyone gathered together?" he asked a woman staring toward the marketplace.

"The chieftain died," she explained, "and the election of his successor ended in a three-way tie. Therefore, we have decided to let Resef choose the new chieftain. Each candidate is standing in the marketplace, and the priests have blessed a pigeon. In a moment, they will let it loose, and whichever candidate it lands on will be our new chieftain. Watch!"

Tanvir could not get through the crowd, so he hauled himself onto a nearby barrel for a rest. He pulled out his water pouch and a loaf of bread and settled back to watch the spectacle. This would make a better story for Mother than the ill-fated battle.

Every gaze was fixed toward the center of town, though the crowd chattered gaily. As soon as the sun reached straight overhead, the crowd fell so silent that Tanvir could hear the click of the key as the priest unlocked the pigeon's cage.

A soft coo echoed, and then a frantic flutter of wings propelled the bird into the sky. The crowd gasped and turned to watch. After circling around the market, the bird dipped, and the crowd cheered. Then the pigeon rose again, and the crowd groaned.

Tanvir took another bite of bread. It made no difference to him who the new chieftain was, but watching everyone was entertaining. The expressions on each face made it clear who supported each candidate, and smiles and frowns alternated as the bird flew.

The pigeon circled the market, and every time it dipped, the crowd held its collective breath.

"Land," the woman by Tanvir whispered, clearly audible in the silence.

The bird shot high into the sky, and the crowd leaned back to follow, shading their eyes from the sun.

"Where did it go?" the crowd muttered. "Can you see it? Did we lose it?"

"Calm down," the priest cried. "It will land eventually. Everyone, wait. If you cannot wait patiently, then pray to Resef."

He bowed his head in example. Half the crowd copied him while the other half searched the skies. Tanvir kept eating, flexing his aching feet to ease them.

Wings fluttered nearby, and the watching half of the crowd inhaled just as Tanvir felt something touch his head. He brushed at it, and it disappeared, only to return a moment later. This time, sharp claws pricked his scalp.

The crowd cheered. "Resef has spoken. We have a new chieftain!"

Tanvir brushed at the pigeon again, but it only pecked his hand and refused to move.

The crowd surged forward, surrounding Tanvir's barrel.

"Come with us," they demanded. "Hear my petition." "Grant my wishes." "Give me justice." The demands increased from all sides, and hands clutched at his robe and boots and hands.

Tanvir kicked and hit until he could stand on the barrel. "Leave me alone," he cried.

The priest forced his way through the crowd. "This is a surprise, is it not?" He chuckled. "You were not among our candidates, but the ways of the Most Holy Flame can be mysterious." Then his face grew serious, and he folded his hands together. "I'm afraid I need to check on a few technicalities, though."

"This was all a mistake," Tanvir explained. "The bird only came to eat my crumbs." He waved the rest of his loaf near the pigeon on his head, but the bird ignored it.

"Are you of the Serafi clan?" the priest asked, eyeing Tanvir's faded scarf.

"Yes. I live on that mountain." Tanvir pointed north.

"Good, good. And you are an adult in good standing?"

Tanvir sighed. "Yes, but I tell you, you have the wrong person."

The crowd protested loudly, and hands pulled at him again.

"Leave me alone!" he demanded again. "I'm going home to my mother."

The priest chuckled again. "No, no, Resef has spoken. You are indeed our new chieftain. We will send for your mother, of course. If you will come with me now, we will get you new clothes before your first meeting."

"*First* meeting?"

"Yes, of course. We have been without a leader for weeks, and everyone is waiting to talk to you. The chieftains of other clans, everyone with petitions, the trade delegations, the farmers..."

The priest kept talking, listing all the meetings, judgements, and duties awaiting the new chieftain. It sounded as if every day of the rest of Tanvir's life was already arranged. He would never have a free moment to himself, but must always try to improve his clan's prosperity and make angry people happy and bad people good. Always trying and never succeeding, for who could satisfy everyone?

"No, no," he cried, burying his face in his hands.

Someone patted his leg. "Do not worry, you have been selected by Resef."

The priest was still talking. There seemed no escape from the doom approaching. Though the sun still shone warm over Tanvir, cold rushed through his veins, and he shivered. Something was wrong with him, for he had never felt like this before.

A voice whispered in his head. "You have learned to shudder. This is the fear you sought." The voice laughed like the crackle of flames. "Now that you have what you wanted, may it enlighten you."

Tanvir wept into his hands. The voice could have been no one but Resef, and if his god had truly chosen him, then there was no escape. He must be the Serafi chieftain, and for the rest of his life, fear would ride him as he had ridden the lion.

His mother had been right. Finding fear had not helped him.

I f you liked this story, you might like the traditional Earth fairytales:
Moti
The Boy Who Found Fear At Last
The Story of a Boy Who Went Forth to Learn Fear

FAIREST

1. INN
(SOUTHWEST ISKRA)

She was the most beautiful in the land.
The Legend of the Fair One

When Ketifa Acharya heard her tormentor's slimy voice around the corner, she pressed herself against the wall and held her breath.

"Your hair is like silk," Virat Kapadia oozed.

Ketifa shuddered. Should she rescue whichever poor maid he had trapped in the hall? But she didn't want the merchant to catch *her* again, either. Her bucket tilted, soaking her robe with dirty water. Quietly setting it down, she dropped her rags to soak up the puddle. Her mother's new husband would yell if he saw the mess in his inn.

Someone giggled, and Ketifa winced. Perhaps the maid did not want a rescue. She checked her scarf to be sure it was tightly wrapped over her black hair. Nothing could be done about her wet robe, but perhaps the filth left from her cleaning duties would discourage the merchant if he saw her.

"I use a special oil on it," Astra cooed.

Ketifa gasped, then covered her mouth. What was her step-sister doing with the slimy merchant? And why had she let him remove her scarf? She was a respectable maiden with a father to protect her, not a defenseless servant.

"And your eyes are so luminous," the merchant continued.

More giggles.

Ketifa shook her head. He had used exactly the same compliments when he found her cleaning his room yesterday. And then he had touched her—

Astra gasped, and Ketifa picked up her bucket. She would risk the merchant's wrath to protect her new sister, despite their strained relationship. Perhaps a dousing would persuade him to keep his hands to himself.

The merchant chuckled, and Astra sighed and murmured something. Ketifa flinched. Why had Astra not slapped him yet?

When Astra moaned, Ketifa gathered her soggy rags and snuck out the back. If her sister *wanted* to be stupid, then Ketifa could not save her.

After dinner, the merchant followed Ketifa into the kitchen.

"Excuse me, sir." She held the stack of dirty plates against her chest as a shield and headed for the sink.

"I asked you to call me Virat." The smiling merchant side-stepped to block her way, reaching toward her.

Ketifa jerked away. "I could not possibly be so casual with Father's best customer, sir."

She smiled the bland smile her own father had taught her to use with customers. Step-Father might not care what his customers did, but Father would have protected her even if he lost a client. And Mother — Mother did what it took to please her new husband.

"But I want to be casual with you." The merchant's voice dropped into his cozening tone again. "You are so beautiful."

Ketifa kept her smile, though her hands tightened on the plates. "You are too kind." And almost as old as her father.

He reached for her scarf, and she stepped backward.

"Sir, please leave the kitchen so I can finish my work." Despite her effort to remain calm, her voice squeaked.

"Come with me, and you will never have to wash dishes again." He winked slyly, waving one hand around the room. Rings on every finger glittered in the lamplight.

"How could I leave my mother, sir?" She moved around him and put the dishes in the hot water, then laid a knife beside the sink as if for the next load. "I'm sure you can find someone else to work for you."

"Silly girl, I'm asking you to marry me." He grinned, shaking his finger like she was a naughty child.

Someone gasped, and Ketifa whirled. Astra stood in the doorway, an angry red staining her white face. The merchant smirked at her and ran a finger down Ketifa's arm. Both women flinched, and Astra fled.

"I will come back for your answer," he said.

"The answer is no." Ketifa picked up the knife, but instead of dropping it in the water, she pointed the blade toward him.

He shrugged, not even looking at the knife. "I will speak to your father." After another wink, he sauntered from the kitchen.

Ketifa finished the dishes with shaking hands. If Mother's husband thought it would increase business, he would marry her to the merchant without a second thought. How Astra could like Virat, she did not know and did not care to ask. The answer was sure to turn her stomach.

After the kitchen was clean, she crept into her tiny back bedroom, dropped her filthy robe into the corner, and crawled onto her cot. As sleep pulled her under, her worries swirled into nightmares.

W hen dawn peeked through her window, Ketifa pulled a clean gray robe from her chest, running wistful fingers over her old embroidered belts. Mother was from the Tetsuya clan, and their gray was considered appropriate for cleaning the inn, but Ketifa was no longer allowed to accent with their teal or with the crimson and emerald from Father's clan, the Farashu. Astra Kukarni pranced around in the steel blue and crisp white of the Heresa, *her* father's clan, but she was not scrubbing floors, either. Ketifa hoped it was only Astra's responsibility to greet customers that explained the difference in clothing. She feared it was not.

The intersection of the three clan's borders made the inn prosperous, even before counting trade from farther away. The nearest town was a day's journey, so everyone stayed here before moving on. Gem merchants passed from the northeast, metalwork and weapons dealers from the southeast, and dyes from the north and west. Virat dabbled in all of it, anything that would turn a profit. There were rumors he would trade in *anything*, but no one had proof of illegal dealings.

And as long as he was here, Ketifa would be glad of her drab gray. She dressed, making sure her scarf covered her hair, and headed downstairs to cook breakfast.

Before Ketifa had all the food set out, Mother hurried into the room, frowning.

"Virat is accusing us of theft." She scanned the table, then ran her hands along the counter. "Have you seen his ring? The big blue stone, he says." Mother bent to search the floor, peering into corners and under baskets.

Ketifa shook her head. "I have been in the kitchen all morning." Alone, thank Resef.

Mother hurried out again, and Ketifa arranged fruit in a basket.

Noise arose in the hallway. Time for breakfast. She rushed to set out the dining hall mats and the plates and mugs, but she was not finished by the time a crowd pushed into the room. Instead of sitting to eat, everyone surrounded her, yelling and shaking their fists. Mother tugged on her sleeve, and Step-Father's face was red. Astra leaned against the wall, eyes dancing.

Ketifa did not have time to wonder about her sister's odd expression because Virat shook her.

"Why did you take it?" he asked.

"Take what?" She looked frantically from Mother to Step-Father.

"My ring," Virat bellowed, shoving a sparkling bit of gold and blue in her face.

"I did not." She tried to free herself from the merchant, but he held tight.

"Stop shaking her," Mother said. "Back up and let her breathe." Once everyone spread out a little, she turned to Ketifa. "Virat's ring was found in your room."

"No! Who said so?" This was a trick of the merchant, surely, to punish her for her refusal to marry him.

Astra stood straight, her lips curving in a sorrowful frown. "I found it, sister dear, in the bottom of your trunk, where you hide everything." Her eyes narrowed, and the corners of her mouth turned up in the tiniest of smirks.

"Astra lies," Ketifa said. "I took nothing."

"I saw her pull it out," her step-father said, face grim. "I have already sent for the guard."

"But I did not take the ring." Ketifa tightened her lips to keep them from trembling and turned to Mother. "Please."

"I do not think she would steal," Mother said timidly, clutching her husband's arm.

"I saw it in her trunk myself," he repeated. "She must be guilty."

Mother turned her face away, even as a tear escaped. Panic and sorrow clamped around Ketifa's chest until she could not breathe. Would Mother not help her?

The merchant rubbed his chin. "There is no need for the guard."

Ketifa sobbed in relief.

"I will take her to jail myself," Virat continued, reaching for her again.

Ketifa cringed away, and Astra gasped.

"No," Astra cried. "The guard will handle her. No need to worry yourself." She reached for his arm.

The merchant smiled. "But the sooner she is in jail, the sooner I can think about other things."

"Oh." Astra grinned. "Other things." She smoothed her robe and fluttered her eyelashes. "Yes, take her away now."

"That would be best." Step-Father frowned at the other guests peering into the room.

Another tear ran down Mother's cheek, though she said nothing. Ketifa fought for breath or another argument, but the truth had already failed. *Oh, Father, why did you die and leave me alone?*

Virat grabbed Ketifa's arm. She yanked back, struggling to free herself, but his fingers pressed into her skin with unrelenting strength. He dragged her to the door, calling instructions to his servants to pack his bags and follow him, hauling her so quickly she could barely keep her feet under her. In the stable, he bound her wrists together and locked her in a stall while he saddled two horses.

"I did not steal your ring," Ketifa choked out between sobs. Panic blanked her mind, and she struggled to think clearly. How could she convince him to let her go?

The merchant merely grinned at her. "Your sister says you did."

He threw packed saddlebags onto the horses and led them from the stable. Ignoring her struggles, he shoved her onto a horse and tied her hands to the saddle. Then he mounted, took both sets of reins, and set off.

"But what about your belongings?" Ketifa asked, desperate to delay.

"My servants know where to meet me," Virat said coolly, pressing the horses into a trot.

That was the last he said, even when she protested her innocence again and begged for her freedom.

Ketifa twisted in the saddle to look at her family. Mother covered her face, but Step-Father watched grimly. Astra waved as if Ketifa left for a pleasant trip.

Ketifa could only weep. Had Astra put the ring in her chest? Why had Mother not defended her? How long would she be in jail for something she did not do? If the merchant felt it necessary to take her to jail in the next town, he must fear her family's influence a little. Surely they would come after her in a day or two.

After an hour, Virat pulled off the road and wheeled his horse to face her. "Time for a chat. First, stop worrying about jail. I have no intention of taking you there."

"Thank you," Ketifa started, but he raised his hand.

"That would be a complete waste when I can marry you instead." He squeezed her knee and smiled.

Her mouth dropped open in shock, and she jerked her leg away. "You cannot make me vow to you."

The merchant shrugged. "True. Fortunately, I do not care about mere words."

Not marriage at all, then. Ketifa crossed her arms, partly for defiance but mostly to hide the shivers of fear that wracked her. "Take me to jail. I will talk to the judge about my innocence."

"No. I will get you settled before I return for your sister." He set both horses into motion.

Her head reeled. "What do you want with Astra?"

"*She* wants to be my wife, and you are both beautiful. Silky black hair, pure white skin, and ruby-red lips." He closed his eyes and smiled dreamily. "Delicious."

"All Iskrins have black hair and white skin," Ketifa argued. "If she wants you, why not marry her and let me go?"

"I have four beautiful wives so far," he said. "Five, with you, all in different towns along my route. Astra will make six. I'm never more than a few weeks from marital bliss. The others love me, but you I think I will take north where I have someone to make sure you stay put until you see reason. Mmm. We should get you there quickly." Virat kicked his horse into a canter.

How could he have five wives? What priest would perform a marriage to an already married man? But they lived in different towns, and he must keep them secret.

What if she could not escape Virat? Ketifa clutched the saddle with her bound hands. The inn and her new father had been tolerable. The prospect of jail was worse. But eventually, she could have left home or defended her innocence in court. Her stomach churned. What were her options now?

Ketifa sobbed for the first day and night, cursing the merchant between tears, but he cheerfully ignored her. He gave her food and water at regular intervals but kept her tied, even when he let her off the horse during breaks. At night, he avoided the inn and pitched a tent outside town. He slept with her in his arms, but, Resef be thanked, travel left them both so exhausted that he did nothing but sleep. Ketifa cried herself to sleep, despair and temporary relief tangled in her heart.

The second day, she rode the horse in silence as the mountains grew closer. The merchant cheerfully talked to her about the bright future he saw for them, warning her not to try to escape lest the wild animals rip her to shreds. Meals were difficult to swallow through the constant nausea, and sleep was riddled with nightmares.

It was obvious her hatred made no difference to him. The third day, she hid her disgust and replied to him as often as she could bear, smiling at him between conversations. If she could gain his trust, perhaps he would loosen her bonds enough to let her escape. She would rather scrub a thousand dirty floors than be his wife for a single day.

Virat talked more that day, but he also touched her more, squeezing her knee or caressing her arm. It grew harder and harder to hide her shudders. At night, he removed her scarf before they lay down, stroking her hair until he slept.

Ketifa took much too long to fall asleep. If she continued her attempts to gain his trust, would his ardor reach the tipping point before she could escape? But if he did not trust her, he would surely prevent an opportunity. Both ways were risky, and she did not know if either could save her. Nonetheless, she must try.

All during the fourth day, she chattered at the merchant as if she were a brainless goose. Desperation forced her to hide her disgust and compliment him, fluttering her eyelashes like Astra always did while she talked about the advantages of being married to a rich merchant. Eventually, she persuaded him to untie her ankles even when off the horse, though he kept her wrists bound and a rope around her waist.

At nightfall, they again stopped outside town. The mountains now towered next to the path. The merchant let her help pitch the tent, and she made sure to appear compliant in all ways. When they went to bed, she tried to slide toward the opposite edge of the blanket, but he slid close, running a hand over her curves.

Ketifa shivered and turned to face him. She pulled her lips into a smile and forced herself to put a hand on his chest.

"There is no hurry," she said. "I'm so tired from riding all day. We can wait until we are in our new home and have enough energy to make the night special." She ran a finger across his shoulder and giggled like Astra had. For extra effect, she wiggled a little. "And the ground is so hard. A proper cot would be more comfortable."

The merchant grinned. "I knew you would relax eventually. I suppose one more night will not hurt me."

He ran his hands down her body again, then pulled her in for a kiss. His lips were slimy and hot, but when she shivered in disgust, he only grinned.

"Just like your sister." Virat closed his eyes. "Tomorrow, my darling."

Ketifa froze until his breathing slowed, then she rolled over and wiped her mouth on the blanket.

One more day. She must find a way out.

2. MOUNTAIN
(HERESA/FARASHU BORDER, ISKRA)

Thought dead, she found refuge with strangers.
The Legend of the Fair One

The fifth morning, Ketifa woke with fear burning along her spine. She had to escape today or it would be too late.

But how? Virat had taken her knife the first day and had kept his out of her range. He controlled her horse and allowed her no chance to slip away. She stiffened her shoulders. Somehow, she had to find a way.

As she folded the blanket and collapsed the tent, she simpered at the merchant. She rolled the tent and knelt to tie it. Her knee landed on a rock, and she reached to brush away the annoyance, then froze at the touch of a sharp edge. Quickly, she tucked it under her gray belt, then fastened the tent.

While the merchant loaded the horses, she asked inane questions about her new house and his expectations for his wives. Once on her horse, she let him bind her wrists without complaint. She chattered for hours as they wound through the wide pass of the western trade route. If she could get away, she could take mountain paths too small for horses or wagons.

Her chance came at midday, when he let her down for a break. Ketifa meekly took care of her personal needs behind a thorn bush, but on her way back, she hid a thorn between her fingers. When she reached to pull herself into the saddle, she drove the thorn into the horse's side.

The poor horse squealed and bucked. Ketifa fell onto the ground, covering her head with her arms as the horse bolted.

"Oh, no!" She waved at the other horse. "Go get him, Virat. I will wait here for you."

The merchant jumped onto his mount and chased the runaway. As soon as he was out of sight, Ketifa took the knife-sharp rock and sawed at the rope around her wrists. She needed her hands free to climb the mountain. The ragged edges cut into her skin, but the pain was better than what Virat planned for her.

Once free, she ripped off a handspan of her skirt to bandage her wrists, which bled too much to ignore, then ran toward the steep mountainside. How much time did she have? Not long, certainly. She hiked her robe to her knees and climbed, thankful for her bland gray robe and scarf against the gray stone.

She was only halfway up the mountain when she heard the clatter of hooves returning.

One more desperate lunge to the next ledge, and she hid behind an inadequate bush, ducking her head low and pulling her knees to her chest.

Please, Resef, she prayed, *Most Holy Flame, hide me.*

Virat rode back and forth, calling her name. When he found the blood, he froze, then dismounted to touch it. After a very long moment, he rose, looking around him with a hand on his sword.

"Bless her soul, Luminosity," he said, "and strike the beast that killed her. What a waste of beauty." He remounted his horse, took the reins of the second, and trotted north.

He thought she was dead! Ketifa stayed behind her bush for a long time, shaking and praying in thanks.

Thirst finally drove her out. Reluctantly, she descended for a deep drink from the stream.

South and north ran the trade route. Somewhere ahead, there was a town she must avoid, since the merchant had intended to install her there as his wife. East and west were high mountains. Where did that leave?

As she scanned, something glinted on the mountainside. Ketifa squinted and took a step sideways. Something shimmered again. Glass. A window on the mountain?

She walked, stretching for a better view. In the shadow of a passing cloud, a wall stood out from the mountainside above her. A small building nestled against the mountain, nearly invisible, gray stone on gray stone. Surely Virat would never look for her there.

Ketifa tightened the cloth around her wrists, hiked up her robe, and climbed again. The afternoon sun beat down, baking her shoulders and drying her mouth. Her legs ached, and her hands burned. The bandages slowly grew redder and damper. What good would it do to escape Virat but die of thirst or blood loss? Yet she kept climbing.

An hour of clambering over small footholds finally led her to her goal. When she pulled herself up the last foot and collapsed onto the small landing, panting, her gaze fell on a wide path stretching down from the other side of the tiny building. A frustrated laugh slipped from her. She could have walked up if she had seen the path.

Once recovered, she peeked into the small window by the door. Other than a tiny table and a single chair, the one-room alcove was empty. Beside the chair, a second door opened into the mountain itself. Perhaps she could find an even better place to hide.

After another look around, she slipped inside. The table held a stack of paperwork written in a terrible scrawl, and a draft whispered beneath the back door. Under the table, a basket of fruit tempted her into snatching a pear. Eating the fruit nearly fast enough to choke, she listened at the door but heard only a distant tapping. She had found a mine.

When she finally gathered enough courage to open the inner door, she saw a rough-cut tunnel leading into the mountain. Now the tapping was joined by the distant sound of voices, and she shrank against the wall.

But no one came. After waiting an agonizing hour, she crept into the tunnel, which slanted downward in the wavering light of periodic oil lanterns. Eventually, she could no longer see the door behind her. Shortly after, the path into the mine split. One way continued downward, straight ahead. One turned left on a nearly level plane. Both were lit. The last path turned right, unlit, and ended at a shallow cave within view of the main path.

Ketifa followed the dead end and discovered the cave had an alcove around the corner, out of sight of the path. A perfect hiding place. She listened, heard nothing new, and scurried to the outer building. After stuffing half the fruit down the front of her robe, she crept back to the shallow cave and tucked herself into the alcove.

After another snack, nothing happened for so long that she fell asleep, sitting against the rock.

Noise woke her. Voices and pounding footsteps. Ketifa pressed herself against the cold stone and pulled her feet closer to herself. The tramping grew louder, passing her hiding place in a steady stream. Men and women chatted and teased in weary voices, and then the door to the building opened noisily.

"Hey, which of you lummoxes sneaked out early and ate the food?" someone bellowed.

Ketifa guiltily touched the fruit down her bodice, but they could get more at home and she could not.

Denials rang through the tunnel, and the miners argued as they exited, taking the lanterns with them. After what seemed a very long time, the door slammed shut and quiet returned.

Ketifa waited in the dark, then pressed her hand to the cave wall and felt her way around the corner, left and upwards. Once to the door, she leaned her ear against it. Silence.

Slowly, she cracked it open. Sunset trickled through the window in the little room, but it was empty. Even the basket of fruit was gone. Ketifa ate an apple from her stash while she wandered down the path. Partway to the foot of the mountain, a stream tumbled into a miniature waterfall, and she took a long drink. In the last bit of twilight, she walked up again, then felt her way back to the alcove in the cave.

When Ketifa woke, all was silent. Her muscles ached from climbing the mountain and sleeping on cold stone, and her wrists burned when she touched them. While she pondered the best strategy, she ate some of her hoarded fruit.

She eventually crept up the dark hall and peeked through the inner door. The room was empty, and the sun was rising. Watching for danger, she opened the outer door and sneaked outside.

After taking care of her hygiene needs, she sat cross-legged at the head of the path and laid her hands on her knees for her morning prayers. Resef deserved thanks for her escape yesterday, though she did not know what to do next. She could not go home, and she dare not trust any town without knowing if it was allied with Virat, but she could not stay here forever.

Ketifa dozed in the sunlight until voices and footsteps alerted her to the miners' return. Before they climbed high enough to see her, she darted back to her alcove. Tramping past her, they sounded like a cheerful bunch, but she dared not show herself in the light of the lanterns they hung as they walked deep into the mountain.

Once their voices dropped to a faint whisper and their tapping began, she tiptoed back to the outside room. It seemed the basket was a habit, though today it was filled with bread instead of fruit. She gladly stuffed herself with rolls before hiding again.

If she was to stay, she needed a better source of water. With frequent stops to listen, she borrowed a lantern and crept down the quieter left-hand path. She had almost given up when she found a battered tin bucket with a hole in the bottom. Good enough. Soon, she would have water.

For the rest of the day, she hid in her alcove, letting the rhythmic tapping soothe her nerves. Tomorrow would be early enough to make a plan. For now, she needed time to rest and heal.

Again, the workers accused each other when they discovered the missing food as they left.

Once every sound of them was gone, Ketifa sneaked to the waterfall and watched the sun set as she patched the hole in her bucket with clay. Now sure of the miners' routine, she slept in the outside room, head pillowed on her folded scarf.

Sunrise woke Ketifa long before they returned, and she repeated her hide-and-eat routine of the day before. While the miners busily tapped below, she borrowed a lantern flame and burned thorny branches carefully in the bottom of her pail until the clay dried well enough to hold water without much leaking. Unfortunately, she had to return the lantern before the miners collected the lights on the way out.

When they left in the evening, the arguing lasted for a long time, finally ending when someone suggested they leave a guard at the bottom of the path to catch the thief.

Ketifa waited longer than usual before she cautiously snuck into the outer room and peered down the slope. The path took too many turns and dips for the end to be seen, so she crept slowly further. A little more. Finally, she reached her rivulet of water and breathed a sigh of relief. She saw no one, so if they had left a guard, he could not see her, either. With relief, she filled her bucket, returned to the top, and went to sleep.

Subsequent days followed her usual routine, with water collection during her evening and morning trips, and the miners never caught her. On one day, no one came to the mine at all. Ketifa spent the day hungry, but she reset her mental calendar and marked the rest day on a tally she scratched on the wall of her alcove. She used that day to wash a little and drink a lot and soak in as much sunlight as she could.

One day, after a week or so in the mine, Ketifa crept out after closing time, feeling her way against the wall in the darkness while she unwound her scarf. Sunlight waited for her, and she wanted to feel it on her face and hair for as long as possible. She pulled on the door, and as a crack of sunlight sprang into the dark tunnel, someone rushed up and slammed the door closed. Hands grabbed her, pushing her against the stone.

She screamed and kicked. Her precious bucket clattered to the ground. A man cursed, and the hands vanished.

Ketifa scrabbled for the doorknob, sobbing, but the door did not move.

"Stop that," his voice said. "If you back up so I can let go of the door, I will light a lantern."

Ketifa slid along the wall and waited for her doom. Flint sparked, then a lantern's glow revealed a dark figure leaning against the door.

"Bright day," the miner said. "Come into the light, please."

"No." Ketifa's voice wavered despite her best efforts.

He sighed and stepped forward, holding the lantern high. He was a young man, of average height but very strong, curly black hair matted with sweat, and covered in dust. His robe was threadbare but well-mended, and his belt was a dirty version of the Heresa steel-blue-and-white.

"A girl!" His gaze traveled from her boots to her dirty robe and uncovered hair. She had long ago lost hairpins and ties, and it hung in a tangled mess to her waist. He flushed and lowered the lantern until he found her scarf on the tunnel floor. "Sorry. Here you go."

Ketifa huddled against the wall and covered her hair with her arms instead.

"Mmm." He tossed the scarf at her feet and backed to the other wall.

"Turn around," she ordered.

"If I do, I think you will disappear."

That had been her plan, but she settled for twisting her hair into a knot and covering it with her scarf. While she worked, he watched only her feet, an unexpected courtesy.

"Have you been taking our food?" he asked. "What are you doing here?"

"Nothing! I took your food, but I hurt nothing." She pressed her hands to her always empty belly. In the inn, she had eaten three meals a day, even in the dry season. Now she divided her stolen food into a meager two meals, and nothing at all on a rest day.

He rubbed one hand over his face. "Please sit. Can we talk?"

Ketifa glanced at the door longingly. "'Tis almost sunset, and I missed the sun today."

His eyebrows shot up his forehead. "Very well. I will go first, and you follow."

Without taking his gaze from her, he opened the door and walked through, holding it ajar until she reached it, at which point he backed up and set the chair against the outer door.

"Now, what are you doing here?" he asked. "You do not look like a spy or saboteur."

He leaned back casually, as if he were not blocking her only escape. She sidled along the wall until she reached the window, then tilted her face to the last rays of the sun.

"I'm hiding," she finally admitted.

"From?"

"'Tis complicated."

He shrugged. "They're not expecting me home tonight. I have time."

She rubbed her dirty hands on her even dirtier robe.

"My name is Tadaki Parikh," he said. "I'm a miner in the Heresa clan, if you cannot tell. We mine jewels, which you will never steal."

Virat traded in jewels, too. She could not trust anyone.

Ketifa shrugged. "I would rather have bread. Or a bath."

His raised eyebrow made her cheeks heat.

"Alone," she added.

"If you tell me your story, I will bring bread tomorrow. And a brush." When he smiled, a dimple peeked from his cheek. Then he sobered. "If you will not talk, I must assume you are a thief and turn you in."

With no other choice, she started her tale. "My mother married an innkeeper after my father died..."

Tadaki listened silently in the lantern light, though his jaw clenched at certain parts of her story. When she reached the end, he rubbed his forehead, leaving dirtier streaks.

"You can stay here," he said. "Or in the village below. My neighbor has a passel of girls. Either way, we will feed you." His dimple flashed. "And let you bathe. Alone." His smile faded. "Or we can send a messenger to your parents."

Ketifa stared out the window at the stars. If she went home, Virat would find her on his next trip, and her family would not stop him. They had already proved they would not.

"Do merchants come to your village?" she asked.

"We usually meet them at the crossroads. The location of this mine is *secret*, you know." He quirked an eyebrow. "And the village is nothing special."

"I will come. For now," she added when he smiled.

Tadaki bowed gravely and moved his chair to open the door. "Allow me to light the way for you."

They walked side by side, and though he never touched her, he reached toward her every time she stumbled. The path was not long, perhaps, but she was hungry and no longer used to long walks. By the time they reached the village at the bottom, she was exhausted.

A woman answered the door of a small cottage. Tadaki gave an extremely abbreviated version of Ketifa's story and asked if the woman had room.

She dragged Ketifa into the house, leaving Tadaki at the entrance. "We can throw another mat on the floor." She pulled Ketifa to the back room, fitting her between two of her sleeping daughters.

"I will see you in the morning," Tadaki called, and shut the door.

Ketifa fell asleep within minutes, feeling safe for the first time in weeks.

3. VILLAGE

(HERESA MOUNTAINS,
ISKRA)

Upon discovering she still lived, her enemy tried to kill her.
The Legend of the Fair One

Ketifa woke to six little girls staring at her. The woman, Rizpah, introduced them during breakfast, then filled a laundry tub with warm water for Ketifa's bath. She lent Ketifa one of her own robes, since even her oldest daughter was much too small, and promised to wash Ketifa's gray robe on laundry day.

Tadaki dropped off two rabbits, which Rizpah made into stew for lunch. Ketifa and the girls spent the morning cleaning the tiny house, cooking bread, and weeding the garden.

Tadaki came by again after midday. In the sunlight, his now-clean hair was unusually light for an Iskrin, dark brown instead of black. "Are you ready?"

"For what?" Ketifa asked.

He grinned. "To earn your keep in the mine."

"I do not know anything about mining or jewels."

"You do know how to empty buckets?"

Ketifa laughed. "I'm an expert bucket-emptier."

As they walked toward the path up the mountain, other miners joined them, talking and teasing. They greeted Ketifa casually, as if she had lived there her whole life, and no one asked prying questions.

Ketifa blinked back tears. What had Tadaki said to make them so willing to hide her when even her own family would not protect her? She sniffled and rubbed her sleeve across her eyes.

Tadaki brushed his hand against her elbow. "We will get you back to your family soon," he said, then immediately began a detailed explanation of her duties in the mine.

As much as she missed her mother, Ketifa felt safer here, among strangers who were kinder and braver than her own family. And all they asked in return was a little work. She took a deep breath and concentrated on Tadaki's instructions so she would not disappoint him.

This time, with lantern light and guides, the mine was friendlier. Ketifa followed her teammates, children too young to wield a pick or hammer, filling buckets with rock debris and dumping it into large carts that would be emptied into a chasm at the end of the day. The children babbled happily, asking many questions about visitors she had met at the inn.

In the evening, Tadaki collected Ketifa almost before she dumped her last bucket. After making notes in the outer room, he escorted her down the path while she munched on an apple. The trip passed quickly with their conversation, seeming to last only a few minutes, though the sun set just before the group arrived in the village. Lantern light twinkled like fallen stars as the villagers split to go to their homes.

Tadaki walked Ketifa to her new home, then promised to escort her in the morning. The girls were already asleep, so she nestled between them and went to sleep, peaceful and happy.

The next two months were always the same. In the mornings, Ketifa helped around the house. Tadaki escorted her to and from the mine, except for rest days. It was more strenuous than her work at the inn, but after a few weeks, her muscles hardened and she stopped falling asleep as soon as her head hit the pillow.

Ketifa gradually moved from the bottom ranks of bucket-emptiers to supervising the children and reporting to Tadaki each night while he scribbled notes in the outer room.

"Are you the foreman?" she asked.

He shook his head and pointed down the tunnel to an elderly man with muscles of iron. "I'm just the only one who can write."

"Oh." She looked at his scribbles. "I can write. Father was a clerk."

Tadaki lowered his chalk and stared at her. "Are you any good?"

She blinked. "Of course."

"Oh, of course." He rolled his eyes and escorted her out, but once on the path, he left her with her crew of children and hurried to talk to his supervisor.

The next day, he picked her up with a wide, dimpled grin. "Congratulations, you have a promotion. Besides directing the buckets, you get to be our scribe. 'Tis wonderful, especially for me. You might have noticed, but I'm not good at writing."

She could not argue with that.

Once at the mine, he let everyone else vanish into the darkness, then sat in the sunshine with her to explain his illegible notes and tallies.

"May I take some time to rewrite these now, or should I stay longer tonight?" she asked.

"The children can work without you," he said, "but if you need my help, it must wait."

"Then tonight," she promised.

They returned the slate and got to work. While she dumped buckets, she marveled at the trust shown her. Not only did she know the location of their secret mine, but now she would have their production details. She could ruin them, but miner after miner offered congratulations as she collected their slag.

At night, the others left, and Tadaki sat with her as she rewrote everything, double-checking her figures.

"Your writing is beautiful," he said.

The sun had set, but the lantern lit their way home, and Tadaki kept a hand under her elbow as they walked. Her blood tingled at his touch, and she was glad the pale light would hide the blush heating her cheeks.

Ketifa blushed again the next day, when the miners also admired her writing.

"Right pretty, 'tis," the foreman said. "Is that what it should look like, eh, Tadaki?"

He elbowed the younger man, who made a rude noise and shooed everyone inside.

The next month, the miners invited Ketifa to go north with them, to record sales and special orders at the market. Rizpah held out an already packed bag.

"But—" Ketifa twisted her skirt.

"I doubt anyone is still looking for you." Tadaki ran his fingers through his dark brown curls, watching her intently. "And we will not leave you alone."

She swallowed and nodded. "They must think me dead. Or still in jail, if Virat did not report my blood."

"Then come." Tadaki held out his hand.

Ketifa took it, cursing her blush, and he led her to the caravan. To her surprise, they were all on foot with only moderate packs. But of course, unset jewels took little space to carry.

The trip took three days, and she spent most of it talking to Tadaki, who was more handsome than ever without his usual coating of dirt. All the miners treated her as they treated each other, teasing her gently and making sure she got her fair share of each meal.

At the market, they pitched a canopy at the base of the mountain and settled Ketifa at the back. Several burly miners at the front with samples of the merchandise blocked her from the view of customers. The first day was uneventful, and Ketifa enjoyed the colorful crowd and rapid haggling. She kept records of everything while Tadaki brought her water and food and entertained her with stories.

When Tadaki was getting food the second day, Ketifa heard a familiar voice that curdled her stomach. Virat! Had he found her or was it only miserable luck? She ducked her head and turned her back, crouching behind the miners.

The merchant left, and Ketifa relaxed, turning back to record his purchases. A woman examining the jewels looked up to ask a question, saw Ketifa, and gasped.

"Astra," Ketifa choked.

She dropped the slate and bolted out the back of the canopy, straight to a path up the mountain just behind her. Astra followed at full speed.

Halfway up the slope, Ketifa tripped. Astra caught up before she could regain her feet.

"I'm so glad I found you," she said, "and that Virat was wrong about a beast eating you."

While brushing off dirt, Ketifa glared at her. "You know I did not steal the ring."

Why had she left the company of the miners? Surely they would have protected her.

Astra waved her hand. "Oh, I'm sorry about doing that. I wanted you out of Virat's sight so he would pay attention to me. But you can go home now, because we are married now."

She blushed and smoothed her fine robe, embroidered around the neck, hem, and sleeves. Small jewels twinkled among the bright thread.

Ketifa struggled to her feet on the narrow path, pressing her back against the rock. "Please do not tell anyone you saw me. He means to marry both of us, unless you pretend you did not see me."

She glanced down and saw her friends starting to climb, Tadaki hurrying in the lead.

Astra turned red. "He does not! Virat loves me. He cannot marry you while married to me."

Ketifa winced. She must convince her sister of the danger. "You are wife number five, and none of them are dead. How much could he love you?"

"Liar," Astra sobbed. "Why do you have to ruin everything? I will ask him. You will see."

"No, please." Ketifa reached for Astra. "Do not tell him you saw me, I beg you."

"He does not want you," Astra cried.

"Please."

Astra's face crumpled into a terrible mask. "He cannot have you." She lunged at Ketifa and pushed her off the mountain.

Ketifa screamed as she rolled down the steep slope. Thorny shrubs caught at her, ripping her robe and skin, but still she bounced over rocks. She kept falling until she slammed into the canopy and collapsed it.

Amid everyone's cries, the world went black.

The ground rocked, and Ketifa groaned. Everything hurt. Everything hurt so much. Why did death hurt?

Someone touched her arm. "Do not move, Ketifa."

She tried to roll over, and someone pressed her down.

"Shh. She's still bleeding. What do I do?"

"Press on the bandage," someone else said.

Someone pushed on her head, sending agony through it, and she whimpered. She tried to push them away, but her arm stabbed like a hundred knives.

"Hold *still*, Ketifa. Can we go faster?"

Was that Tadaki? Her head ached so badly, she could not tell.

"No." The second voice huffed with breathlessness.

She opened her eyes, but all was darkness. "Am I — am I blind?"

"No, 'tis the bandages. I will tell you everything later."

When blackness carried her back to unconsciousness, she welcomed the relief.

Some time later, she woke again. This time, everything was still. The air was quiet and cool, and something heavy pressed her down.

Her whole body ached, but she pushed against the weight. Her arm screamed with pain. Ketifa sobbed, and something rustled.

"Ketifa? Are you awake?"

"What—" Her voice croaked to a stop in her dry throat.

"Wake up. She spoke." Then a cup was held to her lips, and cool water trickled into her mouth. "Hold still, Ketifa. If you move, you will hurt yourself more."

"Who?"

"I'm Tadaki. Or do you mean who hurt you? The woman ran away before we could catch her."

"Astra," Ketifa whispered, as memory seeped into her injured brain.

"Your *sister*? But why?" Tadaki paused as someone murmured. "Yes, come here; she's awake."

Someone removed the weight and gently touched her arms, her legs, her aching ribs.

"I'm going to unwrap your head now," a low voice said.

Calloused fingers wrapped around the hand of her less-aching arm while hands moved her head. Soon, the absolute darkness lightened to mere dark gray. Sparkles of light twinkled randomly above her. She blinked, but the sparkles remained.

"I cannot see anything but sparks," she whispered. "Am I blind?"

Tadaki laughed. "Those are stars. 'Tis night. Two nights later, actually. We will be home tomorrow."

"How do you feel?" the other shadow said. Ketifa finally recognized the voice of one of the other miners.

"Horrible," she groaned.

Cool water touched her head, pushing on the ache, and she sobbed.

"At least the bleeding stopped," Tadaki said gently. "Hush and let us change the bandages."

The torture was fast, and Tadaki held her hand until the end. They made her eat a little bread, then drink more water, then Tadaki lay by her side and murmured softly until she fell asleep again.

The next day, she slept sporadically, and in her fitful wakings, Tadaki held her hand and comforted her.

By nightfall, they were home again. Tadaki and Rizpah settled Ketifa in the front room instead of the crowded bedroom. After chasing out the men, a healer went over every thumb-length of Ketifa's battered body, bandaging cuts and setting bones.

"Too late for stitches," she scolded. "You will have scars."

Ketifa chuckled. "I'm alive. Who cares about scars?" If they would scare off Astra and Virat, she even welcomed them.

"Hmph. I will return tomorrow." The healer gathered the dirty bandages and left.

For a month, Ketifa recuperated slowly. Tadaki visited every day on his way to the mine, bringing the records for her to update once she could focus well enough to read, but spending much more time with her than the records needed. Other villagers stopped by less frequently, and Rizpah assigned one of her young daughters to bring Ketifa water and help in any way she needed.

Astra weighed on Ketifa's mind, and finally she gathered the courage to discuss the matter with Tadaki. "Do you think she will come after me?"

Tadaki shrugged. "You looked dead—" He choked before continuing. "And she ran off quickly. Why would she follow?"

"Astra hates me," Ketifa whispered as a tear ran down her cheek.

Tadaki softly wiped it away. "I do not hate you. You will be safe here. We will be your family."

K etifa was mending clothes a few weeks later, while Rizpah and her daughters gardened in the back, when a knock came at the door. It was a little early for Tadaki's usual visit, but not much. She set aside the worn little robe with relief and shook her aching arm as she limped for the entrance. He would be excited to see her moving around by herself.

When she opened the door, a peddler on the doorstep turned to face her.

"Ah! I found you at last," she said.

"Astra!" Ketifa gasped.

She stepped back to shut the door, but Astra pushed her way into the house.

"I thought you were dead," Astra said, "until someone told me they had seen you carried away instead of buried." Tears glistened in her eyes.

Ketifa touched her arm. "Oh, sister, I know your husband's treachery must have been a shock."

Astra fiddled with the end of her scarf. "I love Virat, you know. In a while, I will convince him to divorce his other wives."

Ketifa grimaced. "I hope you will. I hope you can keep him happily married to you alone."

Calmly, Astra pulled on her scarf until it unwound. "I will. That only leaves one problem. He heard the gossip, too, and he knows that no beast ate you. He is insulted and intent on finding you."

Ketifa shuddered. "Please, sister, do not tell him where I am."

"No," Astra promised.

She threw her scarf around Ketifa's neck and pulled tight. Ketifa gasped for air, struggling, but her healing body was no match for Astra. As she sank to the floor, her sister bent, keeping the tension on the scarf. Her face was as smooth as if she were killing a spider.

Now no air passed Ketifa's throat, and everything went black.

4. MINE
(HERESA MOUNTAINS, ISKRA)

After death, her body was placed into a glass coffin.
The Legend of the Fair One

Air suddenly returned to Ketifa's lungs, and she gasped against the floor.

Rizpah sat her up and patted her back. "Breathe."

Ketifa sucked in air, wincing as her throat protested.

Rizpah picked up a steel blue scarf from the floor and folded it. "I will save this for the constable. Can you tell me what happened? You are lucky I came inside for another basket."

"Sister," Ketifa wheezed.

"Again?" Rizpah slammed the door. "How did she find you here?"

Ketifa shrugged, and the small motion jerked her bruised neck. "Gossip."

Rizpah gasped, wide-eyed and tight-lipped. "That endangers the entire village and the secret location of our mine. I must speak to the elders about this. Will you be all right if I leave you?"

Ketifa scooted over to sit against the wall. "Yes," she croaked.

She folded her trembling hands in her lap and concentrated on breathing. Rizpah nodded and left with the scarf. Her eldest daughter soon came in and sat beside Ketifa to finish the mending. Though she did not talk, she watched the door and Ketifa between every stitch.

An hour later, Rizpah returned with Tadaki and several of the village elders. Tadaki held her hand while the others talked.

"Because Rizpah interrupted your sister before she could be sure you were dead," the chieftain said, "we cannot be sure she will not return. This house — this village — is no longer safe for you, and we cannot risk strangers wandering around."

Ketifa squeezed Tadaki's hand as her heart collapsed. She should have known this place was too good for her.

"You want me to leave," she croaked.

"No," Tadaki blurted. "Not entirely, but we think you might need to stay in the mine for a while."

"I did before," she wheezed through her sore throat.

Her hiding place had been horrible, especially the darkness, but she could do it again, sneaking sunshine in the early morning.

"This time," the chieftain said, "you need to stay entirely in the mine. No coming out to the path where you might be spotted. We will bring you food and water and help you set up a better room."

No sunlight at all. Ketifa already felt wilted. "How long?" Impending tears made her throat ache even more.

"Not too long," he said. "A few weeks, perhaps. We will plant rumors at the marketplace about your horrible death."

"And make a false grave for you," Tadaki added, his dimple peeking out.

Ketifa pinched his finger, then rubbed the spot in apology.

"Once everyone knows you are dead, we will bring you back." Rizpah patted her shoulder.

Ketifa touched her throat. Twice Astra had tried to kill her. Twice she had nearly succeeded. Next time, she might.

Ketifa nodded. What choice did she have?

"I will tell the village," the chieftain said.

Rizpah jumped to her feet and grabbed a basket. "I will pack your things."

"And I will walk with you," Tadaki promised.

The rest of the morning went rapidly, and not long after the usual time the miners left, Ketifa started up the mountain path, leaning heavily on Tadaki's arm.

"It will not be so bad," he murmured. "We will all visit with you."

Ketifa looked toward the sun. "Weeks in the dark," she whispered.

"Resef will understand if you pray without sunlight," Tadaki said.

Ketifa sighed and limped another step upward.

Tadaki patted her hand on his arm. "The time will pass quickly."

When they reached the top and went inside the mine, the other miners had already turned her little cave into a proper room with a thick layer of mats on the floor and a folding screen to give her privacy. Baskets of food and a small barrel of water filled the corner, and a basket of mending sat next to a lamp.

"To give you something to do," one woman said. "Not because you have to earn your keep."

"We will get enough work out of you later," the foreman teased, "when you stop walking like a three-legged goat."

Ketifa threw a holey sock at him, and he brushed it off, laughing heartily. "To work, everyone. Only three-legged goats get to sit around."

The miners chuckled and filed into the mountain.

Tadaki waited until the others were gone, then stepped closer. Giving her plenty of time to move away, he put an arm gently around her shoulders. "I will see you tonight."

She leaned in for a moment, and after he left, she dropped the sock back into the mending basket. Later would be soon enough to work. The trip up the mountain had been difficult, and a nap sounded like a nice way to ignore her burning throat and aching body.

In the evening, the miners stopped by to chat on their way out, and Tadaki stayed longer to eat dinner with her, piling his food on a flatbread so she could use the only plate. She picked at her food and finally handed her mostly full plate to her friend.

"Does your throat hurt too much?" he asked.

Ketifa shrugged, nodded, and shook her head.

He shoveled food into his mouth and squinted at her. After he swallowed, he said, "So, it does hurt, but you're too depressed to eat anyway?"

She stuck out her tongue at him.

Tadaki put down the plate and wrapped an arm around her shoulder as lightly as a butterfly. "I will be back in the morning."

She rested her head on his shoulder, but all too soon, he had to leave, and Ketifa was left alone.

The next several days were monotonously similar and depressingly dark, without even her old morning and evening routines outside. She finished the mending and accepted another basket with a sigh.

Her only happiness was the nightly visits from Tadaki, when they talked about the mine or the village or nothing in particular. She started teaching him to write better, teasing him about his letters being worse than a three-legged goat could scratch with its hoof. He merely dimpled and tried again.

But an hour of talk did not make up for a day of silence. Until she healed more, she could not even return to emptying buckets. More and more often, she found herself merely sitting in her little cave doing nothing at all. She stared at the wall in silence, mind blank. Her body still ached, and she was cold all the time, even when she wrapped her blanket around herself.

Ketifa soon found herself hovering near the door while the miners filed in and out, desperate to catch even a glimpse of sunlight. One ray of sun, a single spark of light. Anything.

"I'm almost ready to die," she admitted one evening, "rather than stay here in the dark for the rest of my life. If I die, please bury me in sunlight."

Tadaki washed her plate and put it away. "You will not die. In fact, I have an idea. What if I found another way to keep the merchant from chasing you?"

Ketifa narrowed her eyes. "Like what? You cannot kill him."

He choked. "I had something else in mind." He cleared his throat and shrugged. "Perhaps we need to change your status."

"I do not understand." She could not muster the energy to think.

Tadaki scooted closer and took her hands. "Marry me, and he will not want you, which makes it safe enough for you to come home with me instead of pretending to be dead."

Heat rushed across her cheeks, and her breath caught. Tadaki had sheltered her from her sister and saved her life. He was kind and funny and adorable, and he did not care if she was beautiful or not. She looked forward to their nightly talks more than anything else.

His idea would solve her problems for her, but what if that was all he had in mind? Her heart, which had soared a moment before, now froze again.

She squeezed his hands before pulling free. "That is hardly a fair deal for you, stuck with a wife you married only to rescue."

Tadaki yanked on his curls. "I'm muddling this." He took her hands again. "Marry me because I love you. And then he will not want you because you will be mine."

He was her best friend, and her heart beat faster around him. Was that love? If they could get rid of Astra and Virat some other way, would she want to live without him? No. The best parts of her day were with him, and she wanted to stay with him always. Yes, she loved him. Tears welled up in her eyes.

He let go of her hands and searched for a clean spot on his sleeve, dabbing at her wet cheeks.

"Never mind," he said in a sad voice. "We will keep you safe another way."

Ketifa pushed aside his sleeve and threw herself into his arms. "Yes."

"Yes, I promise," he said.

She laughed, her heart lighter than it had been in weeks. Perhaps even since Father died. "No, I mean, yes, I will marry you."

"Yes, oh, yes," Tadaki cheered. He hugged her tightly and laughed. "Tomorrow on the rest day? No, I promised my brother I would visit, since we have an extra holiday the day after. Ah! I will send him a message that I will visit next week."

"No, go visit. We can marry in three days, before we start work." She caressed his cheek, then made a face at the grit that came off. "By then, I expect you to be clean."

Before she could anticipate his moves, he leaned forward and kissed her quickly. "I will see you in three days."

Her new betrothed left before she recovered from the shock and delight, and she went to bed with warm cheeks and dreamed of more kisses.

In the morning, Ketifa woke sluggishly. No miners would come today. The door would not open, and no sunlight would reach her, even for a moment. Suddenly, the prospect was too much to bear.

Despite the trade route passing nearby, the mine's location was secret, hidden by good design and effective camouflage. Even the path looked like a simple hiking path, with no cart tracks to betray it. What harm would it do to sneak outside for only a moment? A minute, no more.

Ketifa dithered by the entrance until desperation overcame obedience. She opened the door a crack and slipped into the little outer room. Sunlight poured through the tiny window, but it was not enough. Despite lecturing herself on idiocy, she snuck through the second door and stepped outside.

After so many days in the dark, the light hurt, and she covered her eyes while she let the warmth soak in. Just a minute, then she would go back.

A gasp came from her right. "I knew they lied!"

Ketifa lowered her hand and squinted in the sunlight. A woman stood at the top of the path, panting for breath. Astra!

Ketifa retreated toward the little room, reaching for the door.

Astra grabbed her arm. "They said you were dead, but I knew you were not. I searched all over, and here you are."

Ketifa jerked free and backed up, but she missed the entrance and had to edge around the little building to avoid Astra.

"I have something for you." Astra stalked Ketifa, sharp, thin metal gleaming in her hand.

Half blinded from the rising sun and flailing to stay on the mountain, Ketifa threw her left arm sideways and caught it in a thorn bush. She yanked it back, straight into Astra's hand.

"Ow," Ketifa complained, pulling her hand free. Blood oozed from her finger.

Astra laughed. "Now I do not have to worry about you."

She flicked the needle over the edge and walked down the mountain path.

Ketifa cradled her hand. That was odd. Why would a thorn scratch make Astra leave? Nonetheless, Tadaki had been right, and Ketifa should have stayed inside. She raised her face to the sunlight one last time and returned to her cave. Three days until she could leave with her new husband and never worry about her crazy step-sister and the slimy merchant again. She could last three days, even without the sun on her face.

The day passed slowly, and her finger continued to sting. Lethargy crept over her again, and she curled up in her blanket and slept. Each time she woke, her finger was more swollen and red in the lantern light.

The next day, she barely stirred at all, ignoring the pain that crept up her hand and arm.

By the time the miners returned the day after, she was barely conscious. Despite someone shaking her, she could not move or speak. The voices faded into silence as the familiar darkness swallowed her.

A very long time later, Ketifa woke with sunlight shining on her face. For a while, she lay there, enjoying the warmth without moving or opening her eyes.

Then it hit her. Sunshine. She was outside. Why was she outside instead of in the mine?

She opened her eyes and found herself in a glass box. The mountain towered on one side, and the trade route ran on the other. What in Resef's name was going on? Why was she in a box at the roadside?

Ketifa tried to move and banged into the glass. She hammered on the sides, but they were too close for her to get a good angle or work up any momentum. Running her hands along the walls, she felt only smooth glass. No crack, no catch, no way out. Would she be trapped here forever? With no water, she would last no more than a few days. Which was better than slowly starving, though not by much.

And if she panicked, she would use air too quickly to be replaced through whatever crack allowed it in. She took a slow breath and held it until she calmed. At least she was alive for now, and alive meant she had hope. After all, she had already survived death three times. Was one more too much to ask?

The box was too low for her to sit up, but she managed to pull her hands to her chest. Her left hand was bandaged and stunk of ointment, but it no longer hurt. She unwound the bandage, banging her elbows on the glass a few times, and inspected her scratched finger. Though a little pink, 'twas not swollen.

Ketifa folded her hands across her stomach and closed her eyes. If she could not get out, then she might as well enjoy the sunlight. The warm sun crept under her skin and lit her veins. For the first time since Astra strangled her, she felt well again. Yes, this was what she had missed while hiding in the darkness.

Silently, she prayed both her thanks and her pleas for escape.

An hour or two later, judging by the progress of the sun, a shadow fell across her face. Ketifa opened her eyes just as Tadaki closed his and knelt beside the box, leaning his forehead against the glass.

Oh, what a sweet sight he was. His face was actually clean, and curls escaped from under his headscarf. Most importantly, he was *there*. Love and relief flowed through her warmer than the sunlight.

But he looked so sad.

Ketifa rapped on the glass. "Bright day. Will you let me out, please?"

Tadaki screamed and fell backward, fumbling for his belt knife.

Ketifa tried to cover her ears but only banged her elbows on the box.

Eyes wide, Tadaki crept forward and peered through the glass. She waved, careful not to bump the sides again. A huge smile spread across his face. He jumped to his feet and fumbled with something near the top of the box. In less than a minute, he swung open the lid.

Tadaki touched her sleeve. "Are you — are you alive?"

Ketifa blinked. "Can I talk if I'm dead?"

He ran his hands lightly over her arms and legs, then helped her out of the box. "You were not moving or breathing. We thought you were dead."

As she wobbled on her feet, he wrapped his arms around her and buried his face in her hair, which streamed loose over her neck.

"*I* thought you were dead." His lament was almost too soft to hear.

Ketifa started to reply, but sobs shook his body so she merely held him until he raised his head.

"Now will you tell me why I'm in a glass box?" she asked. "And do you have any food or water?"

"Oh, yes, I should have thought of that." He settled her on a large rock and pulled out his water pouch and a small loaf of bread. "We came back to the mine two days ago, and you were sick. Your arm had red streaks running through it." He took her hand and examined the scratch, then tucked it between both of his. "We thought you had an infection, but Astra said — No, that part comes later. We treated your hand, but it did not seem to help. You got colder and colder and stopped breathing."

He took a shuddering breath. "I remembered what you asked and insisted on this coffin in the sun, at least for a few days before we would have to really bury you." Tadaki looked away and cleared his throat.

"While you were here, your sister and her husband came by. He ranted about the waste of your beauty, and I wanted to punch him. Your death was a waste of your life, not your *face*. Astra told him she protected her own, and that if he did not want his other wives to be poisoned like she had poisoned you, he should divorce them now. So then we thought the infection was really poison and that was why the ointment did not work. But we did not know the antidote, and Astra would not tell us." He cleared his throat again.

"I thought living with each other would be punishment enough for them both, but the elders had them arrested to keep the secret of the mine. They will never be free again." He grinned. "I think the merchant got more than he bargained for with your sister."

"But who got the worst end of the bargain?" she asked sadly. Reasonable or not, she loved Astra.

"If you have no more questions," Tadaki said, "I have two for you. What did your sister do to you, and will you still marry me?" He squeezed her fingers and smiled, though a worried line cut between his eyebrows.

She held up her finger. "Astra grabbed my hand and tried to stab me with something, but I yanked it back before she could. She must have seen the scratch I got on the thorn bush and thought she had succeeded."

"Then 'twas only an infection after all," Tadaki whispered. "Thank Resef the ointment finally worked."

Ketifa examined her finger. Was it even the thorn scratch that had brought her close to death? She remembered the way she had withered in the darkness of the mine, even before Astra found her again. And she had not recovered until they put her in sunlight. But who would believe such an unlikely story?

His second question was easier. "I'm safe now. I do not *need* to marry anyone."

Tadaki looked at the ground. "I know."

"I want to marry someone I love," she said.

He let go of her hand. "I understand."

Ketifa turned his chin so she could look into his kind brown eyes. "So that is why I want to marry you. You bring me life more than sunlight itself."

Tadaki's eyes widened. A dimpled smile crept across his face. He whooped and pulled her off the rock, swinging her around before putting her down again.

She leaned against his strong shoulder, and he wrapped an arm around her.

"I'm glad you said yes. The mine needs a good clerk," he teased.

Ketifa giggled. "You've discovered my secret reason for agreeing. Even a three-legged goat needs to feel useful."

Tadaki dropped a kiss onto her forehead, and she tilted her head to offer her lips. He leaned down slowly, giving her time to change her mind, and she stretched to close the distance. His lips were warm, and his arms closed around her, and time disappeared in his loving embrace.

I f you like this story, you might like the traditional Earth fairytales:
   Snow White
Snow Drop
Bella Venezia
Gold-Tree and Silver-Tree
La petite Toute-Belle
The Glass Coffin

YAY! I LOVED THESE FAIRY TALES!

So it's safe to assume you want more, dear reader?

OF COURSE I DO. BUT WHAT ELSE IS
THERE?

So glad you asked.

Turn the page for two chapters of **Wind of Choice**, the first book in the **Unexpected Heroes** series, which moves forward in history to a time of great upheaval. If you already read the whole series, no worries — I've written another. You can also find information about **Return of the Fae**, a contemporary fantasy set on Earth, and an offer for **free stories!**

WIND OF CHOICE

Much later in Kaiatan's history, other heroes rose unexpectedly to meet new challenges. Here's the beginning of the new tale...

1. AHJIN
(VASI, IOJ)

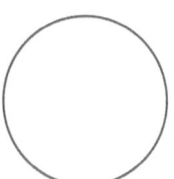

Vasi: Capital city of Ioj. The view from the towering cliffs is awe-inspiring. The main temple of Irajahan, where the sixteen-year-old winged youths present themselves at adulthood, is one of the architectural wonders of the modern world.
The Visitor's Guide to Ioj, 5th edition

Ahjin's feathers whispered in the perfect updrafts. The air was sweet today, and escape was even sweeter. He shoved back his worries about meddling priests and flew higher in the pale orange sky.

When the city on the cliff below was almost too small to see, Ahjin tightened the tie restraining his curls. He stretched his arms and somersaulted into a dive. The wind whistled in his ears as he fell.

After one breathtaking minute, he tucked his arms and legs, spread his wings, and snapped into the roll that started his aerobatic routine. He ran through his old stunts, then added the new tricks he'd learned from spying on the advanced class. Father trained him daily after school and would teach him the rest of the techniques when he became a skydancer.

Ahjin spun into a deliberate spiral. He flew well, and hard work would make him even better. He'd be an asset to his parents and their troupe while he made a living doing what he loved best. All he had to do was stay away from the temple long enough to be forgotten in the vocational assignments, then follow his own skydancing goals without interference.

He ran through his routine three times. If he judged the height of the sun correctly, it would be too late for the priests to ruin his plans now.

To celebrate, he should buy something delicious for Mother. He flew lower and scanned the flying lanes in the market. There wasn't much produce available this early in spring, though, only some fruit and fresh greens.

As he removed his goggles and spiraled for a better look, Father glided from behind a group of shoppers. Oh, no. The market was busy today, with heavy traffic both on the ground and in the air, but not enough to hide Ahjin. He should have flown a little longer. Or a lot.

Father dodged through the airborne crowd with crossed arms and an impressive frown. "You're late. On purpose, I dare say."

Father had been more easy-going before Ahjin's birthday brought the possibility of change to their lives. He had trained Ahjin since his first flight so he could join the troupe at adulthood. Now it was time to follow their long-held plan, and Father still insisted he go to the temple. Why was the priests' approval so important?

"Father, I told you I wasn't going. We already have plans." Ahjin dodged a little girl chasing her pet bird. That had been one of his favorite childhood games, too, when he was younger and carefree.

Father sighed. "I felt the same way when I was your age. Don't roll your eyes — I was young once."

Ahjin snorted. Father's hair had been white from birth, and his body was as strong as ever. Ahjin had seen no evidence his attitudes had ever been young, though.

"Unfortunately for you," Father continued, "the only choice you have left is whether you want to arrive by wing or tied in a carpet. Don't shame our House by making me call the temple guard."

He motioned to the black marble road among the ordinary cobblestone roads made for the convenience of wagons and wingless visitors.

The cobblestone led everywhere, from the market to the Great Library, and between the older houses and the new, three-story towers with landing platforms on every level.

The black marble went only from the market to Ahjin's doom.

"Well, given those charming options," Ahjin scoffed, "I'll go. It won't make any difference. I don't need anyone telling me what to do with my life."

Ahjin slowed to an insulting speed, but whenever he meandered, Father was at his back, too experienced to be shaken. They traveled without wasting their breath on the same futile discussion they'd had every day for the last month.

Vasi was the largest city in the country, but Ahjin could cross it in half an hour at his slowest flying pace. He normally enjoyed the flight and visiting with people. Today, he only had time to wave and smile, hoping to annoy Father and slow the trip.

"Hurry," Father said. "Many of your friends are already there. You can talk to the rest after your interview." When Ahjin waved at a pretty girl, Father tried again. "The Winds won't be happy if you're late. If you cooperate more, they'll have no reason not to give you what you want."

Cooperate. Ahjin snorted. "If I avoid the temple altogether, dear Father, there's *no* chance for them to tell me what to do." He didn't care if Irajahan's priestly Winds were unhappy. The whole tradition was ridiculous. He was an adult now and could choose a vocation himself.

"That never works," Father said. "They'd just assign you something unpleasant later. Do you want to work in the sewers?"

Ahjin clenched his jaw and narrowed his eyes. "Why would they care about one person?"

Father sighed and didn't reply.

Even at Ahjin's best dawdle, they approached the temple too quickly. The grandiose stained-glass windows sat in gray-and-white marble traced with gold, but he didn't appreciate the splendor today. His normal schemes for flying through the high arches and between the towers were replaced with bitter musing.

Ahjin's pretty mother waited for them in front of the temple, her flyaway blonde hair pinned into place. Her pale golden wings were one shade darker than her hair, and her flowing dress hid muscles as toned as the ones displayed by Father's sleeveless vest.

Ahjin and Father swooped down to land by her. Worry eased from her face as she pulled Ahjin into a hug before he folded his wings.

"You're just in time." She smiled at him, but her look to Father was almost a wince.

As they entered the gilded temple, the long line of monthly petitioners waned to the last boy and girl, probably latecomers from the country. The priests gave Ahjin and his parents impatient looks and hurried them to the front of the antechamber.

He had been within minutes of being too late.

It wouldn't matter that Father dragged him here. Ahjin had no intention of cooperating against his own desires. If the official word coincided with his plans, he'd be the model of obedience. He might agree with something only a bit different from what he wanted, if it took advantage of his talents. Messengers, for instance, came from the ranks of talented fliers. Never let it be said he was *completely* unreasonable.

The dark-haired novice at the desk, wearing the empty-circle badge of the lowest priestly rank, had been a year ahead of Ahjin in school. While the novice wrote Ahjin's name in a massive book, his parents went outside to wait in the courtyard.

The novice walked Ahjin to the left-hand room and ushered him in with a scowl and a casual wave. Ahjin hid his own scoff; the incompetent novice hadn't advanced past Doldrums in almost a year.

Inside the room, colorful murals on the high walls detailed the great deeds of Irajahan, God of Air, guardian of their country. Ahjin had glimpsed them before, during required services and his rapid flyovers. If there weren't a row of plainly dressed priests staring at him from behind a long table, he'd examine them now. It would be more fun than this dreary interview. Only the Wind on the far end had even a hint of a smile.

"Come in, boy, and hurry," said the closest priest. "We don't have all day."

Ahjin stomped over and introduced himself — Ahjin Machol, son of Jayan and Aria — followed by his House and the names of his grandparents. Then the inquest began, with the priests taking turns asking arbitrary questions.

"How well did you do in school?" asked a Wind holding Ahjin's record, which made it a trick question.

Ahjin smirked. "I pay attention to things that are worth my while. School qualifies sometimes."

"What were your favorite subjects?"

"I liked flying, gymnastics, meteorology, and geography," Ahjin replied.

"Do you have any siblings?"

"One little sister, who's still too young to fly."

"What profession would you like?" asked the almost-smiling priest.

"I want to be a professional skydancer." Finally, a good question.

"Do you have any special skills or talents?"

"Well, obviously, I'm great at flying." Ahjin was in fair currents here. "I practice daily."

"If you're that good, why didn't you take the advanced aerobatics classes in school?"

Ahjin rolled his eyes and stared at the murals, but one of the other priests pointed to his school record.

"They have academic prerequisites for those classes."

Ahjin ignored that, too. It was stupid to need good scores in math for a flight class. Flying was unrelated and more important.

"Do you have any job prospects?"

Yes, a better question. "My parents want me to join their aerobatic troupe."

Then the questions came faster and more complicated. "Explain the political significance of the recent trade treaty." "Given a right triangle with one side the length..." "What are the major exports..." "Name the last three potentates and their policy differences." "If the barometer falls and the temperature rises..."

Ahjin got at least half of them correct.

"What's your favorite color?"

Ahjin blinked at the change of subject. "Blue." Flirting girls said it looked good on him, but what difference did it make?

The Winds glanced at each other and dismissed him to join his parents outside. At least the stupid question ended the obsolete ritual.

When Mother tried to get him to stand still in the courtyard, Ahjin dodged her grasp. When Father threatened to ground him if he even hovered, he walked back and forth in the corner. Ten steps left, turn, ten steps right, turn. The afternoon sun sank lower as he paced behind the other petitioners and their families.

It seemed forever before the stuck-up novice climbed the outer steps of the temple to the gilded marble podium used for public announcements. He unrolled a scroll and, in a bored voice, read the names of the new adults and their assigned jobs, in the order they arrived that morning. When he got to the end, he sneered at Ahjin.

"Wind." He snapped shut the scroll and swaggered back inside the temple.

Father gasped. "Really?"

No, that had to be wrong. Ahjin wasn't a priest. But thanks to the temple guard, he couldn't ignore it. Ahjin evaded Father's grasp to run after the novice.

"Wait, there's been a mistake," he yelled as he ran into the echoing antechamber. "I'm to be a skydancer with my parents."

He skidded to a stop when he realized the room was filled with priests and priestesses glaring at him.

Ahjin stammered an apology, then gulped and repeated his explanation with shaking knees. If he didn't find the courage to convince the Winds, he'd be trapped as a priest for the rest of his life. His skydancing training would be wasted and his talents ignored. That was unacceptable.

The nearly-smiling priest from his interview stepped forward, without a rank pin, but now dressed in lavish garb that overshadowed his plain gray wings. "Do you remember being asked your favorite color during your examination?"

"Yes," Ahjin said, "but many people like blue." Perhaps it was proof something had gone wrong in the interview or the entire flawed system.

"Hmm, true," the priest said. "There's only one issue. None of us asked you that question."

"I heard you." Why would they lie about something so obvious and irrelevant?

"No. Irajahan asked you." The Wind folded his hands together as he made that outrageous claim.

Ahjin flared his wings and jerked his head around to stare at the large stained-glass window above the temple door. It depicted the god in his ostentatious glory, summoning the winds from all directions. The caption said "Irajahan the Omnipotent." The artist had drawn the powerful god with a sulky face.

"A god has no better question to ask me than my favorite color? What's the point?" He folded his wings and edged away. Perhaps it was time to end the conversation and leave.

The priest grasped Ahjin's shoulder. "The point is that you heard him. Telepathy is an automatic qualifier for the priesthood. Other skills become inconsequential. Your personal desires and your family's needs are irrelevant. You have until tonight to say farewell to your family and bring your things to the temple dorms. Initiation starts tomorrow morning, so don't be late."

He waved his hand at the other Winds, who bowed to Ahjin's captor and filed out of the room. The novice from school scoffed at Ahjin, then simpered at the Wind on his way out.

Ahjin was left alone with the old priest. He had telepathy? When had that happened? Never mind, it didn't matter. "No thanks, I have other plans." Ahjin tried to pull away.

For an old man, the Wind had a strong grip.

"Let me explain. When a new adult is assigned a job, he or she may petition for a change if they truly feel the assignment is unsuitable for them." That blithe half-smile stayed annoyingly on his face.

"I appeal!" It wasn't smart to *tell* him the way out.

"The exception is the priesthood," the Wind continued. "There is no release for telepaths. They are too rare and too badly needed. I'm sorry. Go say your farewells." His hand tightened until Ahjin's shoulder ached. "Please don't make us get you in the morning." He released Ahjin and followed the other priests into the inner temple.

Ahjin's groan echoed in the empty room. He couldn't return to his parents yet. They wouldn't understand why he wasn't happy, but he had dreams he'd worked hard to reach. Did he have no choice but to give up skydancing? Tradition was strict and the priesthood apparently stricter.

How could he fight a god?

2. CHANGES

(VASI, IOJ)

While priests' many duties include administering rites, preaching, and caring for the temple, their most important task is to relay Irajahan's will for his people.
Handbook for Winds

Ahjin held his breath as he glared at the colorful temple window and thought nasty things he hoped were overheard. When he ran out of insults and could pretend to be happy, he set his shoulders and left.

The courtyard was empty. Even Ahjin's parents had gone to collect his little sister from their cousin's house. He flew home slowly, thankful for the chance to think.

How could the priests be so cruel? He had worked hard for his dreams, and he wanted to stay with his family. Father was wrong — Ahjin should have hidden longer. His telepathy wasn't in any record; even *he* hadn't known about it. If he hadn't heard that question, they would have let him be a skydancer. Now everything was ruined. Even if his assignment was a mistake, the Winds didn't care.

His life was over. As a priest, he wouldn't learn any more aerobatics and might not have time to fly for more than transportation. Wonderful flying would be replaced by boring duties. What a waste of his constant practice. Someone would always tell him what to do and where to go, even after Doldrums. He wouldn't be able to live with his family, and might barely have time to visit.

He clenched his fists. How dare Irajahan and the priests destroy his life!

If only his parents would help him fight this. Ahjin snorted. Father would think this great honor was worth changing their dreams. Mother was too gentle to oppose either the authorities or Father. Even if his parents wanted to back Ahjin, they couldn't win against the law of the Winds or the temple guard that enforced the holy dictates throughout Ioj. This was his last evening as a civilian.

Ahjin watched the children play carefree tag above the gardens. He admired the view from the cliffs and waved to an acquaintance among the city guards who operated the pulley platforms used for freight and visitors.

Lee beckoned from his post at the top of the cliff until Ahjin landed by the guards. "Fair winds, Ahjin. How many new soldiers were called today?"

Ahjin had anticipated that question, and the number was high enough to satisfy.

"So, congratulations on your big day. What's your new job?" Lee asked.

"Priest," Ahjin muttered.

Some of the soldiers whistled, but others flinched. Lee glanced at the temple and ended the conversation as quickly as good manners allowed.

Ahjin cringed and turned for home again. Would people always be wary of him now, afraid of his connections? He couldn't read their minds, after all. Could he? If he didn't know, how could they? When his friends and neighbors called to him, he waved and kept going, afraid they'd also pull away.

His stomach cramped as he turned the corner before his parents' modest, one-story cottage. He was out of time, and he'd never live with his family again unless he beat this dilemma.

Did he have to pretend he was happy about his life turned upside down? It could be worse. Garbage collector was worse, wasn't it?

And priests could still marry — in fact, they were encouraged to — if he found a girl who didn't mind sharing him with Irajahan. Some girls thought the prestige was worth the hassle and long hours. It was no consolation.

When he shuffled through the door, his parents jerked their chairs back from the table. His baby sister smiled and reached for him, fluttering her downy wings. Maili's wispy hair was as yellow as Mother's, but she had Father's blue eyes. Ahjin forced a smile and hugged them all.

"There is no appeal," he croaked. He swallowed and tried again. "I have until curfew to report."

Mother handed him the baby and headed to the pantry. "It will be fine. You'll see." Her voice wavered. "Tonight we'll have a feast; tomorrow will be a new day. Do you want to invite friends to dinner?"

"No, I'd rather be alone with you." He spent more time flying than with his friends, anyway. He tickled Maili and listened to her giggle.

Father reached for a traveling basket. "Should I help you pack?"

Ahjin shrugged and carried Maili to his tiny room at the back of the house. She sat on the bed while Father helped Ahjin choose clothes for his days off. The temple uniforms were ugly for the first couple of ranks, but that was the least of his worries.

"Why did you make me do it, Father?" Ahjin hunched his shoulders. "You said it would be better, but look what happened. This is your fault. I should have done it my way."

Father stopped folding clothes and bowed his head. "I had a friend who skipped his ceremony and became a miserable sewer worker. I didn't want that to happen to you."

He smoothed a shirt and folded it slowly, matching every edge. When finished, he handed it to Ahjin, eyes downcast.

Ahjin tucked the shirt into his pack silently. Father was still ruining his life. He glanced at the map he had painted on his wall, with a different color for each country and each direction of wind and current. There was a whole world he'd never see now.

Hmm.

How did this telepathy nonsense work? Could anyone eavesdrop on his thoughts? Until he knew, he should think quietly. He wrapped a small family portrait in the silk scarf Mother had embroidered last winter.

Father picked up Ahjin's surujin and swung the weighted ends for Maili to grab. "Do you suppose they'll let you hunt or continue your practice?" He coiled the rope.

"I'll find a way." Ahjin was good with a bow for a boy — no, he was a man now — and better with his weighted throwing rope. He could take down a goose on the wing or stop a horse in its tracks, although that stunt had almost gotten him arrested when the irate farmer called the city guard. The horse was uninjured, but Ahjin practiced on wild animals after that.

He tucked the weapon inside his pack with his wrist guards and bowstring, and strapped his recurve bow to the outside, looking around his room with regret. There was so much he couldn't take, and he didn't know when he'd return for the rest. Now that he was leaving, Maili would move from their parents' room to his.

He looked again at his wall map. Though it wasn't as splendid as the temple's murals, it was more useful, especially now.

Shh, think quietly.

Dinner smelled ready, so he lifted his sister and his pack and left the room behind Father. Ahjin glared at his parents' House crests hanging on the wall with his ancestor's triple-curled Wind badge between them. Perhaps his great-grandfather was responsible for the "gift" of telepathy. He had been a mid-ranked Squall who married late in life and had only one child, a girl who did not follow him into the priesthood. Ahjin would happily blame him if no better prospect appeared.

He fastened Maili in her baby seat, then sat between his parents. They ate slowly and in silence. Maili pounded her spoon on the table and burbled at Ahjin. These memories of home would be a treasure when he was gone.

When Mother served dessert, Ahjin took a deep breath. "I've heard novices don't get time away for a while."

Every new adult went through an initiation. The soldiers trained before a mock battle. Most entertainers and athletes had a similar display. Farmers grew a garden in summer or wrote a report in winter. Teachers taught a class in public. Whatever Wind novices did at first was a secret.

"I'll miss you so much," he continued. That was true. "Don't worry about me. I'll see you soon." That was the possible lie that made his chest ache.

Father ran his fingers through his short, curly hair. Ahjin regretted, a little, growing out his own hair to look different. Mother's purple eyes, mirrors of his own, filled with silent tears. Both parents tried to smile.

"Do you want us to fly you to the temple?" Father asked.

"This is hard enough," Ahjin said. "Please let me go alone." He pressed his feet against the floor to distract him from his own tears.

Mother squeezed Father's hand. "I know they'll feed you, but I packed treats. Is there anything else you'd like?"

She tipped the small basket to show the contents. Perhaps it was her mother's heart that thought he'd starve without her cooking, but it was handy.

"Do we have any of your dried fruit? Or jerky from our last hunting trip?" Bread would spoil quickly, but she had packed enough cheese and fresh fruit for a week.

"We have both." She wiped her eyes and added his requests to the basket.

It was time. Ahjin shoved away his unfinished dessert. He hugged Maili, tickled her until she squealed, and handed her to Mother. After kissing his parents, he slid his long jacket over his arms. Father straightened the back section of Ahjin's jacket between his wings and laced the sides.

Ahjin slid Mother's treats into his pack and slung it on one shoulder. He took one last look at his family and trudged out the door, hurrying to leave before he cried.

Mother's trembling voice followed him. "Good flight."

Ahjin held his breath until his eyes stopped burning.

This wasn't fair. Perhaps he wasn't even a telepath. The priest claimed nobody in the room had asked that question, but it might be the charlatans' elaborate trick to draft him into servitude. He trudged toward the center of town without bothering to keep *that* thought quiet.

The priests said the god of air was vital to the existence of the world, but Ahjin suspected the Windbag told them that story to justify his extravagant vanity and continued reign. Ahjin didn't like encouraging the fable, especially when it demolished his own ambitions.

Ahjin was *good* at flying. Why didn't the Winds realize that? He had often complained to his parents about life being unfair, but his earlier concerns seemed childish now. The only choice left was not much choice at all.

Whenen Ahjin reached the market, he bought a compass and waved to some girls, then buckled his narrow pack between his wings and jumped into the air. He flew toward the temple with his heart pinched and palms damp. Could he really change his life in so many ways?

He spiraled higher and higher until he saw hints of other towns and villages near the horizon. Below him lay the city on the tall cliffs. Most of the businesses were in the center of town, with the residences along the outskirts. The farms were farther from the cliff, where the ground was less rocky. He waved farewell to his house, then flew west toward the temple. It was beautiful, gleaming in the sunset like an immense opal, more fantastic than the library or the palace.

He kept flying until he passed the cliffs and the lavender ocean was below him, then looked toward the far borders. Stories claimed the northwest forest was infested with giant spiders that trapped foolish explorers in vast webs. Discounting the ridiculous legends, any part of Ioj was within Irajahan's range and thus not safe.

According to the map on his wall, farther out of sight to the north lay deeply forested Darrendra, the land of the shape-shifting tribes. The few people who had visited those territorial folks and returned to tell about it had not gone past the narrow shore allowed to foreigners. There were no stories of how to survive inland.

Ahjin spiraled around and looked to the south, toward the immense desert continent. There were a few semi-permanent camps along the coast of Iskra, but much of the interior was inhospitable. Only the desert nomads knew where to find water in the sand, and a green oasis didn't guarantee a surface spring.

He stretched his wings with pleasure and made a long dive. The night breeze ruffled his unruly curls and cooled his angry flush. He flipped into a series of rolls and ended with an exhilarating loop. Flight was a distraction, but the sport soon palled under the weight of his errand.

Was he far away enough to think openly now? While in the city, he had tried to use his rage and loathing to hide his initial plans from any telepathic snooping. It was too bad he couldn't tell his parents what he was doing, but they would have stopped him. There was no way he'd be a priest, no chance he'd ruin his life.

Besides, he was an adult now. It was time to show he could take care of himself. Once he found how to get around Irajahan's selfish decrees, he'd fly with his family again. He already yearned for that day.

The Nokailana Islands to the west were a garden paradise full of clean springs, fruit trees, lush greenery, and easy-going natives. With wings to reach them and a net to catch fish or birds, the islands seemed his best opportunity for a successful escape. It should be easy to find land with fresh water and shelter until he found a long-term solution. He wouldn't give up his ambitions or his family for foolish priests and a stupider god.

Ahjin flew steadily away from Vasi until the three moons rose. The large, golden moon lit the clear sky with a mellow glow, while its tiny, pale blue companion chased its lavender twin across the heavens.

After three hours, he was tired and far enough from the city that nobody was likely to find him, if they bothered looking before morning. Any searchers would waste their time checking his house and the city before they looked farther. Even if Irajahan found him, Ahjin was out of his territory. The gods barely talked to each other and didn't cooperate for anything, much less the retrieval of one young man.

He searched the dark ocean for somewhere to rest.

A storm blew out of nowhere, with none of the usual warning signs. Clouds drizzled cold rain down his collar. Wind battered his jacket and plastered hair in his eyes. Stronger blasts bent his feathers and scrambled his steering control. His wings wrenched sideways. The drizzle turned into a waterfall. If he didn't land, the wind could blow him off course or snap his wings.

He shoved dripping curls out of his face. Green islands shone on the horizon under the moons, too far away. The only place close enough was a small, rocky islet below him. At least he'd be less at the mercy of the increasingly violent wind and could continue his trip after the storm passed.

He tried to land, but the gusts pushed him back into the air. In desperation, he waited until he was right above the rocks, then furled his wings and fell.

Ahjin missed the islet and fumbled for a hold in the ocean. The wave-splashed rocks were too slippery, and he slid off again and again until the water soaked his wings into worthlessness. He gasped for breath and grabbed a dead branch caught in the rocks.

A horrible scream echoed around him.

He forgot about holding on and covered his ears. It didn't help; the wailing was inside his head and didn't stop. The noise of the tempest rose to compete with the clamor in his head.

Now that he had no handhold, the storm grabbed him again and slammed him into the rocks headfirst.

Everything went dark.

 **Check my website MCLeeBooks.com for links to buy the next story or get the entire series at once.**

When their world is threatened by feuding gods, four teens bury their differences and forge an unlikely alliance. Only the combined talents of a winged acrobat, a mermaid, a shapeshifter, and a fire mage can prevent the annihilation of their world.

Magic, romance, and peril collide in this character-driven fantasy adventure of epic stakes, found family, and the courage to defy fate. Start your next binge-read with the complete **Unexpected Heroes** series, where the truest heroes are often the quiet ones—forged by sacrifice, bound by hope, and wrapped in myth and magic.

Or jump to contemporary Earth and read *Return of the Fae.* **What if Earth has legends of the fae because they used to live here? What if they're coming back...**

https://mcleebooks.com/series/return-of-the-fae/

Book 1: The Coming of the Fae

What if the fae are real?

The fae fled their dying world, taking a magic spaceship toward the vision of a blue planet. Gil is excited they have almost reached their new home and the promise of equality for all races. But when an accident injures the king, he must prevent murderous lords from forcing the commoners back into serfdom.

What if they are returning?

Alexandria wants a happy family, but Dad's PTSD is tearing them apart. No wish on a star can solve this problem, but she continues to watch the night sky. Now a new object in the heavens catches her attention — and Dad's. NASA says it's an asteroid; Dad is convinced it's invading aliens. His paranoia might destroy their family.

The truth will shake the world...

*The Coming of the Fae is a space fantasy that bridges myth and modern reality when magic descends from the stars. It is the first book in the **Return of the Fae** series of clean YA contemporary fantasy with a dash of sci-fi & mythology, from the author of **Unexpected Heroes**, and is best read in order for the most enjoyment.*

Still want more? Get free stories by joining my newsletter. Every two weeks, I chat about my current writing or my life and offer book news and deals. And did I mention free stories?

Sign up at MCLeeBooks.com

Free story #1: The Cat's Fortune

On another world, so long ago that truth has faded into legend, a cat and a boy seek their fortune together. You think you know the story, but do you?

Orphaned and homeless, young Aktar travels to the city of Rapata for a better life.

But it seems the rumors of gold-paved streets are false. Can he find a home and a job before he starves? Maybe with the help of a foundling kitten.

A retelling of Puss in Boots and Dick Whittington, with timeless themes of belonging, courage, and self-discovery, set on the fantasy world of Kaiatan, home of the **Unexpected Heroes**.

Free Story #2: Spotting the Fae

Zak is considered too young to navigate the spaceship, even though he's the best among the fae.

On Earth, Gaby loves math and helping her astronomer Mama with her data.

When Mama spots a new asteroid heading toward Earth...

Everything will change.

The author of **Unexpected Heroes** *returns with a startlingly plausible blend of sci-fi, mythology, and the modern world.* **Return of the Fae** *is a clean YA contemporary fantasy series where fae from space don't match Earth's legends.*

Please leave an honest review on any retailer or reader site. Seriously, it would really help me. :)

If you found a typo, you're welcome to report it at mcleebooks.com/report-a-typo/

CHARACTER LIST AND PRONUNCIATION GUIDE

IF YOU ARE INTERESTED IN THE
MEANINGS OF THE NAMES,
PLEASE SEE MCLEEBOOKS.COM

Name (Pronunciation) Identity

<u>People</u>

Aerilyn (AIR-uh-lin) Iojif, Solana's daughter
Akoni (Uh-CONE-ee) Nokai, Tua's eighth sister
Ala (ALL-uh) Nokai, Tua's mom
Aran (AH-run) Darrendrakar, bully to Kokoro
Arcelio (Ar-SEE-lee-oh) Iojif orphan boy
Astra Kukarni (ASS-truh Koo-KARN-ee) Iskrin, Ketifa's step-sister
Avari Masiela (Uh-VAHR-ee Mass-ee-ELL-uh) Iojif, Fala's fiance
Darravani the Omnifarious (DAR-ah-VAHN-ee) Darrendrakar Goddess
of Earth
Ekewaka (ECK-uh-WAHK-uh) kraken
Erardo Kaoru Shekeda (Err-ARE-doh Kay-OH-roo Shuh-KAY-duh)
Darrendrakar, Kokoro's father
Esen (ESS-en) Iojif, Solana's brother
Fala Ilmarinen (FALL-uh Ill-MARE-in-un) Iojif, young woman
Hanini (Huh-NEE-nee) Nokai, Tua's eleventh sister
Hasana Senjor (Hah-SAHN-uh Sayn-JZOR) Iojif, princess
Honi Erroldin (HOH-nee) Darrendrakar, Zienna's little sister
Ipolani (Ip-oh-LAHN-ee) Nokai, Tua's second sister

Irajahan the Omnipotent (Ear-AH-jah-han) Iojif God of Air

Kahoni (Kuh-HOE-nee) Nokai, one of Tua's mothers

Kamaka (KAH-muh-kuh) Nokai, Tua's third sister

Kamalalokelani (Kuh-MAHL-uh-LOW-kay-LAHN-ee) "Kamala" Nokai, Manami's girlfriend

Kanagan Errolsin (CAN-uh-gun) Darrendrakar, Zienna's little brother

Ketifa Acharya (Ket-EE-fuh) Iskrin, Fairest inn drudge

Kini (KEE-nee) Nokai, Tua's tenth sister

Kokoro Dayandi Shakeda (KOE-koe-roe Day-YAHN-dee Shuh-KAY-duh) Darrendrakar, Goat boy

Lanakila (LAN-uh-KEEL-uh) Nokai, Tua's oldest sister

Leimomi (Lay-MOE-mee) Nokai, one of Tua's mothers

Lono (LOHN-oh) Nokai, Tua's dad

Mahi (MA-hee) Nokai, Tua's fourth sister

Makanavailea the Omniscient (Mah-KAHN-ah-vie-LEE-ah) Nokai Goddess of Water

Manamikamoku (Muh-NAHM-ee-kuh-MOE-koo) "Manami" Nokai, Kamala's boyfriend

Mililani (MILL-ee-LAHN-ee) Nokai, Tua's seventh sister

Molimo Kumaser (Moh-LEE-moh Koo-muh-SEHR) Darrendrakar, Bear forester

Nashoba Erroldin (Nuh-SHOW-buh) Darrendrakar, Zienna's little sister

Netra Hemalata Zerrano (NET-ruh Hem-uh-LAHT-uh Zerr-AH-no) Darrendrakar, Goat girl

Nohea (Noe-HEE-uh) Nokai, Tua's fifth sister

Olkan Errolsin (OHL-can) Darrendrakar, Zienna's little brother

Pekelo (PECK-uh-loh) Nokai, Tua's father

Pomaikai (POME-eye-kie) Nokai, Tua's ninth sister

Raisa Kordairo Dayandi (RAY-suh Cohr-DEHR-oh Day-YAHN-dee) Darrendrakar, Kokoro's mother

Resef the Omnificent (RESS-eff) Iskrin God of Fire

Roukan Errolsin (ROO-can) Darrendrakar, Zienna's little brother

Sahali (Sah-HOLL-ee) Iojif, horse breeder

Siroko Kyveli (Sur-O-ko) Iojif, nobleman

Solana (Soe-LANN-uh) Iojif, lady of the house

Tadaki Parikh (Tuh-DAHK-ee Puh-REEK) Iskrin, Heresa miner

Tanvir Sahira (TAN-veer Suh-HEER-uh) Iskrin, Serafi young man

Tikani Erroldin (Tih-KAHN-ee) Darrendrakar, Zienna's little sister
Tuakahakina (TOO-uh-KAH-hah-KEE-nuh) "Tua" Nokai boy, 12 years old
Uilani (OO-ee-LAHN-ee) Nokai, Tua's sixth sister
Virat Kapadia (VEER-at Kuh-PAID-ee-uh) Iskrin, merchant
Zafrir Kyveli (Zaff-REER Kie-VELL-ee) Iojif, Avari's enemy
Zienna Erroldin (Zee-EH-nuh ERR-ohl-din) Darrendrakar, Wolf girl, 13 years old

<u>Groups, Locations, Languages</u>

Akasha (Uh-KAHSH-uh)City in south central Ioj
Chiharu (Chi-HARE-oo) Iskrin clan, specialty: perfume
Darrendra (Duh-RREND-druh) Northern country
Darrendrakar (Duh-RREND-druh-car) People of Darrendra, shapeshifters
Darrendran (Duh-RREND-drun) Darrendrakar language
Heresa (Herr-ESS-uh) Iskrin clan, speciality: gems, precious metals
Ioj (EYE-ojze) Eastern country
Iojif (Eye-OH-jziff) People of Ioj, avians
Iojo (Eye-OH-jzo) Iojif language
Iskra(ISK-ruh) Southern country
Iskrin (ISK-ree)People of Iskra, desert-dwellers
Iskrit (ISK-rit) Iskrin language
Itziri (It-ZEER-ee) Iskran clan, speciality: raw metals
Kazuki (Kuh-ZOO-kee) Iskran clan, speciality: spices
Nokai (NO-kie) People of Nokailana, aquastrians
Nokailana (NO-kie-LAHN-uh) Western islands
Noki (NO-kee) Nokai language
Serafi (Seh-RAH-fee) Iskrin clan, specialty: coal, mining
Soreka (Soh-REEK-uh) Iskran clan, speciality: fruits, wine
Tetsuya (Tet-SOO-yuh) Iskrin clan, specialty: weapons & metalwork
Tukiko (Too-KEE-koe) Iskrin clan, speciality: healing
Vasi (VAHS-ee) Capital of Ioj

ACKNOWLEDGMENTS

Thanks to my amazing alpha and beta readers, Annabeth, Becky James, Carol Malone, Christie Powell, Donna Gonzales, Eryn Yavingque, Gail Porter, Karen Dimick, Kat Gollihugh, Laci Felker, Lea Carter, Laura Drake, Mari Molen, Mary Jenkins, Matt Peel, Michelle Henrie, Molly Morrison, Paula Barreto, Peter Thomson, Rachel Roy, Ria Gollihugh, Robin Cranney, Sarah Markle, Somer, and Virginia Cummings

ABOUT THE AUTHOR

Marty C. Lee told stories for most of her life, but never took them seriously until her daughter asked her to write this one. Between writing and spending time with her family, she reads, embroiders, paints-by-number, and gardens.

She has lived in five states, seven cities, and ten houses so far. She currently lives in the West, but not in a tropical paradise. She doesn't like flying, even in an airplane. She wishes she could produce her own fire to warm her hands. She's glad she didn't have to wait a year to marry her sweetheart, who also wishes she could warm her hands.

You can find her at
    MCLeeBooks.com and on Facebook and book sites

www.ingramcontent.com/pod-product-compliance
Lightning Source LLC
Chambersburg PA
CBHW031213020726
47499CB00002B/565